THE HOMEWARD BOUNDER
and other sea stories

THE HOMEWARD BOUNDER
and other sea stories

by
Floyd Beaver

THE GLENCANNON PRESS

Copyright © 1995 by Floyd Beaver
Published by The Glencannon Press
P.O. Box 341, Palo Alto, CA 94302

First Edition

Library of Congress Catalog Card Number: 95-75695

ISBN   0-9637586-3-2

Contents

INTRODUCTION

Floyd Beaver has been a writer throughout his life, from a young man's newspaper stint in Osage County, Oklahoma to a post-war career as an advertising man in San Francisco. The writing of fiction and the sailing of boats have provided refuge from the stress of the corporate-merger era.

Beaver's stories search out the places where fate opposes fate, where the only safety lies beyond the reef, where there is no place to go but forward, forsaking what is left behind. In "Breaking Seas" we find a man in love with his brother's wife, willing to risk himself, his ship, his crew, his brother and Sally herself for a chance at getting her to the doctor she desperately needs. In "The Slop Chest" we find an unyielding old captain risking his ship and driving himself to the grave to impose his will on a common seaman of an uncommon stripe. Later, the narrator wonders, "if there was aught to be learned from it at all." The question places Beaver's sea tales squarely in the tradition of Conrad, no friend to neat resolutions, who once declared that, "I love humanity, but I know it is unimprovable."

As a human undertaking, sailing is as moody as the weather. It is as mindless, or as contemplative, as the sailor. The summertime sea breeze really howls across Beaver's home port, San Francisco Bay. In the highrise city, the wind ships seabirds sideways past the cut-stone face of the Pacific Stock Exchange. In the mid-Bay, downwind from the Golden Gate, whitecaps break against the bleak face of Alcatraz. And across the Bay, to the north, the scarfaced hills are hunted by hawks that enjoy open range all the way to Portland. From the helm of a boat (preferably kicked back and steering with one toe) there are views of the whole panorama.

The same Bay in winter is cool and soft, a place for dreaming, for summoning voices out of the air. It is a place where the outlines of city, hills and even Alcatraz are softened. Rocks and hazards and highrises seem far away. In Beaver's stories, the truth is in the simplicity, and the simplicity is in the truth. He has a voice for the young apprentice, and the wizened veteran.

In another age, seamen did not learn to swim. There was no need. Fate would find them when fate was ready. Toward the end of that time, as steam replaced sail, many of those same seamen found they could not swim in the new age of steel-hulled, piston-pounding schedule-keepers. Neither could they abide the diminutions of the machine age which called a man down from the rigging, where he might commune with the Southern Cross, and oblivion, to put a coal shovel in his hand. Beaver, the signalman, flies their flag, too.

Kimball Livingston
February 1995

FOREWORD

For those old enough to remember when popular
magazines regularly published sea fiction, these little stories
will be a warm revisiting of what seems now a much simpler time.   For those too young to remember, they offer
what may be an intriguing look back into a time when
home entertainment was something other than electronic
noise, laugh tracks and flickering images.

It was possible then to go to newsstands anytime one
liked and to find stories very much like these. The magazines in which they appeared could even be ordered for
delivery to one's home. Readers could sit down for quiet
evenings with writers who took them through the oceans of
the world and introduced them to characters, some of whom
— Colin Glencannon and Tugboat Annie, for instance —
became familiar friends and are remembered still by those

who knew them long ago in the pages of the old *Saturday Evening Post.*

Typically unpretentious, the stories were written under the rigid constraints of magazine space, for the entertainment of their readers. They did, nevertheless, sometimes reach impressive levels of artistic merit.

Modern readers, steeped as they are in violence and profane sexual exhibitionism of what passes now for entertainment writing, may find these stories amusingly quaint.

They hold almost nothing of sex, for instance. In only one of them, "Letter to a Priest," is so much as a blow struck — and that in a moment of delusion in which violence serves to create the dramatic dilemma rather than to solve it. The only cuss words are an occasional "bloody" or "damn."

There is no longer any periodical market for such stories. Those who wrote them are gone on to other fields now or left to practice their vice in the obscurity of the private indulgence of an inexplicable compulsion to write, untroubled by the demands of editors or the strictures of markets which no longer exist. The only possibility of publication lies in the hands of perceptive publishers who may find and gather them together in collections such as this one.

Oddly, this enforced isolation can lead to higher achievement in the ways of creativity. Confined only by the limits of their own skills and the fences of their own imaginations, writers are left free to sail whole new courses into unexplored seas. This not only can result in a greater beauty of writing and more inventive stories, it is also a lot more fun for the writer.

In the present collection, for instance, some of the most evocative stories, "The *Caleuche,*" "The Slop Chest," "The Homeward Bounder," were written with no expectation at all of magazine publication or television production. Their former markets no longer existed. The choices of voices and scene, of tone and tempo, could all be made with no thought of whether an editor might like them or not, or if readers and viewers would spurn them for some perceived lack or excess. In a perfect world, writers might well settle for this comfortable state of affairs.

Unfortunately, the world is not perfect and this sublime freedom to create is wedded to a not-so-sublime absence of money, something individual writers may or may not be able to stand with much aplomb. The ego-stroking stimulation felt when one's work is read and appreciated is lacking, as well. Only the most determined, or deluded, of writers will persist in the absence of readers. The quantity of work produced is bound to be diminished.

None of this is meant to be a criticism of current popular entertainment writing. Tastes change. It is futile to complain of what passes for entertainment writing now. It is also arrogant in its implication that what earlier generations liked is somehow superior to what is enjoyed today. But it can hardly be questioned that modern popular writing is different from that represented in this collection of stories.

Still, not all of earlier generations are gone. Some continue to live who find in fluid and graceful writing some satisfaction and who can read into the tone and tempo of words more of beauty and meaning than is contained in the stories themselves. The rhythm and placement of words can add flesh and depth to scene and character in ways sometimes hard to define, but which are real and gratifying to writer and perceiving reader alike.

Anyone can tell what happens in a story. It is the way of the telling which separates out the writer from the reporter. The untutored voices of the narrator in "The Slop Chest" or of Paddy O'Rourke in "The Coming of the Cat" are quite different from the urbane speech of the educated Royal Naval officer in "To Show the Flag," but, in each instance, idiom and inflection are used for very much the same purpose of establishing time, scene and character, utterly different though these three specific examples may be. The Chilean priest in "The *Caleuche*" is made to speak with faint over-tones of both Spanish and biblical coloring for similar pur-poses.

Whether all this works, of course, depends upon the reader. Writers can never know with much certainty if they have succeeded or not — other than for the evidence of checks in the mail — they can be sure only of what they have <u>tried</u> to do.

In this case, these stories were written, over a period of many years, for the purpose of entertaining readers. At the same time, they were meant to show something of the beauty and mystery of the sea, even for those who know it well, and of the marks the sea life leaves on those who live it.

That which is gone is often best left gone. If there is a pity in the passage of popular sea fiction, it is in the fact that so many are unaware of the lack at all.

Floyd Beaver
Mill Valley, California

BREAKING SEAS

T he winter of 1861 was one which sailors off the California coast were a long time in forgetting. For weeks on end, gale followed gale until the Pacific itself grew tired of its torment and tossed in enormous confused seas which made survival alone goal enough for any vessel caught off that coast. And it was that winter, through one of those gales, that schooner captain Johnny West sailed his ship for the Golden Gate.

He didn't have time to lie off and wait for the storm to abate for, below, in the big comfortable berth in his own cabin, a woman lay sick to the point of dying.

So, with reefed staysail and double-reefed fore and main, Johnny West drove his three-masted schooner *Islander* to the outer limits of wood, cordage, and canvas. Sometimes, when the schooner was swept by great smothering

1

masses of broken water, he wasn't sure he hadn't driven her beyond those limits.

It had been three days since he had snatched a tentative sun line. Four days since his last honest three-star fix. For forty-eight hours this quartering southwest wind had been skewing the ship about so as to make steering a true course all but impossible.

The Gulf of the Farallons is a chancy place to make a landfall, even in conditions far less malignant than those facing Johnny West that tumultuous day. From Point Reyes on the north to Montara on the south, the cruel coast offers nothing but lee shores with the rocky fangs of the Farallon Islands themselves stuck right in the middle of it.

Still, on her bunk below, Sally West lay sick and Johnny meant to bring her to help. True, there would be little help for Sally, or for anyone else on board, if he drove the ship on the shore which lurked unseen somewhere before them. That way lay death itself. But that way, too, lay at least a chance of saving Sally.

His tired mind recognized the irony of such an ending as this for what had begun as little more than a pleasure run to the Pacific Islands in his father's schooner, with his younger brother, David, and David's wife, Sally, along as a celebration of their recent marriage. Johnny's mouth twisted in a wry grin at the thought of that. Lovely Sally who, had things gone differently, might have been his own wife.

They planned to do a bit of trading — copra, mother-of-pearl, some raffia work — just enough to justify the voyage, they thought. And they did that, and a bit more, to tell the truth. The voyage stood, in fact, to make a good deal of money; but the main purpose was to show David and Sally the islands.

Neither of them had ever been to sea. David was a mathematics teacher in a San Francisco school and Sally a New Yorker but recently come to California. Although timid and somewhat apprehensive at first, they had come to love the sea and found the islands fascinating.

Sally, especially, was caught up in the wonder of the whole thing and looked at Johnny as he went about his duties on board with a rapt awe which brought a lump to his throat when he saw it. Johnny loved Sally from the first moment he saw her dark hair blowing in the wind, but unlike Johnny, David was home all the time. He didn't disappear for weeks and months on end. Johnny came home from a voyage to find them married.

For a time Johnny reacted with a cold sense of betrayal, but he was honest enough to admit that that was not fair of him. He had never said anything of his feelings to Sally, content to enjoy their time together when he was home. There was never anything formal between them. Sally didn't owe him anything. Besides, the life of a sailor's wife was a hard life, and Johnny could not bring himself to think of leaving the sea.

David, though young, was solid, with a good future ahead of him. He would be able to give Sally things Johnny could never give her. Sally would at least be in the family. He could love her that way, he told himself, and see her from time to time.

Anyway, the voyage had been a great success. Idyllic tropical nights, bright tradewind days, and exotic runs ashore on islands whose peoples remembered Johnny and his father from earlier calls and all but bankrupted themselves in entertaining the young people. It had been one long picnic — until an island fever struck down old Captain West in one horrible night of suffering, leaving Johnny master of the *Islander* and David and Sally shocked into a stunned grief.

Even so, death itself is accepted in time and the homeward passage became as pleasant as might be until Sally, too, was struck down by some lingering island sickness for which they could find no remedy in the schooner's limited medicine chest.

Then, as they came upon California's coast that storm-wracked winter, racing for the help of San Francisco's doctors, the weather and the sea itself seemed to join in a malevolent union to keep Sally in her terrible peril. Johnny missed the steady strength of his father as he never missed it before. It was all on his shoulders and he was not nearly so confident as he tried to appear.

Johnny felt rather than saw the presence of David at his side. "Where are they? Where are the Farallons?" David shouted over the screaming wind.

Twenty-eight hours and more, Johnny West had stood the deck without leaving. Hours in which rain and spray soaked through to his skin, in which wind flayed his face, and noise had rasped his nerves raw. Fatigue and hurt and a growing doubt of himself and his ship dulled his mind.

"How in the hell do I know," Johnny lashed out at his brother. "It's been three days since I've seen the horizon, let alone . . ."

David recoiled from his brother. He was young. He wasn't a sailor. He had no business being out there, Johnny thought. He was a teacher of mathematics, for God's sake. He ought to be back in his bloody schoolroom. He and his sick wife, too. Without them, Johnny could snug down and ride out the storm well offshore. He could take his time and bring his ship home safe.

Johnny saw the hurt in his brother's face, and he reached out to grip David's arm in contrition. "Sorry, Davy," he shouted over the wind's roar. "How's Sally?"

David shook his head without speaking and looked away.

It was a southwest wind they ran before, and the seas marched from that quarter. But there were cross motions, too, and, if Johnny were right, those cross motions were reflections off Point Reyes. He had seen them before

4

in lesser storms. If so, they were already within the arms of the Gulf. That is what his reckoning told him. The confused seas were further evidence.

If he were right, he would know within the hour if it would be the Farallon Islands he fetched, with a chance of running for the Gate, or if it would be the vicious lee shore which curved for forty miles to north and south, and from which a sailing vessel stood little chance of clawing off in such weather.

"We will make it, won't we, Johnny?" David said then.

"It's chancy, Davy. It's chancy," Johnny said without taking his eyes from the white and gray-black nothingness which churned ahead of them. "We'll know shortly."

David tried to smile. "It will have to be shortly, Johnny," he said. "For Sally, it will have to be shortly."

"You better lay below, Davy," Johnny said then. "No sense in you getting wet, too. Stay with Sally. It's going to be rough. She'll need you."

As his brother left the storm-swept deck, Johnny West called for his mate. Even under those conditions, he kept to the etiquette of the sea, more probably for his own reassurance than out of any sense of propriety. "Mister Carver"

It seemed incredible that any human voice could be heard above the storm, but Carver appeared, as though by magic, at Johnny's side. Blurred, wet-shining figure that he was, Tom Carver was a seaman. He knew what was faced. He knew what must be done. Johnny West, young captain that he was, felt a lessening of his own burden in the mere presence of Tom Carver.

"We're coming up on the Farallons," Johnny screamed over the noise of wind and storm sea. He held his voice firm and commanding, admitting nothing of the doubt which chilled his own insides at the thought of what would happen if he should be wrong.

"Best rouse out the watch below, Tom," Johnny said. It was a small ship, too small for continued formality. They were friends as much as master and mate. "Once we make our landfall, we'll have to round up smartly. I'd be obliged if you'd take the main. Get Carl Austen for the fore. We can't let the sails flog in this wind. We'll have to sheet in fast. All right. Get the men up."

Carver hesitated. He knew about Sally West lying sick below. "Johnny," Carver said, "you're not thinking of making for the Gate are you?"

"Why, Tom?"

"Meaning no disrespect, Johnny, but I know about your brother's missus down below. I know how bad you want to get to Frisco."

"So?"

"Johnny, I been over the Frisco bar. Many's the time." Tom Carver motioned with his head at the seas tearing past. "Seas like them'll be breaking over the bar. And over this deck, too, if I'm not mistaken."

"The *Islander*'s been pooped before, Tom."

"Not on the Frisco bar, she ain't. Not with less'n eight miles sea room and a lee shore. Not . . ."

"That's enough," Johnny snapped. "Nobody's said anything about going on in. There's a landfall to be made first. Now, get forward and rouse out the men."

As he watched the huge moving masses of water hurling themselves about his ship, Johnny knew the Mate was right. Such seas <u>would</u> be breaking on the bar. Especially so should the tide be ebbing. On a flood maybe it could be done. But 1861 was before a ship's master could know in advance what the tide at a strange port was up to.

Still, there was Sally, lying sick below. Johnny cursed to himself. His only comfort was the feel of the ship in his hands, the solid sight of her in his eyes. Like a great, living body she was, driving through the crashing waters as though with a life and a will of her own. And an intelligence, too, to know what her captain expected and must demand of her. Good ship, the *Islander*. Johnny felt a pride in being her master. The pride helped. It made him feel better.

Then, even as his spirits lifted with thoughts of his ship, he saw the South Farallons, not a quarter-mile off the port bow. And after two whole days running before a quartering gale. Four days without a sight. Johnny felt the warmth of professional satisfaction. By God, he'd done it. No mistaking that island, coming and going as it was through the storm murk. There it was.

Johnny was honest enough, even then, to realize that it was, in truth, literally "by God" that he had made landfall on the islands rather than on the waiting lee shores lost somewhere in the storm wrack ahead. Either that or dumb sailor luck. In any case the result was the same, and there was work to be done.

The schooner was on a broad starboard reach, near a run, with main and fore booms well out to port. The mizzen boom was secured inboard, its tightly-furled sail under double gaskets. Both jibs were furled as well, and the forestaysail reefed. Even so the seas threatened to board.

Mister Carver ran aft then, his shouts half lost in the wind noise. "The Farallons." His voice sounded cracked and twisted, "Yonder, Captain." He flung an arm to port where the rocky island already had disappeared.

But Johnny had sliced down a bearing off the steering compass. He knew where the island was then. He could feel it, too, in the tiny lee it made in the sea.

"Stand by the foresail, Tom!" he shouted.

"If we try to run the bar in these seas, we'll . . ."

"Mister Carver! Stand by to take in the fore. I'm going to try to hold her here in the lee 'til it lets up."

Openly relieved, the mate returned to his station by the foremast and signalled he was ready, his sodden sailors at the sheets and halyards, all staring aft at Johnny with varying shades of fear in their eyes. Few had seen anything like this storm.

Johnny himself spun the wheel and the *Islander* came up into the wind with a great thundering clatter of wood and canvas and water. She shivered as though in animal terror and staggered drunkenly as the seas took her on the bows.

Fore throat and peak halyards were let run on Johnny's signal. The heavy fore gaff dropped, pressing its sodden canvas down into the lazy jacks. But Johnny could not hold her into the wind. She fell off on the port tack and the hands wrestled desperately to smother the sail.

Johnny let her run for a time to gain steerageway. "Standby main and staysail sheets," he screamed over the noise of the storm. Then he brought the ship again into the wind. "Sheet home." he shouted. "Close haul."

Men ran off with the two sheets. Double-reefed main and reefed staysail snugged in so that when the ship again paid off she was close-hauled and heeled well over, forming with her high weather bulwarks a kind of lee in which the lowered foresail was, at last secured.

After what seemed a very long time, the *Islander* rode more easily, jogging into and over the great seas which were then taking her on the starboard bow. She was virtually hove-to but being driven, Johnny knew, steadily to leeward. It would not be easy to hold her in the lee of the small islands, but the life of the ship depended upon his doing so. Were they to be caught again in the full force of the seas, they would inevitably be driven over the breaking bar.

Lying to was a surrender, Johnny knew, but a surrender for which he could think of no alternative. Driving the ship under would not help Sally or anyone else.

Once all was secure forward, Mister Carver came aft. "She'll hold like this, Johnny," he said. He was breathing hard from the work just past. "And, when it comes on to lay a bit, we can . . ."

"It's all right, Tom," Johnny said. Both men knew they were putting right what had happened between them. It takes a good mate to set his captain right. And a smart one. Johnny knew that.

"There's a log to be seen to, Tom," Johnny said then. "Put a good man on the wheel, if you please. Hold her in the lee, best you can. Keep the islands in hand, you understand? We have to keep the islands in hand."

Johnny paused at the foot of the companionway ladder, leaning for a time against the lee bulkhead. The warmth of below decks acted as a drug in him, making him feel suddenly faint. The roar of wind and sea seemed something far off. It would be easy simply to . . . But he wrenched himself suddenly erect as though ashamed for being tired after no more than twenty-eight hours on deck. He pushed open the door of his cabin.

David West straightened beside the broad double berth on the starboard side of the cabin. There was fear in his face. Not for himself, but for his wife. He looked at Johnny fiercely, as though he might cry out. But he didn't.

Johnny, bulking huge in his wet sea clothes, a puddle of water staining the flowered carpet under his boots, his face wet and red with wind and water, nodded toward the bunk. "How is she?"

"No better," David said. His voice all but broke. "You've changed course, Johnny. We've slowed down. What happened?"

Johnny did not answer. He brushed past his brother and stood looking down at his sister-in-law.

"Hello, Johnny," Sally West said weakly. She tried to smile. "You look tired, Johnny."

Johnny's red face softened. He brushed back a strand of hair caught in the sweated wetness of her forehead.

"We've raised the Farallons, Sally," he said gently. "We're lying off. As soon as the wind . . ."

"The Farallons," David cried. "The Farallons. That means we're only twenty-five miles from the Gate. Twenty-five miles from home! You hear that, Sally? Twenty-five miles! Three or four hours and . . ."

"Shut up, David," Johnny cried, his face twisted with torment. In the shocked silence which followed his outburst, he went on. "The bar is breaking, Sally. We can't go in. I don't know when we can. It depends on . . ."

David West stood as though physically stricken. "She's sick, Johnny," he said. "Sally's sick, and we're twenty-five miles from home, and you say . . ."

"We're not going to help Sally by driving the ship under, David," Johnny said.

David said nothing, but the expression in his face stopped Johnny. "She'll die, Johnny," he breathed at last. "She'll die."

Johnny and David stood then for a time during which neither spoke and only pain passed between them. "I'm going to get some coffee," Johnny said then and without looking at either David or Sally, he went into the schooner's tiny saloon and closed the door behind him.

The coal stove there and the dryness and the warm glow of varnished wood were all a comfort to him. The sounds of the storm seemed far away. Even the clash of water against the ship's sides was muted. But any comfort he found was a comfort for his body alone. There was no comfort for his spirit.

"Here, Captain. Get a little of this down," Spook Avery, the schooner's combined cook and steward, handed Johnny a thick mug of something steaming. "Make you feel better."

Sensing his captain's mood, Spook went back into the little pantry off the saloon. "Anything you want, I'll be right in here."

For a time, Johnny hunched over the saloon table, his hands wrapped around his hot mug as though to squeeze from it the warmth it held and to take the heat into his bones. There was only the dull crash of the sea against the ship's thick wooden sides, and the complaining of timbers and fastenings. And, from time to time, the shifting of the deck as the ship again was brought about to hang in the tenuous lee of the islands.

The door to the big cabin opened then and David came out. He sat down across from Johnny. "I, I'm sorry, Johnny," he said. "I had no right. I . . ."

"It's all right, David," Johnny said.

"No. I shouldn't have said what I did. You've done everything anyone could have done. I know that."

The cook returned then and placed a bowl of stew before Johnny.

Johnny began to eat without appetite. He ate as a steamer takes on fuel.

"Johnny, is there anything, anything at all we can do?" David said. Panic showed again just below the surface of his young voice.

Johnny continued eating, but a new purpose seemed to be growing in his face. "I've been thinking, David," he said. "Remember how you used to play around with measuring the tides in the Bay? How I used to take you around in my boat and you would take measurements at different times and places, Remember that?"

"With old Crazy Zack Miller? The one that was going to make up what he called a tide book, so sailors could tell the tides for any day or time? I remember that."

"You remember how, on an ebb, the water'd get rough? And, on a flood, it'd flatten right out? Especially in the Gate. You remember that?"

"Yes." David was still puzzled.

"I've been thinking, David. If we knew what the tide was doing over the bar right now . . . If we knew, for instance, when maximum flood hit the bar, we might . . ."

David's face lit with comprehension. "Of course! On a good flood, it would make all the difference in the world."

"Yes. Yes, it would," Johnny said carefully. "It would. If we knew when it would be. But we'd have to <u>know</u>, David. I can't run the ship in there and look first. We'd never be able to work clear again. You understand that? Without <u>knowing</u>, I'd be guessing. I can't do that, David. You understand that?"

David did not reply at once. His own face was busy with purpose. "Suppose, Johnny, suppose I could tell you when it will be maximum flood on the bar? Would you go in if I could tell you that?"

Johnny hesitated. "We've been out three months. Almost four. How are you going to know what the tide's doing now?"

"Johnny, if I know what the tide's doing at any one time, I can tell you what it's doing at any other time. I can, Johnny. I swear it."

"But we don't know what the tide was doing at any one time, David. It's been more than three months . . ."

David's tired face burned with an eager new hope. "When we sailed from San Francisco, we sailed on an ebb, didn't we? You logged the time, didn't you?"

Johnny rose and fetched the ship's log from his desk. He thumbed through the pages. "Here. Here it is. Slack water at eleven-ten. Underway eleven-thirty on the ebb."

David snatched up paper and pencils from Johnny's desk. "Eleven-ten," he muttered, half to himself. "That was daytime. What was the date?"

"September seventeen."

David noted that, too, and dashed back into the cabin where Sally lay. Feverishly, he tore an oilskinned packet of books from its place under the berth. Within minutes, he had the saloon table heaped high with books and papers which persisted in sliding off with the schooner's motion so that he had constantly to retrieve them.

"You're sure you know what you're doing?" Johnny asked.

David waved him to silence without looking up from his calculations. "This is going to take some time. Leave me alone."

"You know what will happen if you are wrong, David?" Johnny said then. "You know what will happen to Sally?"

David did look up then. His face was sober. "Yes, Johnny," he said. "I know what will happen if I'm wrong."

Johnny left his brother then and returned on deck.

There had been no slackening in either wind or sea. The mate, Carver, stolid and taciturn as ever, had the wheel himself, easing the ship as much as possible. He pointed without speaking, and Johnny could see a whitish blur of rocks to windward. "Farallons," Carver said. "Time to bring her over again."

Johnny took the wheel. "Best get below, Tom," he said. "See the hands get something hot. Yourself as well." With sail shortened as it was and all sheets self-tending, Johnny could handle the schooner alone. He felt a great need to do so.

Again and again, he brought her into the wind and onto the other tack. He lost track of how many times. The lee of islands as small as the Farallons is small, at best. From the wind, there was virtually no relief but the islands did break the racing seas and made for the schooner a slight protection. Hanging on shortened sail as she was, the *Islander* made way enough only to hold steerageway. Even so, she passed through the relatively sheltered waters quickly and had to be brought about.

Twice, Carver moved close to relieve him but Johnny waved him away. Some of the older hands came, too, to

13

help but Johnny would wave them away, as well. And they, in turn, seemed to sense Johnny's feeling, leaving him to his lonely fight, contenting themselves with huddling in whatever shelter they could find so as to be near at hand in case of need.

How long this went on Johnny never after knew. He knew that night came and he had to hold his place under the islands from the feel of the sea itself. All was black, save for the ghost white of sea foam and blown spray. He was aware of Mister Carver approaching once more with an offer to help but before Johnny could reply, David burst from the companionway hatch, a sheet of instantly wet paper in his hand.

"I got it, Johnny!" he shouted. He had not bothered with either hat or coat, and was instantly soaked. The paper went limp and as he sought to hold it in the binnacle glow for Johnny to see, a gust of wind ripped it from his hands. It was gone in the wild night.

"Never mind!" David cried. "It's perfect, Johnny. We're in the second hour of the flood. At the Gate. That means maximum flood in about an hour and a half. About four hours until it turns."

Johnny said nothing. Mister Carver was openly puzzled. He was alarmed, as well.

"Johnny! Listen to me," David shouted. "We're twenty five miles from the Gate. With a wind like this, we can make it in a couple of hours. Even shortened down the way we are. Maybe an hour to the bar. Close to maximum flood. That's what you said you wanted, Johnny. That's what you said."

"What is this, Johnny?" Mister Carver said. "What's going on? You said we wouldn't be going in 'til the wind lays."

"It's the tide, Tom," Johnny said. "Davy has calculated the tide. It's flooding now. If it is, we might make it."

"You said if the tide was flooding we could make it, Johnny," David said. "And it's flooding. It's flooding right now."

"I said if the tide was flooding we _might_ make it. There's a difference, David."

"Not to Sally, there isn't," David said. "She's unconscious. She doesn't have much more time, Johnny."

But Sally West was not the only one on the schooner. There were nine men, as well. Johnny did not count himself. They had to be thought of, too. Still, if the tide were flooding . . .

"Johnny, you said . . ."

"I know what I said, Tom," Johnny said. "The tide's flooding. We can make it. Call the hands, Tom. We're going to run for the Gate."

"But, Johnny . . ."

"There's a lady down below, Tom, who is near to dying. I mean to save her, if I can."

"You'll not be saving her by losing your ship. Have you thought on that?"

"I've thought on it. Now, if you'll be so good, call the hands and stand by to make sail."

After but a moment more of hesitation, Carver moved off to call the hands and Johnny and David were left alone on the tilted deck. "You'd better get below, David," Johnny said. "Get into some dry clothes. Do what you can for Sally. I'll be busy from now on."

Carver and the schooner's oilskinned crew came then before their captain. "Listen up," Johnny cried. "The tide is flooding over the bar. It will be near maximum flood by the time we get there. That will lay down some of the sea. It will be rough. But, under the circumstances, I think we can make it. I wanted you to know what we're getting into."

"But, Captain," Erling Carlson, the schooner's boatswain, called. "Seas the like of these'll be breaking on the bar, flood tide or no flood tide."

"But not so bad. Not so bad," Johnny said.

"Bad enough," Carlson insisted. "We'll broach, Captain. We'll be swept clean and . . ."

"We won't broach, Erling," Johnny said. "Not if we carry enough sail to keep her ahead of the seas. And we'll not be swept. Not if we drive her fast enough."

"Captain, I've seen that bar break," Carlson persisted. They ain't a ship been built that can . . ."

"If you've been on the bar you know how a flood settles it down."

"I know no such thing, Captain. And, meaning no disrespect, I don't know how you know what the tide's doing over the bar now. It's been three months since we left here. Who's to say what the tides . . . ?"

Johnny talked to all of them then. "As you know, my brother's a mathematician. His hobby is the study of tides. I used to help him when we were boys. He has calculated the time of maximum flood. It is time we move, or we'll miss it." And, pressing on, he gave his orders, the orders which would mean a chance of life for Sally West — or death for them all.

"I want the fore set again, Tom. Single-reefed. And a reef out of the main. We'll want all the speed we can get to stay ahead of the seas much as we can."

"We'll fill away on the starboard tack. And I'll want the fore over on the starboard side, main to port. Once we're squared away, take in the fore staysail, lay aft and take shelter under the lee of the after house. Do you have that clear in your minds? We cannot afford delay or confusion."

Mister Carver made no show of hesitation in front of the hands but Johnny knew he was still doubtful. Carver hustled the men forward, though they, too, were dubious.

16

Johnny put all that out of his mind. Once committed, none of them would have any choice in the matter. They would cross the bar or they would die. All of them. But Johnny would not let himself think of that, either.

"Ready for'rd." Carver's drawn-out halloo sounded ghostlike in the rushing roar of the gale, but Johnny heard it.

"Ready on the main." Carlson's voice was stronger for it was closer.

"Stand by throat and peak halyards." Johnny cried over the storm's bellowing, peering through the wrack to see that the hands heard. On their signaled acknowledgment, he brought the big schooner into the wind with a violent clattering of sails and gear.

Without further orders, the single-reefed fore went up. The second reef in the main was thrown clear, and that big sail, too, rose, flogging and flailing about until the ship fell off on the starboard tack, staggering drunkenly under the hammering of the gale in her suddenly enlarged canvas. She could not have stood much more and lived. And, while all this was going on, the fore staysail came down and was secured with double gaskets.

Johnny eyed the barely-seen islands to port and bent over the big brass binnacle to fix in his mind the compass course to be sailed for the invisible Golden Gate somewhere off to the northeast. Content, he straightened. "Stand by to gybe foresail," he shouted. He felt in himself a tightening of muscles. Gybing a sail in a gale of wind is not lightly done. The shock has been known to rip out chain plates and shatter masts. But, in Johnny's mind, he must gybe either fore or main and the fore was best done for it could be handled in some part in the lee of the main.

To run for the Gate with both booms to one side would be to invite an accidental gybe, with virtually certain disaster to follow. At best, such a set of the sails would make steering a sure course difficult to the point of impos-

sibility. Wing-and-wing, setting of fore and main to opposite sides of the ship would give Johnny some measure of
balanced force, which should, in turn, make the schooner
more manageable in the rough following seas then prevail-
ing.

"Lively now," Johnny shouted. "Keep the slack out
of the sheet." He put his helm up, bringing the schooner's
stern into the wind, but being almost delicately careful in
order that the main not gybe as well.

The main sheet was let run. And, blanketed by the
main as Johnny put the ship before the wind, the fore came
in, hanging all but limp for a moment before the wind
caught the peak of the gaff. Viciously, the spar whipped
over. The sail itself followed, coming up with a shock
which shivered the ship to her keel. The boom followed
then, snubbed so gently that the gybe was completed far
more comfortably than Johnny had dared hope.

Mister Carver and Carlson may have gone into the
evolution reluctantly, but they were seamen. Johnny blessed
them under his breath. Given such men, he might still
make the Gate.

The great seas, right astern then, rose dismayingly
high behind the *Islander*. Johnny could hear the tumbling
rush of their crests. He worked desperately to anticipate the
yawing thrust of them under the schooner's stern.

But, as the fore came to draw, the schooner surged
forward. Her rudder took a firmer bite of the water and she
stood up straighter. Her speed became more that of the
seas themselves, and she seemed more content with her
course. The relative speed of the wind dropped as the ship
sped before it. If the rigging held, they might make it —
to the bar, anyway.

"Tom. Erling." Johnny shouted to the men busy about
the two forward masts, securing halyards and making all
fast. "Get the hands aft. Get them under cover."

Johnny kept his eyes fixed on the two great straining sails, alert to catch the first hinted flutter of leach or lift of boom. All else was forgotten in his terrible concentration upon those two vital telltales of disaster.

"Hands under cover, Captain," Tom Carver reported. He stood next to Johnny, ready to lend a hand should his help be needed.

"Cut away the boat, Tom," Johnny ordered then. The ship's boat hung in wooden davits off the stern. Should they be swept, Johnny had no wish to have the heavy lap-strake craft crushing him against the wheel.

"And get some canvas, Tom," Johnny added. "Heavy canvas. Rig it aft of the mizzen sheets. Lead out the ends to the after corners of the house." With the mizzen sheets serving as a strongback, such a rig would break the force of boarding seas better than a solid structure would do. It would give at least some protection for him at the wheel.

After that, there was little else to do, except to wait for the bar. Torments of white water frothed under and over the schooner's bows as she dug into the back sides of the seas. She sagged back against the drive of her sails as each sea slipped from under her, causing her to reel and sink sickeningly before the next sea lifted her and drove her on in a wild, terrifying careening down the foreslope of a foam-streaked mountain of rushing water.

The bar could not be far away. The seas seemed shorter, steeper, already to have lost the longer and more regular rhythms of the open ocean. The crests of tumbling white and black waters came ever closer to the *Islander*'s fleeing stern.

Then, there it was. Stretching for as far as Johnny could see to either right or left, a great gray-streaked wall of water raced before his ship. It was moving away from them and Johnny realized it was the after slope of a breaking sea. Such a breaking sea as he had never seen before.

The wall of water seemed to stay before them for a long time. Johnny felt a panicky urge to spin the wheel, to turn away and to flee. He wanted to order the sheets hauled in to slow the schooner and to keep her from riding up on that monstrous wave. But he knew none of those things could be done. To do them would be to kill them all.

And, slowly it seemed, the schooner did ride up on the hissing giant. Her jib boom pointed to the unseen sky and wavered there as she faltered and slumped back against the mighty push of her sails.

Then, without ever having climbed the great sea, the schooner seemed to slow, the wave to melt from under her and Johnny became aware of a new and still more terrifying sound behind him. It was as though a waterfall had suddenly been loosed. He did not dare look back. Chillingly, he felt a definite lessening in the force of the wind, a lessening which could come only from their being in the lee of a huge sea. Johnny waited for the blow to fall.

But, again, the schooner rose. With a speed which caused Johnny's knees to buckle slightly, her stern shot up. And, although white water boiled to the level of the bulwarks themselves, none boarded in any amount. The schooner dashed forward as though in terror before the thing which had all but engulfed her.

As the collapsing, wind-tousled crest of the sea passed, the schooner slumped again into the tangled waters of its back side. Even with the full force of the gale in her sails, she staggered and seemed to hang without motion. Until, again, there came that great clashing of waters from astern.

The *Islander* lurched and surged ahead. But not quickly enough. Johnny felt the falling masses of water before they actually hit him. There was a rushing of air before them. And a shutting off of the storm wind. He fought to hold the schooner steady so that she might take the blow fairly.

Only the stout canvas, rigged beforehand with the mizzen sheet as strongback, saved Johnny and Carver from being swept away. As it was, they were pressed to their knees and salt water smothered them for what seemed a long time in a great, roaring wet tumult.

When the sea at last was gone, the deck Johnny saw before him looked strange. The top of the after house was swept clean. Saloon smokepipe, skylight, fire buckets and life rings, all were gone. The deck itself was awash to the depth of a man's waist and tons of water sloshed heavily from one straining bulwark to the other, completely beyond the capacity of the spewing scuppers.

Twice more the seas swept the schooner. Burdened as she was with the weight of water on deck, she rose but slowly. And so deep were the troughs between seas that Johnny feared she would strike bottom. They must then have been on the bar itself. It was a time during which Johnny came close to despair, saved only by the terrible knowledge that he must hold the ship dead before the wind, else they all die.

In the end, the laboring vessel rode free, beyond the bar. As though spewed from a millrace, she straightened and shot forward into relatively smooth water. The great breaking seas through which they had passed lost their awful purpose and fell quickly into a confused chop through which the schooner burst like a terrified wild animal let free of danger.

Wings of white spray spread from under her bows, to be caught by the wind and hurled ahead of her in a swirling white mist which blotted out all sight of anything which might lie ahead. The sidelights shone red and green in the mist, lighting the still-streaming deck in an eerie glow.

Carlson and the other hands appeared from under the lee of the after house, moving wonderingly, as though puzzled at finding themselves still alive.

"There.   There," a man shouted, pointing to port. "Bonita! There's Point Bonita."

Johnny looked. He could see little more than vague black shapes through the rain and spray but he saw enough. It was indeed Point Bonita. They were inside Point Bonita, with Lime Point little more than a mile beyond, and the anchorage off Sausalito waiting for them but a mile or two beyond that.

Already, the great seas grew less in the lee of the point although the wind became fractious as they neared the Gate itself and Johnny was hard put to avoid gybing one sail or the other.

But the *Islander* moved steadily, as though conscious of having done something proud.

Within half an hour Johnny rounded up off the lights of Sausalito and let go the starboard anchor. Within minutes more they had bundled Sally in a great mound of blankets and lain her gently in the stern sheets of a shore boat which had answered their signal.

Johnny leaned on the bulwark and looked down at his brother's foreshortened figure in the boat. "The tide was flooding, wasn't it, Johnny?" David called from the boat.

"Yes. Yes, Davy, it was flooding," Johnny said. He did not mention that the *Islander* was swinging, settling to her anchor, her stern to the Gate, riding to the growing pull of a strong ebb. Tom Carver made as though to point this out, but Johnny stopped him with a hand on his arm. "Leave it be, Tom," Johnny said. "Leave it be. It's over now. Best get some rest, all of us."

THE SLOP CHEST

T he slop chest it is on a ship what provides a sailor with the little needs and comforts what come up during a passage. Tobacco, like, or new socks and drawers and such like. It's like a little store, is what it is, that the Old Man keeps for the hands, docking their pay for the things they buy on passage, so that when they come to signing off, many's the time they get a smart surprise at what they got coming.

At a time when masters in sail was paid as little as six pounds a month, I guess it ain't too surprising that some captains made a good thing out of the slop chest. It wasn't like they had no competition or nothing. They could bloody well charge what they wanted for their truck, and some of them did.

I mind one ship I was in one time with an Old Man that was worse than anything I ever seen in that line. I'd been with him for two or three voyages so I knowed what to expect, but it was rough enough on the new hands before it was over.

We was in an outport in the south of Australia at the time, loading bagged grain for the Channel for orders. Three-masted barque, the vessel was, and well enough found, though we was coming to the end of sail then and none of the ships was what could be called first rate. Not in the sense they was in the old days, anyways.

It was the time of the big pearl boom up around Darwin and we lost just about the whole bloody lot we had for a crew. There was just me and the cook and the boatswain and old Sails left. Even one of the apprentices took it in his head to try his luck in the pearl luggers.

The ship was loaded, and the Old Man was going bloody crackers with the shipping masters and all, trying to come up with a crew for the passage home. He even paid the fines for some that was in gaol but we was still short when it come on time to sail.

The lines was all singled up and the tug standing by when the sorriest excuse for a seaman I ever saw in my life come off in a hired boat. He hailed the Old Man and asked if a hand was needed. Well, I guess the Old Man had the fellow figured just about the way I did, but he wasn't in no position to be choosey, as the saying goes, so he had me help him up over the mizzen chains.

What with getting underway and all, there wasn't no time for discussion. The boatswain put him to work on various kinds of idiot work, coiling up lines and striking stores below and the like. But I did notice the fellow didn't have no kit at all, not a blessed thing. And I remember even then thinking the Old Man had got hisself a live one for the slop chest that time, for certain sure. I could see the old crock looking at the new hand like he was already counting up his take from slops.

Parish-rigged is what we called hands what come aboard like that. I didn't never know where the saying come from, but that's what we called them. And I hadn't never seen nobody that come aboard any more parish-rigged than that fellow was, and us heading for a winter passage of the Horn.

A man could easy die just of the cold and wet without he had the proper boots and oilskins. I'd seen men do it, sometimes even they <u>was</u> proper rigged. But I knowed this Old Man had stuff like that in slops, so I didn't give it no more thought at the time. We was busy getting underway, you see, and short handed at that.

Once we was clear, though, and the mates selected their watches, me and this character both wound up in the port watch.

I wasn't none too happy about that. You get a weak sister in a watch, all it means is more work for the others; and this fellow looked to be just about the weakest sister you ever seen in your life.

His name was Ian Dunne, I remember that. And that night, in our watch below, he told me he was from out Perth way and working his way back to Edinburgh where he was going to go to University. I'd already seen he talked real good, more like a gentleman than anything else; and his hands sure didn't look like he'd ever done a lick of work in his life.

Even his clothes, though they was old and pretty well worn out, was better than workingman's clothes. You could see that right off. But the ones he was standing in was the only ones he had to his name in the world. So I asked him how come he was shipping before the mast and not going passenger, like.

Well, it turned out he was married and had a baby. He left every penny he had to keep his family going until he could get his education and come back.

I didn't know how much of that I was ready to believe. Seemed to me like he could have took his family with him. Running off halfway around the world in them days was not something you done easy, like. There was a bloody good chance, for one thing, that he'd cop it off the Horn and never live to see Edinburgh, or his family neither.

But that was his pidgen. He was old enough to know what he wanted, and I guessed he'd settled it all with his wife before he left Perth. I helped him all I could and showed him how to do things and come in out of the rain and stuff like that.

It wasn't that he didn't try. He was willing enough. It was just that he didn't know a blessed thing about a ship. And sailors in them days was a rough lot for the most part. They didn't make things no easier for Dunne, what with ragging him and everything, but I come to like the little fellow pretty good. He was a bloody sight better than some of the others, and it wasn't long before he was holding up his end pretty good.

It wasn't long neither before him and the Old Man tangled.

It was over the slop chest, like I figured it would be. There was some things Ian just plain had to have. A knife, for one, and a change of clothes and blankets and such like.

Well, the Old Man had all that stuff. I never seen a ship with a bigger slop chest than that one. But I never seen one neither that charged more for it, and that's where Ian and the Old Man got into it. Ian figured the prices was too dear, by far. He had left all his money with his family, and he would need his pay for when he reached Scotland. He wasn't of a mind to give it to no greedy old bastard like the Old Man.

The Old Man, of course, saw it different, and I could see his hard eyes squinting even harder. He didn't say nothing, but you could see he was thinking.

Things wasn't too bad for the first couple of weeks or so. We was blessed with uncommon good weather across the Bight of Australia and over the top of Tasmania. Ian managed pretty good with the bare minimum of stuff he got out of slops, but we all knowed that kind of weather wasn't going to last, not in that part of the ocean, it wasn't.

But it did. It lasted a lot longer than we had any right to expect. It wasn't until we was well past New Zealand and running down our easting for the Horn that we got any kind of a dusting at all. And that wasn't bad. Not bad enough to make Ian nor any of the other new hands buy nothing much out of slops.

I used to see the Old Man watching Ian working about the decks in his by-then-frayed gentleman's clothes. The old pirate would look at him and then up to the bland sky which, by all rights, should have been a roaring gale. You could just see what he was thinking . . . God's weather was cheating him out of his slops profits.

And, sure enough, after a couple of weeks and it was beginning to look like the good weather would last forever, the Old Man started shaping his course farther south.

Normally, ships kept well to the north for most of their easting, shaping south only in time to clear the Horn. It kept them clear of the ice, for one thing, you see, and made for an all-around more comfortable ride. There wasn't no call to suffer more'n you had to. Them old ships was bad enough in good weather.

I think I knowed right off what was in the Old Man's mind. If he went south the weather, sooner or later, would turn cold and, if it turned cold enough, the hands would bloody well come to him for coats and boots and oilies. And beg to pay him his price, too.

Well, he was right in that, of course. A man gets cold enough, he ain't going to argue too much about price. A reasonable man ain't, anyway. But that ain't to say that Ian

Dunne was at all reasonable. Not when it come to money, he wasn't.

As we moved down to the south, the weather did turn cold, and with the usual wind and snow and the like you expect there. Day after day the howling westerlies blew, and snow drifted into odd corners about the deck, until the boarding seas washed it off. Things was not what you could call comfortable at all, and the others petitioned the Old Man to open up slops and lined up to pay his robber's prices for what they needed.

They all did, that is, except for Ian. That poor fellow went about his work with blue hands and a drop hanging from his nose, most times. He got some scrap canvas off of Sails and made hisself the most God-awful looking suit of foul weather clothes you ever saw in your life. He coated them with tallow he scrounged from the cook to keep out the water a bit, but the smell was bloody awful. And he wrapped canvas about his regular boots and tied it about his shins.

At first, the hands kind of admired Ian for what he was doing, I think. They all hated the Old Man's guts and they was ready to see something good in anyone that had the nerve to stand up to him. Some of them even slipped him bits and pieces of gear when they could, gloves and warm socks and things. They come to talk to him in the mess, too, and let on like he might be human after all.

Ian, for his part, he wouldn't take nothing big like seaboots or proper oilies or nothing. But little things he would. And he come to take part in talk with the hands, but he never said nothing bad about the Old Man or nothing. It was like he knew what the Old Man was doing and he wasn't blaming him or nothing. He just wasn't going to have nothing to do with it his own self.

But, I tell you this: I never heard talk in any ship in my life the like of what I heard from Ian them times. Seemed like they wasn't nothing in the world he didn't know. Especially about stars. That's what he was going to Edinburgh to study, it turns out.

There ain't nobody, I reckon, that gets more chance to see stars than sailors do. But I ain't never seen nobody, except for the officers that use them for navigation, that knows less about stars than sailors do.

Now, sailors don't normally take to being taught nothing. They seem, in my experience anyway, to kind of resent learning anything that don't have nothing to do with their work. But the way Ian talked about stars, them hands just set and looked up at him like pups at a dinner table.

Ian told us not just how to tell one star from another one and how to find them in the sky. He told us how far away they was and what they was made out of and everything. It was hard even for me, his best friend on board, to swallow everything he said but I reckon he knowed what he was talking about. He even tried a couple of times to explain to us how he knew all that stuff, but that was way over our heads and we just come to take him on faith.

I don't know about the others, but I come to look forward to those times in our watch below when Ian told us about the stars. Even old Sails and the boatswain come to drop around. And the second mate stopped by once in a while. Them was some of the best times I ever had at sea.

But Ian still wouldn't buy nothing from the Old Man's slops. And, by that time, we was in the Southern Ocean for fair. Sleet and freezing rain turned the rigging to black ice. It was all your life was worth to move out on the footropes, and Ian was doing it in them jury-rigged boots of his, his handmade foulies bagging and filling with wind like to blow him right off the yard.

The hands all knowed, of course, why we was so far south. They knowed the Old Man was trying to freeze Ian into buying stuff from slops. And they didn't like it none too much. They wasn't nothing they could do about the Old Man, but they was things they could do about Ian.

At first they tried to talk some sense into him, but that didn't work no better for them than it had for me. Then they even offered to take up a collection for him to use in buying enough to make the Old Man come north a bit. That didn't work neither because Ian said it was "a matter of principle" by that time. He wouldn't give the Old Man the satisfaction.

Well, I don't know nothing about that, but we was all getting bloody cold. The sailor's life ain't all that comfortable in the first place. It didn't make no sense at all to make it worse than it had to be. And, before long, the hands was taking it out on Ian. A bloody big Finn even knocked the little fellow about in the mess one night before we could stop him. And the others done little things to make his life miserable.

The funny part was the Old Man was just as stubborn as Ian was. And I don't think it was all on account of slops, neither. The two of them just plain didn't like each other. They had their horns locked, seemed like. Nothing was going to stop until one or the other of them broke.

Most ships even in them hard days let the watch on deck take shelter as best they could when they wasn't actually working the vessel. There was places where we could get out of the wind and still be ready to hand if we was needed. But the Old Man seen to it that our watch wasn't never not busy. He had us out in the worst of it and we knowed it was all because of Ian.

Most times, the Old Man had Ian in the eyes of the ship, keeping watch, though God knows they wasn't likely to be another ship in a thousand miles. Nobody else would be crazy enough to be that far south when they wasn't no call for it.

But Ian wouldn't bend. I used to have to help him into the fo'c'sle after his watch and bundle him in his berth, throwing some of my own blankets over him in trying to get him warmed up a bit before we had to go on watch again.

I used to fear he would come down with pneumonia, or something, but he was a tough little bugger.

You got to give the Old Man credit, though. He stayed on deck as long as Ian did. He was bundled up, of course, and he had a nice warm cabin for his time below; but he stood right out in the open on the break of the poop for every minute Ian was on deck.

It wasn't natural, in a way. It was like a weird duel of some kind. The old captain stood brace-legged on the poop, staring down at the little Aussie in his outlandish outfit of tallowed canvas. And the little Aussie stood and stared up at the Old Man. Sometimes they'd stand like that for minutes at a time, like they was daring each other, neither one moving except to sway with the wild moving of the ship. It was enough to make your skin crawl, sometimes.

But it was getting old for the rest of us. I got to thinking they was both crazy. I had got to liking Ian, but enough was enough. It was just bloody money, after all.

I don't know how much longer it would have gone on like that. The Old Man would probably have sailed us right up to the South Pole, I reckon. But, one black night, we got in the ice.

It was blowing a howler, like it usually was down there, and snow was gray pencil marks on the black slate of the night. It was the port watch on deck, and Ian was back out there on the main deck staring up at the Old Man. The rest of us was in the lee of the poop, but it was still bloody cold and wet.

We was so miserable, I guess, that none of us was keeping much of a watch.

I had just been called up to take my trick at the wheel when the second shoved me away and started spinning the wheel, like he meant business, yelling "Ice," as he done it.

I scrambled back on my feet and followed the second's scared look forward to where a bloody great gray cliff rose up, so high I couldn't see its top, and so wide I could see no end to it either way.

We was rushing down on it at speed and I couldn't see no way we was going to miss it. But, somehow, we did. Slowly, the bowsprit come to slide across the great mass of ice, and the ship heeled, sickening like, what with the force of wind in her sails, even though she was shortened down and all.

Someone on deck thought fast and threw off the lee braces, and the ship came up. We raced along the face of the ice, feeling its cold in the wind and thinking to feel, at any minute, her keel bite into one of them underwater ledges that icebergs have sometimes. The wind, of course, jumped up when we rounded from a dead run to reach. There was a terrible noise of sails and gear, but we was clear of the ice and sailing like a demon was after us.

All hands was on deck by that time, of course, and things was put right in a little while. The ice was some place astern by that time and we was still racing to the north. I was back at the wheel and just fixing to start breathing again.

That's when I noticed Ian and the Old Man. They was still standing where they was before the ruckus started. They hadn't moved a muscle, near as I could tell.

The other hands seen them, too, and they drew back from them like they was, all of a sudden, afraid. The two of them was left like they was, just staring at each other. Even the mates didn't come close to the Old Man. He had to raise his voice to order the second to put the ship back on her course.

The second didn't say nothing, but you could see he wasn't of no mind to do that. We had just escaped destruction by the tightest of margins. There wasn't no reason in the world to think we would be so lucky next time. But tradition at sea is a powerful force, and mutiny a scaring word.

"Your course, Mister Mate," the Old Man roared. "See to your course, sir."

"But, Captain . . ."

The Old Man then turned on the second such a baleful glare that the man cringed before it. He gave me the course to steer and saw to the trimming of the sails. And we tore off before the howling wind again, blind as some huge bat and racing, but scarcely in control, through black waters we knowed then to hold ice.

Both watches still was on deck following all the commotion, and despite the wind's roar, they heard enough to know what was going on. An ugly defiance took hold of them. Even the mates on the poop drew together and spoke to each other. And, still, the Old Man and Ian stood as they was before.

When, at last, the starboard watch was told off to lay below, they went sullenly and with many a look back at our crazy Old Man. It was one thing to get cold and wet, a man could get warm again. But ice was a different story. We bump a berg, and there wouldn't be any getting warm, not ever again.

Yet, there we was, tearing through the black water and not knowing from one minute to the next when another one of them big white buggers would loom up ahead of us, and us without room to turn, or nothing.

It's hard, times like that, to keep track of the time, but somehow the watch did end. Froze to the bone, I went to fetch Ian and get us below for what little comfort there was there before we would be back on deck again. This had become a habit with me, I guess, from when the Old Man had kept Ian in the eyes of the ship so much. Lots of times up there, a man might not even know when his watch was over.

This time, though, Ian was right there on the main deck, staring up at our crazy old captain. I took his arm and moved as though to lead him below, but he would not come. He shook off my hand and continued to stare at the Old Man.

Well, I had had just about a bellyful by that time. I was wet and cold and I didn't much have it in mind to stand there in the weather and argue with no crazy man like that. I give Ian a pretty good sense of what I thought about both him and the Old Man and went to get my head down.

It's hard now to remember just how bad them old fo'c'sles was. There wasn't never no heat in them and though we stuffed the hawseholes, water still got through and we was sometimes up to our ankles in cold seawater that sloshed back and forth hard enough to get our bedding wet. But at least we was out of the wind and, most times, we slept.

That time, though, I didn't. I kept thinking about Ian standing out there in the wet and the cold. One four-hour watch was bad enough. To stay out there for more than that just didn't make no sense at all. He'd brought it on hisself, of course, but he was still my friend.

I got up once and went to the fo'c'sle door. There wasn't no light but the weird greenish-blue glow of phosphorescence from broken water alongside. It lit the careening masts and rigging overhead but I had to wait for my eyes to adjust before I could see Ian. He was still standing where I had left him. And the Old Man was still at the break of the poop.

I kind of shuddered, and it was not all because of the cold, and went back to turn in for what was left of my watch below. I had the most awful feeling that something terrible was going to happen. I wasn't thinking about ice then, neither.

I never seen nothing before like what was going on aboard of us that night.

Anyways, Ian did spend the whole of that second four-hour watch out in the weather like that. And two more as well.

And, like I said before, the Old Man stayed right there with him. I reckon they was both out of their heads by that time. I seen the mates two or three times go to the Old Man and try to talk him into laying below, but he wouldn't do it. And, if the Old Man wouldn't quit, neither would Ian.

The steward then brought hot stuff to drink for the Old Man and things to eat. And I done the same for Ian. But they was both getting weak. Especially Ian. The Old Man had his heavy coat and good seaboots, while Ian didn't have nothing but his old tallow-daubed canvas stuff. But Ian was younger, so it was hard to tell which one was worse off.

I happened to have the watch below when it ended and didn't see it happen. But one of the starboard watch stuck his head in the door and yelled that the Old Man was down. I jumped up and ran out. We slept all standing then, so there wasn't no need to dress, or nothing.

The weather was just like it had been for days then, blowing like stink and cold as the hinges of hell. Both mates and the steward was bent over the Old Man's body on the poop, and I knowed from the minute they picked him up and carried him below that he was dead. You can tell when a man is dead, just from looking at him.

I turned then to Ian. He was still standing where he was when I last saw him, but he was staggering a good deal just to keep from falling, the way the ship was going. I don't think he even knowed the Old Man was down. I don't think he could see at all. His face was all white, and he looked kind of crazy.

Old Sails come up to us then, and together we carried Ian into the fo'c'sle. He was beyond walking by that time. We put him in his berth and piled blankets over him and tried to get him to drink something hot. His teeth was chattering so loud we could hear them, and his arms and legs shook like they was going to come loose from his body.

It wasn't no way easy, but after a while we did get Ian to warm up a little bit. They was even some color come back in his face, but he never did get to breathing just right. He never said nothing, neither, and about noon the next day he died.

Man and boy, I had been to sea more'n forty years when all that happened, but I never seen nothing else like it. And, lots of times since, I've wondered if there was aught to be learned from it at all.

Coal From Clydeside

C aptain Carl Mathison, gaunt and grimed by two unbroken days on the coal-blackened decks of the *Ailsa Craig*, leaned on the coaming of number three hatch and looked down. For a moment his eyes, narrowed against the glare of a flat tropical sea, could see nothing in the darkness below. He closed his eyes, letting himself rest, if only for the moment. He felt many times his age of twenty-seven years.

"They'll not be up to it much longer," Thompson, the vessel's saturnine first officer growled. He was sodden and blackened with coal dust, wet with his own sweat. He pulled a rag from about his head and wrung black water from it. "A man's not born to take heat like what's down there." Thompson, an older man, took little trouble to cover his impatience with captains given their commands long before their times.

Mathison did not answer. He opened his reddened eyes and looked again down into the hold where two cadaverous men stumbled about shovelling coal into canvas bags to be hoisted on deck by the old-fashioned steam-spewing winches. Seen through the heat, masts, kingposts, the old ship's rigging shimmered and wiggled weirdly. Mathison felt his own face tighten as he looked down. He moved back from the hatch. The men in the hold moved slowly, awkwardly, as though drugged by the thick, wet, coal-stinking heat which stood up from the open hatch like a solid thing capable of being touched.

Nor were the men on deck, the men who took the coal as it was hauled up from below and dumped it on deck, in much better shape. They had had their turns below, and they moved as men move who have lost conscious volition.

The decks all along and between the three forward hatches were stacked high with coal. Stacked so high that as the ship rolled sullenly to long ocean swells bits of coal tumbled over the bulwarks and splashed audibly in the still water alongside. Huge windsails sagged, useless, in the rigging.

"No more room on deck for coal anyways," Mister Thompson said. "No point in killing ourselves digging the stuff out if we got no place to put it."

"No place to put it, <u>sir</u>," Mathison said, stiffening.

Thompson's lip curled. "No place to put it, <u>sir</u>."

"If you have no place to put it, Mister Thompson," Mathison said, "be good enough to throw the bloody stuff over the side."

"Over the side?" Mister Thompson said unbelievingly. "All of it?"

"All of it," the young captain said.

"All of it?" Thompson repeated again. Then, suddenly comprehending, and becoming angered at comprehending, he stiffened. His bleared eyes burned in the shadow of his coal-dusted brows.

"All of it, ye say, Captain?" Thompson screeched, his voice becoming thick with the tones of his native Scotland. "All of it, ye say! And I'm supposing you think we can do that with shovels and our bare hands, I'm supposing?"

Mathison met the angry man's eyes squarely, trying to make allowances, trying to remember the man's condition. "You'll do it, Mister, or you'll burn. That's the choice you have. That's the only choice you have."

"Aw, no it ain't, <u>Sir</u>," Thompson said bitingly. "We can bloody well get on the wireless and take to the boats."

"The boats?" Mathison's tired brain tried to cope with this new task of arguing with a man whom he half suspected was right.

"Aye, the boats, Captain." Thompson swept an arm behind him. "Look at yon sea, man. Flat as the Clyde at Glasgow, it is. And, like as not, a dozen ships within a day's steaming of us. Aye, the boats, Captain. It's a fool's thing we're trying to do here, emptying out a vessel of this size with hand shovels. And her cooking her insides out with hot Clydeside coal."

Thompson paused and glanced back at the scarecrow figures of the men on deck who had stopped their work and stood watching and listening to this clash of their leaders.

"Aye, she'll blow, Captain. Long afore we can get the coal out of her. She will, and ye know it, Captain. Ye know it for a fact. Ye've heard about Clydeside coal."

Captain Mathison met Thompson's eyes again, measuring the man's remaining strength, sounding his desperation. Then he looked past Thompson to the sailors standing in silent but unmistakable support of him. He looked forward, too, to the other hatches whose crews had stopped work as well and who stood looking aft, waiting.

Mathison turned back to Thompson. "Turn the men to, Mister," he said. "I'll hear no more talk of boats."

The mate's middle-aged face twisted, much as a child's face might twist before it cries. "Aaaaaaaagh!" he screamed suddenly. Then, again, "Aaaaaagh!"

"Stop it!" Mathison shouted. "Stop that, Mister!"

And, touched by an iron in his young captain's voice, the mate did fall silent. He breathed deeply. His face still was twisted under its coating of coal dust, and his fists knotted hard

39

against his legs, but he didn't say anything more.

Mathison felt sympathy for the man. He was older. He must have been near the end of his tether, but so were they all. As master he must not soften. To do so would be to invite wholesale insurrection and the loss of his very first command.

"Listen to me," he shouted then, raising his voice to take in both Thompson and the work parties alongside the other hatches, as well. "Listen to me!

"I have just talked with the Chief. The engines are near ready to go again. It won't be much longer. Once we get way on, the windsails will cool down the holds. We can make it if we can but get way on the vessel again. You hear me there?"

Thompson did not speak. Nor did any of the others. They stood and stared their sullen disbelief at Mathison.

"I know you're tired," Mathison went on. "We're all tired. But — if we can but hold out a bit longer. A few more hours.

"We can make it, men. Every shovel we take out cools her just that much. Every shovel gives us a bit more time."

The captain paused then, letting his eyes run over the men, letting them feel the force of command he hoped still was his. "All right. Once more. Let's have a go at it. Men on deck, lay below for your trick. Men below, lay up on deck."

"You're lying, Captain," Thompson growled hoarsely, but in a tone that could not be heard by the others. Some residual of the officers' code remained in him. "But if she blows while we're still on board, it's the blood of us all that'll be on your head."

Mathison held down a sudden cold realization of the truth of the mate's words. But so long as there was a chance, a chance at all, that the vessel could be saved, he felt himself bound to try. "Thank you, Mister Mate," he said dryly.

"Aye," Thompson said then, his face hard against his young captain. "It'll be a fine feather in your bonnet if ye save her, but for the likes of us, Captain, it's our bloody asses in a sling, and nothing to show for it but sweat and the chance to be blown to Kingdom Come."

Mathison did not answer for a time. He let his eyes run along the deck where some men were laying below, and others heaving themselves on deck to take their turns there. "Keep the men at it, Mr. Thompson," he said as evenly as he could. "I'm laying aft to see how Mister Wharton-Taylor is getting on."

Coal had been piled even on the weather decks flanking the superstructure of the old ship, and Mathison slipped and stumbled his way aft. "How's it going, Mister?" he asked, once he reached the after deck.

Third Officer Terrence Wharton-Taylor, thin and youthful, started at the sound of his captain's voice. He straightened and half-lifted his hand in a vestigial salute. "Well enough, sir," he said, in a voice whose gentility was incongruous on the coal-piled after deck of the *Ailsa Craig*. "Well enough, considering, sir."

"Lads standing up to it all right, are they?"

Wharton-Taylor nodded toward the shade of an overhang at the after end of the deck above. "Harper's down," he said. "Heat exhaustion, most likely. Others about what's to be expected, sir. Under the circumstances."

Wharton-Taylor was young. His body could better take the heat and the work and the loss of sleep. And his mind, largely innocent of what a cargo of Clydeside coal, too long under hatches, could do to a vessel once spontaneous combustion started, was free of the leaden fear dragging down on the rest of them. He seemed damned-near cheerful, Mathison thought.

"That's good, Mister," Mathison said briskly. "Keep them at it. No need to tell you it's important. Get as much out of her as you can. Over the side with it when you run out of room on deck."

"Right-oh!" the younger man said. Then, turning back to his men: "Here, there! You, Younkman! Bear a hand, man. We don't have all day, now do we?"

Mathison smiled within himself. The boy was all right. He would do. Mathison turned then and pulled himself up the ladder to the next higher deck. Once out of sight of his laboring men, he allowed himself for a moment to let fatigue take over. He leaned against a bulkhead and closed his stinging eyes, figuratively beating at his brain for some way out.

It all wanted a word with the chief. Thompson and the men had knuckled under this time, and young Wharton-Taylor had his lot in charge, but it was not a condition likely to last.

The men were nearing their physical limits, there was no mistaking that. The heat alone had been enough to sap a strong man's strength, to say nothing of the brutal hard work and loss of sleep, and the knowing in each man's mind that some thousands of tons of good Clydeside coal was steadily growing hotter, was steadily growing closer to that point when it would ignite of its own will and blow them all from the face of the earth.

The captain walked to the forward end of the house and looked ahead over the black-heaped deck. The forecastle head, the masts and rigging wavered uncertainly in the heated air rising from the open hatches. The great canvas windsails, blackened with coal dust, slumped from their supporting lines as though discouraged by being useless in the windless calm which held the world. They looked like grotesque religious figures with arms outstretched in a futile kind of benediction.

The sea itself, beyond the ship, was that special blue white so often seen close under the Line when there is no breath of wind for days on end, when the sun burns from first dawn to night in a sky scorched clean of clouds. The only movement was that of a long, low, indolent swell out of the southeast. The swell lifted the drifting ship only to let her down again, and then moved on as though reluctant to stay in that dead ocean.

Funny, the way things turn out, Mathison thought to himself. A man wouldn't have picked this kind of thing to have happened. Not the night he joined the *Ailsa Craig*. That was in the Firth of Clyde, in the raw roads off Greenock. A cold

Scottish rain was skidding down forty knots of wind off the Western Ocean, and the old *Ailsa* glistened black in the rain wet.

Even then, in the blowing night, he could see his first command was not a thing of beauty. At least forty years old, she must have been. With most of her recent time in the eastern Mediterranean trade, her good Glasgow owners had not seen fit to convert her to oil, what with coal so easy to come by in her ports of call. But her working rigging looked sound enough and she rode the wild night in a good honest way. And she was his first command, there was that to be said for her.

Mathison, young and ambitious as he was, was honest enough to own to himself he would not even have had the *Ailsa*, poor old thing that she was, had not her former master gone sick and there was a paucity of men with papers ready to hand. The owners, though dubious about Mathison's age and lack of experience, were reluctant to hold up the ship to wait for a more qualified man. She already had been delayed for some weeks.

Nor could Mathison say he had not been warned. His first officer, already middle-aged and bitter at his lack of advancement, let show his resentment at being asked to serve under what he clearly felt to be an inadequate master.

"Six weeks, yon coal's been under hatches whilst the main engine's been down. And loaded wet when it come on board," the mate growled, sourly. "Proper thing'd been to unload her during the down time, but no bloody fear. Too dear a thing for our owners, you see. 'Course, the owners ain't sailing with us."

Mathison was disgusted by his mate's grousing, but he had seen failed men before and knew that they could be good officers, properly handled. If what Thompson said were true, the coal would want watching.

It is practice for vessels carrying coal to make regular log entries of hold temperatures. Clydeside coal, loaded wet and kept long under hatches, had a reputation for being worse than most. Right off, Mathison became aware that heat was building down in the blackness of his cargo. Less than four days after taking departure from a green Irish headland, he ordered the hatch covers thrown back. There was little sea running at the time and opening the hatches would give, at the least, a bit of surface ventilation.

When the heat continued to grow, the captain ordered the rigging of windsails, great tubes of canvas with widespread arms to capture cool sea winds and force them down into the cargo holds. The windsails had helped. It was only when the sounding thermometers were thrust deep into the coal that dangerous heat was found, as though driven to cover. There it lurked, waiting for its chance to move out and destroy them all.

They might have reached port in that way, with the windsails forcing fresh air into the holds with the speed of the ship itself. Any kind of weather, of course, could have forced the closing of the hatches, but the time of the year was right for a smooth passage. Only one other thing was to be feared — and it was what did happen.

On the second day after crossing the Line, in the afternoon watch, a harsh metallic thrashing about sounded through the fidley gratings and the *Ailsa Craig* shuddered and drifted wearily to a stop. She hadn't moved since.

Now they were in the doldrums and, once the ship lost her way, there was no air. The big windsails hung slack in their rigging and, almost at once it seemed, the cargo temperature began to climb alarmingly. It had been rising every day since, and now it could not rise much farther without dire consequence.

To this point, Mathison had relied heavily upon his good and able second officer, an atypical blonde Welshman named Evans. But Evans had gone sick one night and died a few hours later, leaving Mathison alone with only the surly Thompson and the eager, but untried, Wharton-Taylor for support. And Chief Engineer Fergus Adams.

Returning to the present, Mathison turned, went to his cabin and rang for the chief engineer. He felt old. His unshaven face felt thick and stiff under its layers of sweat-soaked coal dust.

He was tired. He poured himself a glass of John
Crabbie's best export Scotch whisky, and a second glass for the
chief, who presently appeared at the door.

Fergus Adams was true to his type, a Scots marine engineer, with all the gruff fustiness of the breed, but with its
dedication to "principle," as well, and an unbending loyalty to
his "employ," meaning his ship and its owners. He was a short
man, no longer young, with muscles long since reduced to thin
wires of strength, and a skin rinsed white with the sweats of a
hundred firerooms. He took his Crabbie as a matter of right,
but gave the impression, nonetheless, that no more than the
single glass would ever pass his lips whilst on duty.

"How goes it below, Chief?" Mathison asked in that
particular balancing of protocol required of the master of a
steamer when talking to the man who is king of the engines.

"Eight hours, I'd say," Adams answered. "Kin ye gi'e
me eight hours, Captain?"

Mathison shook his head, his eyes bleak.

"It's the condenser," Adams went on. "There's tubes
still out, but we're making do. We'll have way on her inside
of eight hours. Nine at the outside."

"We don't have eight hours, Chief. She can blow at any
time now."

"Ain't they getting the coal out of her? I thought . . ."

The chief had his breed's distrust of deck men.

"Not fast enough," Mathison said morosely. "The deeper
we go, the hotter it gets. The men can't take it, Chief. We're
doing the best we can. We . . ."

"My bloody engineers could do it . . ."

Suddenly furious, Mathison slammed his glass on his
desk so hard it shattered. He looked down, stupidly, at the slow
welling of red between his fingers. He felt no pain. But the
sight alone was enough to bring back his control.

"Sorry, Captain," the old engineer said, as though realizing he had gone too far.

Neither man spoke for a time. Disparate in temperament, separated by a generation of age and experience, they nevertheless liked each other and had arrived at a healthy respect, each for the other. The old engineer had lost a son on the Murmansk run during the War. Brian would have been of an age and a size with this young captain.

Mathison wrapped a startlingly white handkerchief about his bleeding hand. "Is there anything we can do below, Chief?" he said. "Anything else, I mean. Anything . . ."

"Aye, certainly, Captain," the chief said, reverting to his natural truculence. "We can order us up a lot of new tubes, we can. And we can order in some dockyard navvies to set things right. Then, maybe . . ."

"There's no call for sarcasm, Chief," Mathison said. "I know you're doing your best. I . . ."

Before Mathison could go on, a commotion sounded forward, followed by shouts and the sounds of running feet on deck.

"What is it, man?" Mathison demanded of the gasping man he met in the alleyway outside his cabin door. "What is it?"

"Gas," the sailor blurted. "Gas in the holds."

Mathison pushed past the man. He ran to the coaming of number three hold and looked down. Two bodies lay sprawled on the coal. A third man lay retching on deck beside the hatch.

"What happened?" Mathison demanded of the mate.

"It was him, Crane," Mister Thompson said, indicating the man on the deck. "We thought he passed out from the heat, like the others. His mate got a line on him, and the second man went down to help. It's gas, Captain. It's gas, right enough. It got the both of them." There was a kind of gratification in the mate's voice. He had been confirmed in his opinion they must leave the ship.

"Get them out of there," Mathison ordered.

"No bloody fear. Sir." His fear had made Mister Thompson bold. "Sending a man down there now is death for him. Ye might as well knock him in the head and be done with it. No point in getting anybody else killed, I say."

Before the mate had finished talking, Mathison had whipped a line about his middle and, after taking a deep breath, he let himself quickly down into the hold.

A man on deck had presence of mind to throw down other lines which Mathison bent onto the two men lying on the coal. His lungs already felt as though they would burst. He looked up, his eyes burning, at the blinding square of light which was the open hatch and signalled for them to be hauled up.

"Hurry! Hurry!" he screamed as he felt his lungs sucking in the deadly air. The men on deck bent into it and he was all but clear when, at last, the air burst from him and the gas-tainted air rushed in. He felt a quick nausea and spat out the air. Then he was on deck and the clean sea air was his to breathe.

"Bloody fool," Mister Thompson muttered, but he supported his young captain gently to keep him from falling.

"Get word — get word aft," Mathison gasped when he could speak. "Tell the third to get his men up. Tell him there's gas."

He looked forward and saw that work already had stopped in the other two forward holds. He glanced at the two men who had been hauled up with him. "Dead?" he asked.

"As mackerels," Mister Thompson answered. "Now, I guess we'll hear something about boats, eh, Captain?" He spat into the hold. "Or do we just hold our breath and shovel her on out? That the ticket, Captain?"

"What's going on here?"

Mathison straightened as best he could. It was the old chief engineer. "Got a little gas in the hold, Chief," he said. "Lost two men. Another one down with it."

The chief nodded, looking at the poor dead bodies lying on the cluttered deck. "You went down and got them, I reckon," he said to Mathison.

Mathison did not answer.

"Did I hear somebody say something about boats?" the chief growled, looking directly at Mister Thompson.

"Aye, I said something about boats, Chief," the Mate blurted. "Seeing as how we got gas down there now, and seeing as how there ain't nothing else we can do, seems to me like the sensible thing's to get off while the getting's good." He paused and looked to the men flanking him as though for support. "Long as there was a chance, the lads and me, we worked willingly, we did. Long as we could see we was doing some good, we . . ."

The old chief looked at the mate with contempt in his eyes.

"I am fully aware of how willingly you have always worked, Mister Mate," he said chillingly.

Thompson bristled at the old engineer's sting, but he chose to ignore it. "Well, that's neither here nor there," he said. "Thing is, we're standing on a bloody ship what's fixing to blow up any minute now. I say it's time we got off a wireless and took to the boats."

"Mister Thompson!" Mathison struggled to stand erect, still groggy from the gas in his lungs. He fought to put into his voice the terrible power of Queen and Country and honored Tradition. It was one thing for a ship's officer to argue a point privately with his Captain. It was something else entirely to foment mutiny on the open deck before a mob of wharf sweepings. Most of them were not even British, so low had the mighty merchant Navy of England fallen.

"Shout all you like, Captain," the mate said insolently. "When you get a bit of time at sea, you'll know what's what. If you want to stay here and get yourself blown to Kingdom Come, that's your pidgen. I just don't fancy going along with you. Eh, lads? You with me?"

The men held back, pressed hard between their pending destruction by explosion and fire and their bred-in superstition about the power of a gold badge on a cap.

"Here, now, lads," the mate said, sounding like a politician. "It's not mutiny we're thinking of here. It's not mutiny to get off a sinking ship. The Board of Trade'll lay to that, lads."

"The vessel is not sinking," Mathison protested. "The sea's calm. The engines are all but fixed. We'll be underway in no time, I tell you." Then, realizing he was pleading with men of lower station, and that to do so was demeaning, he fell silent.

"All right now, lads," the mate took over. "It's into the boats with you. Lively, now. Jenkins, you run up to the wireless and have Sparks get off an SOS. Right?"

Mathison moved as though to interfere, but a new wave of the gas nausea wrenched him. He would have fallen had not the chief engineer gripped him.

The mate was off then, followed by the sailors. They made quite a row of it, stumbling and falling over the heaped coal on decks. Nor were they any quieter or more disciplined in rigging out the boats and readying them for lowering away.

Mathison recovered from his nausea, but he was still so weak that he slumped against the hatch coaming when the chief loosened his hold. He knew he should get his gun from his cabin and shoot that bastard, Thompson, but he couldn't move. His arms were too heavy. He could hardly hold up his head.

"Captain! Captain, are you all right, sir?" It was young Wharton-Taylor, scrambling forward from his post aft.

Mathison straightened. "I'm all right, Mister Wharton-Taylor," he said, forcing his voice steady.

"Are we abandoning, Sir?" The young third's voice held such a note of incredulity that Mathison grinned inwardly at hearing it. "Mister Thompson's lowering the boats."

He remembered a time, not all that long ago, when his own reaction would have been much the same. It was heartening to see that such young men still followed the sea. But, outwardly, he kept his face firm. "No, Mister Wharton-Taylor, we are not abandoning. Mr. Thompson has chosen to leave the vessel, we are going to save her."

Mathison felt the chief's grip on his arm tighten. "Captain," the chief interrupted. "It's going to take a good eight hours. Maybe more. I . . ."

Mathison seemed stiffened by a sudden new resolve. "You said it's your condensers that are the problem. Right?"

"Aye, sir, but . . ."

"The condensers change steam back into feed water. Correct me if I'm wrong."

"Aye, that's right." The old engineer sensed a purpose in his captain's voice.

"Actually, an engine will run without condensers at all. Isn't that right."

"Aye. Long as you got feed water. Locomotives do it ashore all the time. There's harbor tugs that do it some places."

"How you fixed for feed water, Chief?"

"Tanks topped up, boiler full." Fergus Adams studied his young captain. "What you driving at, Captain?" he said.

"Chief, listen to me," Mathison went on. "You got your bloody engine back together, right? It'll run now? It'll move the ship?"

"Aye," the chief said, dubiously. "It'll move the ship, but . . ."

"Even without your condensers?"

Fergus Adams stood stock still, as though utterly aghast at what his young captain was suggesting. "Are ye daft, man?" he blurted. "Ye're suggesting I discharge live steam in an engine room where men are trying . . ." He shook his head violently. "No, Sir! It can't be done. It'd boil the men alive. It'd . . ."

"Even if we rigged windsails and . . ."

"There's no place to rig windsails."

"There is, if we pull away the fidley gratings and hang windsails from the triatic stay. We could rig canvas screens around the engine. That would dampen the worst of the steam. We could . . ."

The old chief engineer did not answer at once. His face wrinkled with the force of his concentration but, slowly then, comprehension showed through.

Mathison pressed quickly. "You give me eight knots, Chief," he said, "and I'll put enough wind down there to blow a man off his feet. All right, is it a go?"

"Aye. It might work . . ."

Mathison grinned again within himself. "It won't work," he said severely, "it bloody well won't work if we don't step lively and make it work, will it?"

Fergus Adams was off before Mathison was finished speaking.

"Mister Wharton-Taylor," Mathison ordered, "you will hook onto the fidley hatch with a cargo boom and rip it clear. You understand? Then stand by to give me a hand with rigging two of the biggest windsails we have. Lively now."

Even though the *Ailsa Craig* rolled no differently than she had for the past days, to Mathison she seemed to have come alive. He glanced at his departed crewmen, lying off in the boats but there was no time for them. Using a heaving line, he passed lines over the triatic stay and rigged guys to spread wide the wings of the windsails. He heard the tearing crash of the fidley hatch being torn away, followed almost at once by Wharton-Taylor's eager rush to help.

When the sails were rigged and their chutes passed down through the fidley, Mathison called down to where he could see Adams and his men scurrying about in their maze of gratings. "Chief! Can you hear me, Chief?"

"Aye. Aye, Captain. I can hear ye."

"Ready on deck, Chief. Give me what you can. All right?"

The chief passed from sight, but almost at once there was a cheery ringing of engineroom telegraph bells.

Now they would know. Great, wet, scalding billows of white steam filled the engineroom. Until the ship built to speed there would be no escape from it.

"Get to the bridge, Mister Wharton-Taylor," Mathison ordered then. "Maneuver to recover boats."

Slowly, then, the *Ailsa Craig* began to move. Her soggy sideways rolling ended and she moved counter to the sea, imposing her will once more upon the waves.

The great windsails stirred. Their wings lifted and their long tubular bodies filled, and into the suffocating heat of the engineroom, cool sweet sea air rushed down.

It was still hot in the engineering spaces, so hot men could endure only brief turns. But it was bearable under the gushing spouts of the windsails. The canvas screens about the engine kept the men clear of the worst of the steam.

With the help of off-watch black gang men, and Wharton Taylor alone on the bridge, Mathison recovered his boats and his sullen crewmen who were given the choice of returning on board or staying where they were.

By evening, the *Ailsa Craig* was making a steady eight knots. Her rigid windsails were gushing cooling air into both cargo holds and engineering spaces. Cargo temperatures already had begun to drop. Before ten o'clock, the engine was stopped briefly to bring the restored condensers back on line.

The ship came back to her normal life.

Only then did Captain Mathison return to his cabin.

"Thought I heard you come in, Captain." Chief Engineer Fergus Adams stood in the open doorway of the captain's cabin, a bottle of John Crabbie's in his hand.

"Best get your head down, Captain, I'm thinking. Bit of sleep'll do ye good," the old engineer said. "But, first, a touch of Crabbie'll do ye no harm."

"Come in, Chief," the young captain said, his voice slurred with fatigue. "Thank you. Glasses there on the chest." But before Adams could get the glasses and return, Captain Mathison lay back in his berth and was asleep.

Fergus Adams pulled his captain's legs onto the berth and drew up a blanket to cover the sleeping figure. Then, his eyes wet suddenly with thoughts of his son lost on the Murmansk run, he went out and closed the door behind him.

THE COMING OF THE CAT

I t gets dark of nights down along the Liverpool docks. Especially so of a rainy night when the black shapes of the warehouses press in close on the narrow streets and there's no noise save that of dripping water and of distant traffic where the rest of the world comes and goes.

It's not a cheering place, there's that to be said for it and Paddy O'Rourke, on his way to join his ship, hunched his wet coat about his ears and walked doggedly, his boots splashing in puddles, his mind lost in a fog of alcohol and resentment for a world turned hard against him.

You'd think a man's shipmates would stand him to a drink. A man would think that. And the night before sailing, too, with weeks of nothing staring him in the face.

But, then, there's shipmates and there's shipmates. Paddy could remember no time when he had sailed with a less likely lot. He would say that. It was a wonder he had not signed off and been done with all of them a long time ago. But berths are not easy come by. Not when the white-faced men in the shipping offices have it in for a man and find all kinds of excuses for not finding him a spot. Aye, there's little justice in such a world.

In thinking such thoughts, Paddy found a snug doorway and settled down to finish the scrap of rum that was left. He had meant to save it for the following morning when the moving of the ship would be a living torment in his head. But that was a trouble of a future which might never come. The dark and the wet were troubles of the now, and Paddy sat down to ease them in the only way he knew. He took the sloshing bottle from his pocket and pulled its cork. The rum tasted good in his mouth. It felt warm and good going down his scarred gullet. His condition was such at the time that he needed but a topping off to make things seem considerably better.

It was while he was sitting in the doorway that the cat came. It was a black cat with a white mark on its face, and its fur was wet in little spicules which gave it a comically pathetic look. It came, morose and silent, to sit in the dry doorway with Paddy. Cat-like, it kept its distance.

The cat's coming pleased Paddy. His befuddled brain saw in it a kindred spirit. Paddy knew what it meant to be alone and friendless. He knew the sting of it when a man's own shipmates won't so much as stand him to a drink. His wreck of a face cracked into what he meant to be a smile.

"Here, Puss, here," he said in his croaking voice. "Have a go at this, huh, Mate?" He proffered the rum bottle, but the cat didn't respond.

"Aye, that's the ticket," Paddy agreed affably. "Stop away from the stuff, Puss. There's no good in it. I can tell you that. Naught but ruin and degradation, as the blokes in the Mission have it."

Paddy put his bottle down carefully and rummaged through his pockets. There was a bit of cheese there somewhere. He remembered having picked it up in a pub. He had wanted it for a snack before turning in. A bit of cheese goes good, it does. Ah, yes, there it was.

Paddy pulled the cheese from his pocket with the careful deliberation of the very drunk. It was furred with lint, and there was a coin half-buried in it. But it was cheese and cats like a bit of cheese.

"Here, Puss. It's cheese, it is."

The cat would not come, though. Paddy moved the cheese closer, being careful to keep his own distance. And, after a time, the cat did come and nibble delicately at the cheese.

"There, that's the nice puss," Paddy said approvingly. His voice was ludicrous when he tried to make it gentle. "Make you feel better, it will."

Paddy forgot his rum in watching the cat eat. The rain still spattered the paving just beyond the sodden toes of his boots but it was dry in the doorway and there was a bit of warmth, it seemed.

The cat finished the last of the cheese and daintily licked its forepaws. Its fur was beginning to dry by that time, too, and to fluff out a bit so that it no longer looked so woebegone.

"Aye, feeling better, are we, puss?" Paddy said. "Come on. Let's have a go at drying you off, eh?"

The cat did not resist as Paddy slipped his hand under its belly and drew it to him. He unbuttoned his coat and pulled out his shirttail to wipe the creature dry.

It was good there in the doorway then. The cat relaxed under Paddy's hands. It began to purr. Paddy could feel the rumble of its purring in his fingers. And, for a reason he didn't know, tears formed in his bleared eyes and spilled down his rumpled cheeks, making them shine in two long streaks.

"Ere, now. W'ot's going on 'ere?"

Paddy started as though suddenly touched with something hot. But he knew, even before looking up, that it was the voice of the Law he heard.

"Come on," the Bobby went on. "Come out of it now. Can't be loitering about, can we now? Come on, out wi' ye— Oh, it's you, is it, O'Rourke?"

"I ain't doing nothing," Paddy protested. "Just in out of the rain for a bit, I am."

"Likely story," the Bobby said, with absolutely no faith. "Come on. Off wi' ye now, before I run ye in."

Paddy recognized the futility of further argument. He knew this copper, just as he knew most of the policemen who manned the dockyard area. He had done business with them before. He got unsteadily to his feet, holding the cat gently and slipping it under his coat to keep it dry.

"'Ere, now. W'ot you got there? Huh?"

"Ain't naught but a cat," Paddy said. "He's mine, he is. Ain't no law against having a cat, is there?"

The policeman seemed to consider the idea for a time as though hoping there might be. "No, I reckon not," he said at last. "You got a ship, Paddy?"

"Aye, and sailing with the morning tide."

"Then get yourself aboard of her. I see you on the street again, I'll run ye in."

"Thanks. Thanks to your bloody highness," Paddy said sarcastically, but the policeman did not do him the respect of a reply. Paddy listened to the official boots echoing down the empty street. "Come on, Puss," he said then to the cat. "It's on board for the two of us."

Paddy was unsteady on his feet and he squinted his eyes tight in his concentration aimed at getting back to the ship. The paving was rough and the glistening tram tracks a menace, but he carried the cat as though it were both precious and fragile.

The crew's mess was warm and dry and full of good smells after the cold wetness of the night outside. Paddy stumbled over the coaming in coming in, saving himself from falling only by putting out his free hand to the table.

"W'ot's that you got there, O'Rourke?" the boatswain said, looking up from his cocoa. The boatswain was a lonely man, given to late night cups of cocoa by himself. Paddy was glad no one else was there. "W'ot's that you got?" the boatswain said again.

Paddy's broken and ill-mended face reflected suspicion and puzzlement for a time. Then it brightened, almost childishly. "It's a cat, Boats," he said proudly. He pulled it from under his coat. "See? It's a cat. It's mine. I got it on the beach."

The boatswain looked upon the stumbling Paddy with a kind of rough resignation. Seamen, by nature, drank. It was a natural thing. To be expected. Especially was this so for Paddy O'Rourke. But the boatswain brightened at the sight of the cat. "Ah, so it's a cat," he said. "'Ere, let's have a look at him." Paddy's face darkened at once. He drew the cat close to him and half-turned as though to deny even its sight to the boatswain. "No," he blurted. "It's mine, it is."

The boatswain laughed. "I know it's yours, you bloody Harp. All I want's a look at him."

But Paddy would not relent. He thrust the cat under his coat and stood as though ready to fend off a physical attack. "You don't like me," he said drunkenly. "I know you don't. But Puss does. Puss likes me."

Paddy crouched then, keeping his eyes on the boatswain, as he sidled to his bunk in the shadowed forward part of the forecastle where the sides of the ship came together and where he slept alone with a buffer of empty berths between him and the rest of the crew.

The boatswain growled a careless curse and turned back to his cocoa. Paddy slowly relaxed and placed the cat on his berth. He pulled old shirts from his seabag and fixed a nest for the cat in a corner of his berth.

"There you are, Puss," Paddy said. "Stop there, like, and I'll fetch you a sup of milk, I will."

Paddy was on no better terms with the cook than he was with anyone else in the ship and it took a bit of doing to get a saucer of warm milk but, in the end, he did. He brought it back, with elaborate caution, to the cat.

It was warm and dry there in their berth. The forecastle, like a hundred others of its kind, was the closest thing to a home Paddy had known since longer than he could remember. He smiled as he watched the cat lap at the warm milk. He felt a return of the peace he had felt so briefly in the doorway where he had found the cat. The boatswain was deep in his own thoughts. There was no one else in the forecastle. The others apparently were still in the public room from which they had hooted Paddy earlier. Well, let them stay there, and be damned to them. Paddy had a mate, he did.

"There. Cozy-like, ain't it, Puss?" Paddy said softly. "No more rainy nights on the streets for you, Puss. No, and no more rubbish cans, either. Not while ol' Paddy's got a berth." Paddy laughed easily. "Smart as paint, ain't yer? Lapping up that milk like yer was born to it, eh?"

It was not often that Paddy laughed. Nearing fifty, he was beginning to feel the effects of alcohol and disease. He seldom felt fit anymore and there was little in common between him and his shipmates. But it was only to himself that he admitted his life was not as he would have liked it to be. It would be nice to sit and share a gam and a pipe with some of the old ones. But, ah, well, the young whippersnappers shipping out nowadays took a lot of getting used to, they did. They had little respect for a man what had been sailing when they was still sucking milk out of their mothers.

Little did they know, or care, about the things which can make a man what Paddy had come to be. The war, for instance, and the things Paddy saw during the war. Royal

Navy, he was, until the bottle got hold of him. But a man needed alcohol then, just to keep going through the cold weeks and months and years of fighting Hitler's U-Boats.

Aye, it was the war that started it. And, when it was over, the Navy had no place for a man who could not handle his drink. A pension, they suggested, but Paddy was a proud man then, and it was into the Merchant Navy he went.

A hundred ships, and more, he had sailed in, since that time. With a hundred crews. And with the war memories always there in his seabag. The war memories — and those of Lal. Lovely Lal, who had sworn her love so sweetly in the park before Cardiff Castle one night. And who had married a bloody Yank aviator. Aye, there were memories of Lal, too.

Softly, gently, Paddy stroked the purring cat. The milk was gone by that time and the cat stretched out, its eyes closed, in the nest Paddy had made for it in his berth.

Lost in his own thoughts, with the rum fumes still swirling in his brain, Paddy became aware of the crew's coming aboard only slowly. Horseplay and scuffling there was at the accommodation ladder, and a clamor of drunken voices. Instinctively, Paddy tensed. He drew the cat to him, turning to face the door into the forecastle as though confronting an enemy.

Ginger Harper it was who came in first. Big and young and strong and flushed with drink, his red hair awry, Harper paused for a moment just inside the door, swaying as though the ship already were at sea. He seemed puzzled at finding no one in the forecastle. The boatswain had gone, unnoticed by Paddy. Then Harper spied Paddy and his face lightened.

"Aw, and look what we got here," he cried out to his mates who crowded in behind him. They had all been drinking. They jostled each other good-naturedly, as shipmates will.

"You what's new," Harper cried. "You what's new, have a look what's there. It ain't often you see yon Irisher on board afore sailing time. And standing on his own two feet, like. Aye, a bloody miracle it must be. Aye . . ."

Harper laughed at his own ugly wit, half-losing his balance as he did so. "Here, now, O'Rourke. What's that you got there?"

Paddy pushed the cat behind him, in the gesture of a wild animal protecting its young. "Nothing," he blurted, "I ain't got nothing."

Ginger Harper staggered to Paddy's berth and pushed him easily away. "Don't tell me you ain't got nothing, you bloody Harp. I can see, can't I? Ah — it's a cat you got."

Paddy threw himself upon the younger, stronger man. "Leave it be," he cried. "It's mine, I say. I got it on the beach."

Harper held Paddy off with little effort, laughing at him. He held the cat up by the scruff of its neck. "Aye, so it's a cat all right," he grinned. "And a proper mess it is, too. The poor blighter's half starved, it is. Ain't you got the brains to see it wants feeding, O'Rourke? Ain't you got the brains to see that?"

"I did," Paddy protested. "I did feed it. Now, give it me. It's mine. I found it."

There was humiliation in the abjectness with which Paddy begged, but he didn't care. He couldn't bear the thought of losing the cat. He didn't have much. It wasn't too much to ask to have a cat. It wasn't.

The other crewmen had the decency to become uncomfortable. The fun was gone from the joke. "Aw, come on, Ginger," one of them said. "Give him the bloody beast."

"Aye, like as not, it's alive with fleas. Same as him."

Harper laughed, but no longer with mirth in his laughter. There was no sympathy in Ginger Harper for Paddy O'Rourke. In the strength of his youth he could find no understanding for what Paddy had let himself become. Aye, and in the shallowness of his experience. But there was little sport in so spineless a target. Carelessly, he tossed the cat to Paddy.

"Aye, O'Rourke," Harper said. "It's your cat, it is. But let's see if you can keep him, like. What say, afore we're back, he'll be my cat. And of his own mind, too. You hear?"

"He's mine," Paddy said stubbornly. He clutched the soft warmth of the cat to him and turned away from his shipmates, his mind already chilling with the terror which came of the thought of losing the cat. There was little doubt in him that Harper would win the cat away from him. Paddy had lost too many other things to have hope of holding anything.

"We'll see, O'Rourke," Harper laughed. "We'll see."

Before Paddy could reply, an AB pulled a smuggled bottle from under his sweater and Harper hurried to join the tumult of getting cups. For a time there was a great commotion and Paddy, seeing his chance, tucked the cat under his coat and slipped unnoticed from the forecastle.

Paddy had a place for such times. There was a little house on the poop. The donkeyman and the engineers used it as a storehouse, but there was a trick to opening the lock and Paddy had found an unused corner of the place where he could be alone. It was a kind of sanctuary and recognized as such by the crew. Paddy, once he reached this place, was left free of torment. And, except for when he had a bridge watch, it was the only place he was.

Here it was that Paddy came with his cat. He lay down on a pile of burlap bags, cuddling the cat to him and talking nonsense to it, his eyes moistening at the comfort it gave him to hold something which was content to be held by him. The soft drumming of the cat's purring was something Paddy needed.

The sea is a lonely life. Lonelier still when made so by the devils of alcohol and the kinds of memories which lived in Paddy O'Rourke. The little cat, simply by staying with Paddy and by not laughing or cringing away, did much to make the sea a less lonely place. Paddy felt again a sudden rush of terror as he realized what it would mean to him to lose the cat. He looked about him in the darkness, his eyes wild, as though expecting Harper and the others to burst in on him, there and then, and wrest the cat away from him.

Paddy's hands closed about the cat, clutching hard to hold it against the threat of its loss. The cat squirmed in pain, and Paddy, feeling guilt at having hurt it, released his grip and became even more tender. "There, Puss," he said. "There, now. I didn't mean to hurt you."

Reassured by the cat's return to purring content, Paddy relaxed. It was as though he already realized the crew would never let him have the cat. Perhaps more out of cruel play than from any mean intent, they nevertheless would not leave him alone as long as he had it. Especially Harper. Maybe the others would, but Harper wouldn't. Paddy knew that. Still, for the moment, the cat was his.

It was nice there in the little house on the poop. Paddy could hear the engineers doing whatever engineers do before a ship gets underway. There was the clatter and clank of the steering chains, for one thing. And the warm scent of stack gases as steam was raised. Even after all his time at sea, it was a time which Paddy found stirring, the time of readying a ship for sea. The mates would be around soon to see to singling up the lines.

With these familiar sounds and scents all around him, Paddy felt an ease come over him he had not known for a long time. He caressed the little cat and spoke aloud to it of things he had not put his tongue to in years.

Paddy told the cat about the things which had happened during the war. The Murmansk run. The cold and brutal fights off Iceland. Fights in which, often as not, friend and foe alike disappeared in the deadly cold neutrality of the sea.

He told the cat about Lal, too. "Lal had a cat, Puss," he said. "Aye, not much bigger than you, it was. But different in color. And some older, I'd say. Used to sleep in her sewing basket, it did. I remember it well. I'd come in and it'd . . ."

Paddy's voice tapered into a remembering silence and his face contorted as though with a relived pain. "Aye, I remember it," he said. "Funny little bugger, it was. And Lal that crazy about it."

The cat's purring sounded loud in the silence that followed Paddy's voice. The cat itself was soft and warm in Paddy's hands. He could feel the quick little beat of its heart. He could feel the trust in the cat, and the love, it seemed to him.

A sudden shower spattered against the steel sides of the house as though to remind Paddy of the night waiting outside and he felt again the terror he had known before at the thought of losing the cat. Maybe, if he asked Harper, they would let him keep the cat. Maybe, when they had sobered up, they would see what the cat had come to mean to him and . . .

But Paddy knew they wouldn't. The Navy. Lal. A hundred ships and more. These things had broken more in Paddy than the lines of his face. It was as though Paddy, in meeting mischance so often, had come to expect mischance again. It was as though, in a way, he were ready to meet disappointment half way. As though, in a way, he were somehow relieved at knowing nothing had changed.

Paddy took up the cat. He got to his feet and felt his way out onto the weather deck. There was no one about just then. The deck was wet and shining in the dock lights. The rain misted down about the lights and dimpled the puddled waters.

Paddy was no longer drunk. He walked erect and without pause to the accommodation ladder and down onto the dockside. He put the cat down. His voice was gruff. "Off with you now, Puss! Off with you, I say!"

The cat stood without moving, lifting first one foot then another from the cold wet paving and looking up at Paddy as though puzzled.

"Off with you! Off with you, damn it!" Paddy croaked again. And, when the cat would not go, he stamped his boot in a puddle so that water was splashed onto the cat and it finally then did scamper away, its tail in the air, to disappear in the shadows.

"Off with you, Puss," Paddy said again. But his voice this time was little more than a whisper, a hoarse croaking kind of a whisper. Then, after a time in the rain, Paddy returned on board. There was still time for him to get his head down for a bit before the ship sailed.

THE HOMEWARD
BOUNDER

I t is a sad thing when men outlive their times. The same can be said of a calling, I suppose, and a doubly sad thing it is, indeed, when the two come together.

I mind once, 1927 or thereabouts, when I shipped apprentice in one of the last sailing vessels to call along the West Coast of South America for nitrates. Three-masted barque out of Liverpool, she was. Captain Lloyd Jones, Welshman, commanding, a man of near seventy years at the time.

Iquique, it was, where we came to take on our cargo, a port our captain, judging from things he said, knew well from the great days of sail. But the time of which I write saw us the only sailing vessel present. All else was steam.

I was but a boy at the time. Apprentice, as I've said. But, being a boy, I was able to see things in our Old Man he would most likely have kept from a grown man. He would talk with me sometimes in the night watches, or when I, with the other boys, might row him ashore. He would tell of things the way they had been before, when Iquique and the other nitrate ports were alive with square-riggers and the waters off the Horn not so lonesome as they are now.

"Aye, and it's gone, they are," the Old Man would often say of the lofty sparred ships he had loved. "And gone the ways of them, more's the pity."

Boy though I was, I could hear the loneliness in his voice.

At an age, had things remained the same, when he might have expected an honourable command in a good employ, he was reduced to talking with boys. And to command of an old barque with sprung spars and sides more rust than paint.

Little wonder then, it may seem, that he might take to drink on occasion. The warmth of spirits must have been a rare comfort for him. I mind one time when we boys had rowed him ashore in the early afternoon and were kept waiting until near midnight — without our suppers, I might add — before he came roaring down to the landing.

"Bloody stinking steamers," he cried upon making us out. "Naught in the whole bloody ocean but bloody stinking steamers."

Whereupon he slipped and would surely have fallen had not Derry Baxter and Ginger Rhodes caught him and set him right. With but a momentary loss of dignity, he set his bowler straight and readdressed himself to the sorry state of maritime affairs when a decent commander in sail could not repair to the beach for a mutually satisfying and profitable discourse with his colleagues in the great fraternity of the sea.

"Aye, just a few tots, it was, I was after," he said despairingly. "Just a touch to take the saltpetre taste out of my mouth. Aye, that and a word or two with a sailing man."

Gingerly, we helped the old gentleman off the landing and into the boat. I say gingerly because, in my day, apprentices did not touch the persons of their captains lightly, not even in the way of helpfulness. But we needn't worry that night about the niceties of discipline. The Old Man was well beyond caring by that time and suffered us to get him settled in the stern sheets without complaint.

Whatever his failings, Captain Jones was always good to his apprentices. "Young gentlemen" was his unfailing term for us, and we knew he would see we got our supper on getting back to the ship, if he didn't fall entirely to sleep first.

For the moment, he was muttering in his beard. "Know naught," he mumbled. "The lot knows bloody naught of the sea." He said a good deal more in the same vein all the way out to the ship. And when we fetched him alongside, he heaved himself up and over the bulwarks, still grumbling at the depravity of steam sailors.

I never learned exactly what happened ashore that night but I gathered from a number of things I heard later that the steamer officers had made sport of the Old Man and had taunted him with the shortcomings of sail and of those who still followed it. Young sailors, just like young men in other callings, can be cruel and insensitive to old men.

Whatever it was, it affected Captain Jones deeply and he seldom spoke after that. Not even with Asah Mowbray, first mate. Asah was nearly of an age with the Old Man. They had been together on the coast in the old days. Before the "bloody steamers" came. I know that whilst I was in the ship the Old Man and his mate were very close, drawn together, I suppose, by their shared memories and limited prospects.

But something went out of the Old Man after that night ashore. All of us, even the boys, noticed it. Most put it down to a passing frailty of old men but it was more than that. I suspect he came to a realization that night that his world was indeed ended. He even took no notice of the loading, a vital thing in the last days of sail for a proper load could mean the difference between a paying voyage and a losing one.

Time, it was, that was the problem. It was a slow thing at best, working cargo in sail. And all ship's work. We did it ourselves, off-loading coal in baskets, lifted out by whips and dumped in lighters alongside. Then, filling the single vast cavern that was a sail-ship hold with bag after bag of eye-burning nitrate. Sometimes, months it was that we worked that way. It was that as much as anything else that killed sail.

The voyage of which I write now, for instance, steamer after steamer arrived, filled, and sailed whilst we rode to our anchor with the lighters alongside and the crew working themselves into dusty, red-eyed ghosts of their former like-nesses.

When all the ships were sailing vessels, or nearly all, it was not so bad. They were together in port long enough for the officers and, sometimes, even the men to get to know each other and a lively society often developed. The apprentices were especially gregarious, for it was they who rowed their betters from ship to ship and came to know each other whilst waiting on board.

That is probably why the homeward bound ceremony took such hold on ships off the West Coast of South America. The sailing of a homeward bounder was an <u>event</u>, earned first by the hard and hazardous passage of the Horn on the way out. Then, even more so, by the long months of hot and dirty working of cargo, most often coal off, and nitrates on, both nasty things to handle.

At any rate, the homeward bound ceremony, though practiced to some extent in other trades — notably the tea clippers out of Foochow and Shanghai — was never so honored in its observance as it was in the nitrate trade.

I knew none of that, of course, at the time of which I write. It was only as we neared the time of finishing our loading that I even heard of it.

Some days before we topped off our cargo, the Old Man stirred somewhat from his sad lethargy and set about various mysterious activities which he didn't trouble to explain to any of us. Only the mate, Mister Mowbray, himself an aged and most taciturn man, gave the Old Man a hand. The second, much younger, but a strangely bitter man, was excluded entirely from whatever it was the Old Man and the mate were up to.

It was a queer thing to see the two of them at work, both of them bent and stumbling a bit with age as they were, puttering with hammer and saws and bits of wood and line. Naturally, we were all dying of curiosity, but we were told nothing.

Oddly, though, the Old Man seemed a bit more his old self whilst working at his strange tasks. He even joked a bit with his "young gentlemen" and sent us sometimes on errands for him. Sometimes, he would rest himself and gaze out over the anchorage for a pipe or two, and my feeling was that he was not seeing what was there, but what had been there. High spars, for instance, instead of blackened funnels, soaring bowsprits and jibbooms instead of plumb iron stems.

The rest of us were working as hard as ever in getting the last bags aboard, but we looked from time to time to the two old men on the poop. Even our sardonic second could not contain his curiosity and lowered himself to ask us boys what it was the Old Man was up to.

It was commonly thought in sailing vessels that the apprentices knew more than most about what was going on. They rowed the Old Man about, you see, and the theory was we overheard things. But, in this case, at least, we didn't know any more than anyone else. Only "Sails" had a clue.

Sails was an old man, too, all stove in from a fall aloft when he was young, but not embittered at all and content to reign from his little kingdom of canvas and ropes and tar and beeswax. He knew what the Old Man was up to.

"Going to cheer the bloody homeward bounder, he is," Sails growled to us one evening in the still which follows a long day of hard work. "Aye, that's what he's fixing to do. Seen it, many's the time, right here in Iquique, I have."

"What is it, Sails?" we all cried. "What do you mean: 'Cheer the homeward bounder'?"

"You'll see in good time," old Sails said. His eyes glinted with merriment. He enjoyed keeping us in our ignorance, but he looked at the figures of the two old men on the poop with a sober sympathy. "And I don't want to see you young goslings doing aught to spoil it, you hear me?"

"We won't, Sails," we all cried. And it was true. We all loved the Old Man. It sounds an extreme thing to say, I know, but he had been good to us in a hard world and we sensed, I suppose, the great lonely sadness in him. "But tell us of it, Sails. Won't you now?"

"All right, then," Sails said after a pull at his pipe. "I'll tell you the way of it then. But you're not to let on, you hear? The Old Man's to do it his way, you understand?

"Anything he wants you to know, he'll tell you."

We all nodded and the old sailmaker went on to explain what it was that was meant by cheering the homeward bounder. "And that's what the Old Man's doing," he finished. "He's getting ready to cheer the homeward bounder."

"But why doesn't he tell us, Sails?" we asked. "We would help. Honest, we would."

Sails shook his gray head. "Aye, I know you would, lads. But it is a hard thing that has happened to men like the Old Man. A hard thing, indeed. Their calling's being taken away from them, you see, and with none left to understand what it was that's gone."

"You mean the steamers, Sails?"

"Aye, lads. The steamers. There's no time in the world anymore for the likes of the Old Man. Or for the cheering of the homeward bounder, either, come to that."

With the sensitivity that falls sometimes to coarse men, old Sails took his scarred pipe from his mouth and pointed with its stem to the old men on the poop. "Aye," he said sadly. "And that's why it's not for us to question the why of anything the Old Man wants to do. You hear, lads?"

"Yes, Sails," we said. But, being young, we did not understand. For the few remaining days before the last bag was to be hoisted aboard, we watched the Old Man and the mate go about their preparations with little more than idle curiosity.

Sometimes, we even made cruel jokes about him.

There can be little doubt now, I suppose, that the Old Man was a bit balmy by that time. The years of frustration and loneliness and thwarted ambitions must have left him less than whole in his head. And that's to say nothing of all the cheap rum he had taken in search of comfort.

Still, in the matter at hand, he moved with a sure purpose and when it came time to hoist aboard the final bag, he acted with the true confidence of command. It was easy then to imagine what an imposing figure of a man he must once have been.

The crew, scrapings and dregs as they were, with little feeling for the sea and its ways at all, would have hoisted in the last bag with no more thought than had been given to all the dusty thousands of its fellows already stowed below, had not the Old Man stopped them.

He was standing at the bulwarks, a wispy old man in heavy black clothes despite the heat, with a hard bowler set square on his gray hair. He had a folded Red Duster in his hand. The mate was with him.

"Hold it!" the Old Man shouted to the men on deck. Then, as the hands stood in puzzled silence, he turned to the mate. "Very well, Mister Mate," he said. "Will you be good enough to cheer the last bag aboard?"

Whereupon the mate took the folded flag from the Old Man and let himself down into the lighter alongside. Once there, he pushed past the dusty seamen of the lighter detail and made his way to where the final bag lay already fixed in its sling in the seemingly vast emptiness of the lighter.

With the careful awkwardness of his age, the mate settled himself astraddle the bag, holding to the hoisting line with one hand while shaking out the Red Duster in the other.

"Are you ready, Mister Mate?" the Old Man called down from the bulwarks.

"Aye, Captain. Ready," the mate called back.

The Old Man turned then to the hands on deck. They had, of course, all gone to the bulwarks to see what it was that was going on down in the lighter. The Old Man frowned at them and ordered them back to their hoisting stations. "Aye, that's the ticket," he cried. Then, "Handsomely, now. Up with him!"

And, waving the flag with all his might, the scrawny old mate was hoisted high for all the ships in the harbor to see. And, while he was there, he shouted out at the top of his unfortunately badly-cracked voice: "Three cheers for the captain, officers and crew of the *Solano!*" That being the name of our ship.

This part was not like old Sails had told us. In the old days, it would have been the youngest lad on board who would have been hoisted up with the last bag. But everything else was just as Sails had said it would be.

Three times, then, the Old Man had the mate lowered and hoisted while, all the time, the Red Duster was waved about in mid-air. And, just before both mate and nitrate bag were lowered into the last open hatch, the mate cried out: "Three cheers for all the ships in harbor!"

Whereupon the Old Man stood to the bulwarks and cheered as lustily as he could for each of the steamers anchored about us. It was, in fact, a poor show, his being so old and all. But he seemed content with the effort and went below without so much as a glance at what, by that time, was all hands gathered on deck in open-mouthed wonder at what was going on. That included the second, as well.

So far as I could tell, few of the surrounding steamers even noticed all this. The clamor of their winches and cargo gear probably kept them from hearing and I doubt that anyone noticed the mate being swung about in our rigging. But it all had a deep effect on our own people. They were all somehow subdued and went about the final chores of making ready for sea in an uneasy quiet.

As for the Old Man, we didn't see him again until well after dark. By that time, the hatches were all closed and the water mixed for the fire barrels and the crew cleaned up as best they could manage under the circumstances. But they stayed on deck, leaving only for supper and returning at once after the meal, poorly concealing their curiosity as to what their crazy Old Man would do next.

Then, at exactly eight o'clock, the Old Man came onto the poop and whanged the living daylights out of the ship's bell mounted there.

According to Sails, in the old days, every other ship in harbor would have followed suit, until every poop and forecastle bell in the lot would have been ringing like mad. The din would have been so loud as to echo off the hills ashore and while it was going on, the homeward bounder would have hoisted a wooden framework aloft on the foremast. Lanterns would be fitted to the framework in what was fancied to be the form of the Southern Cross, that most beautiful of constellations.

And, sure enough, at the time of which I write, there was the mate, heaving at a line forward while the Old Man kept on at the bell.

I and the other boys moved as though to help the mate, but Sails stopped us. "No, lads, leave him be," Sails said softly. "It's them that's doing it."

And, slowly and haltingly, the framework with its lighted lanterns swayed and bumped its way aloft for all the harbor to see.

The Old Man left off the banging of the bell then and in the sudden silence which fell upon the dark, still waters of the night, we heard his thready old voice singing a chanty of long ago.

And a moving thing it was, too.

In the old days, Sails said, the forecastle and poop and midship house and every high place would have been manned with men holding high, flaring saltpetre torches so that the decks and rigging and surrounding waters would have been lighted in an eerie light.

It was at this point that the Old Man led the mate in cheering the other ships in harbor. "Three cheers for the *Ailsa Craig*!" he shouted. (We will imagine that to be the name of the nearest ship.) And he and the mate cheered as loudly as they could, which was not very loudly at all.

In the old days, according to Sails, the crew of the *Ailsa Craig* would have returned the cheers, though being careful not to name the homeward bounder, but to refer to her only as the 'homeward bounder'. It was bad luck to name a homeward bounder.

At the time of which I write, of course, the dolts on the anchored steamer did not cheer us back. We could see them, crowded at doors and lifelines, but their interest was, I'm sure, more that of curiosity at the noise of the bell and the shouting of two old men than any evidence of understanding.

The Old Man was not dismayed. I suspect he had expected little else. At suitable intervals, he called out for cheers for each successively more distant vessel until they all were cheered, to their profound consternation, I'm positive.

I noticed some of them calling away boats, probably in the belief we had some emergency on board.

At this point in the proceedings, Sails said, there would have been fireworks in the old days, and the Old Man would have sent a boat round to the nearer ships — especially to her chum ships, which is to say, ships with masters who were friends of his — with a bottle of drink for each.

By ten o'clock, say, the fireworks would all have been done and the anchorage returned to quiet, save for the odd outbreak of cheers and song. The homeward bounder herself would be surrounded by a fleet of boats, for the Old Man would be entertaining all the masters in harbor, along with their womenfolk and certain people from the shore.

The half deck would be filled with apprentices who had pulled their captains' boats alongside and who took advantage of the chance to say good-bye to friends made during the long months in harbor. Letters and parcels were handed over for delivery in far-off England. It had been a gay time, according to Sails. You can just picture it, can't you? The mingled joy and sadness at a parting, with, in the instance of a sail ship's departure on a passage 'round the Horn, the special poignance of certain hazard to friends and loved ones.

Of course, there was none of that at the time of which I write. For that time, no one cheered, save two old men with cracked voices. Nor did any boats come alongside. Nor was there aught of partying or extravagant farewells.

No, at the time of which I write, there was only the slow lowering of lighted lanterns from aloft. That, and the silence of a night time anchorage where the ships of a new age had listened without caring to the last songs of a ship from an older one.

We, none of us, then seemed to know what to do. Slowly, the hands drifted away to get what rest they could against tomorrow's sailing. But I stood for some time, lost in a deep sadness as I watched the Old Man and the mate on the poop who were, themselves, lost in who knows what memories.

Finally, according to what Sails had told us, there was but one thing left to be done. The Old Man saw to that himself.

Drawing up as though for one final effort, he led the mate in singing that sweetest of all sea songs: the Homeward Bound song.

"O, fare you well; good-bye, fare you well!
Good-bye, fare you well; good-bye, fare you well!
O, fare you well, my bonny young lassies!
Hoorah, my boys, we're homeward bound."

Then, slowly, the hands who had gone below came again on deck and listened. And, one by one, they took up the haunting melody until the night filled with the song, and things were, for a little while, as Sails had said they had been a long time ago.

As it happened, the Old Man did not survive the passage home. He was buried in the sea, and became as dead as the ships in which he had for so long sailed. But I shall never again hear the song "Homeward Bound" without thinking of him and the mate and Iquique in the night.

JU-JU MAN

Whole books have been written about the ingenuity shown by ships' engineers in meeting emergencies at sea. Jury rudders have been built and shipped, engines virtually built anew, and all under the most trying conditions. But I saw an old Scots chief one time do something you'll find in no book.

I was going third assistant then, and a good long time ago that was, in an old coal-burning tramp out of the Clyde ports. Our chief was a Glasgow man, small in stature, with all the color cooked out of his skin by twenty years and more in ships' engine rooms. But a better man never took a turn out of an engine, and it was the chief who saved us.

We were trading out of the East African Arab ports, carrying general cargo, mostly, with an occasional go at coal or ore of one kind or another. One trip, we even carried a deck load of pilgrims for Mecca.

It's a hot and dirty coast, the East African, in the low latitudes. Most of our calling was at open roadsteads where we lightered off and on, and where we had to keep steam up, not only for the winches, but also to be able to get clear in the event weather made up. It made for a damnable situation in the engineering spaces, what with the ship stopped so much and no wind at all coming down the vents. It was a problem finding men for such work.

Our good Glasgow owners were cautious with their pay and we manned for the most part with natives. They could stand the heat better than white men, you see, and they worked for a good deal less. But even they had their limits, and we lost them frequently. Which brings us to our story.

We had just discharged off a mud village and the carpenter was knocking in the hatch wedges. We were in all respects ready for sea and I was catching a breath on deck when the second came and reported a trimmer gone sick.

The second was not an unkind man but he did share the Britisher's unhappy habit at the time of calling all natives "wogs."

"Got another bloody wog down, Third," he said off-handedly. "Better get yourself ashore and see what you can scrape up to fill in, like."

That's the way we shipped men then. A man went sick on you, you went ashore and found another one. No mucking about with shipping commissioners or hiring halls or the like. And, since I was sailing third assistant and the job quite likely to be a nasty one, the pleasure of poking about in an African village was all mine. And that at a time when the infidel was considered well within season in that part of the world. But it was the way things were, so I called away a boat and ashore I went, taking Ngor along as interpreter.

You have to know something about British shipping practice of the time to understand Ngor's status on our ship. In the first place, he had no status, not officially anyway. You see, we shipped our crews pretty much by chance. The result was likely to be a truly remarkable grouping of races, nationalities, religions and tribes.

One resulting practical problem was that of languages. Most ships out there carried a man like Ngor. A man who could speak most of the coast's tongues and who was adroit enough to thread a way through the tortuous paths of religion, custom, and prejudice without getting his throat cut. And all this while yet getting work out of the lot.

We were lucky in Ngor. He was a plump little man, Kikuyu, I believe. He was of unfailing good humor under the most harrowing circumstances but he wielded his authority with a will and, except for this time, I recall no crew trouble at all which could be laid at his feet.

At any rate, Ngor was with me when I landed on the beach. The village stretched for a hundred yards or so along the sea, with native boats drawn up on the sand and some dhows riding at anchor offshore. A few palms stood about in hard black spatters of their own shade, but mostly the place simply lay there in the cooking sun and stank. For the job in hand, there was nothing for it but to give Ngor his head and see what happened. But I won't deny a certain apprehension. The ragged, narrow-eyed citizens of the place seemed all to be eyeing me in the manner of housewives passing a butcher's shop in the High Street.

Ngor, as was his wont, seemed perfectly at ease and walked with a pronounced swagger, intended, no doubt, to impress the locals. He appeared to be enjoying himself immensely. So much so that I felt called upon to prompt him to a greater diligence. The ship was waiting for our return to sail, you see.

At any rate, we presently came upon a mud-walled resort where as rascally a looking lot as I ever expect to see squatted about their water pipes. Ngor made known our problem, and we were beset at once by a press of vari-colored men, each asserting, according to Ngor, his great experience and skill in tending fires aboard ship, to say nothing of loyalty which would put the Prophet to shame.

Somehow, out of the babble and screech, Ngor arrived at a decision and came up with his man. The fellow was like all the others there, a wiry caricature of a man with strap-thin arms and legs emerging from a loosely-fashioned wrapping about his waist of cloth which must at one time have been white.

It had been our practice to give Ngor his head in shipping new hands, but it seemed exceedingly unlikely to me that the fellow standing before us was physically capable of doing what a trimmer had to do in a ship at sea. I said so and asked Ngor to have another go at finding something more suitable.

"What's the matter with that one?" I asked, pointing to a magnificent brute of a man lounging by the door. He stood easily six foot tall. Although he had the long bones of a negro, he was muscled well and had a look of strength about him.

"No. Not that one," Ngor said quickly. There was a flash of fear in his face, I thought, and he took hold of his chosen scarecrow and moved as though to leave.

"Hold on, Ngor," I said. "That joker's not going to last a watch in a bunker. Look at him, man. He's half starved, for one thing."

Ngor looked about the room. "Good as any others," he said and moved again to get out of the place.

"He's not as good as yon big man," I said. I was getting a bit stiff-necked about it. It doesn't do to argue with natives, you know.

Ngor looked again at the big black. He shook his head sullenly, which was not like him at all. "No. Not that one."

The big black, though I very much doubt he could have known what we were saying, seemed nevertheless to sense the meaning of our argument. He stood boldly, almost insolently, his skin so black that little tints of blue showed in it. It might have been the frightful tribal scars on his face which gave him such a malevolent air.

But, at the moment, I was not interested in malevolent airs. The brute had the arms of a stevedore, and that is what is wanted in a trimmer. Besides, the ship was ready to sail. I brusquely told Ngor to take the big fellow and to come on back to the ship with me. It was clear he didn't want to, but there was little he could do about it in the face of my stiff neck — and white skin.

Back on board, we got the fellow signed on. "Conakry," he grunted when asked his name. That was all that was needed for the articles. He couldn't write, of course.

"Conakry," our old chief said, having a bit of trouble getting the foreign name past his Scots tongue. "Conakry it is then. Ye'll stand watch with the third, ye hear? Ye'll hae nae trouble, not so long as ye keep coal on the floor plates."

Ngor passed this news to Conakry in a language they both spoke and sent him along with an off-watch stoker to find his place in the mess and all.

"Bad, Mister," Ngor said then, once the fellow was gone. "That one is bad man."

"Why?" I said. "He'd make two of any of the others we saw. What's wrong with him?" We were making our way below at the time, and I confess I paid Ngor's protests little mind.

"He ju-ju man," Ngor said solemnly, as though that made everything clear.

"Ju-ju man? What the hell's a ju-ju man?"

"Ju-ju man talk with spirits," Ngor said then. "Bad on ship. Bad other mans. Bad. Bad."

Sailing as we did, then, you came to know the Africans and their ways. Superficially, at least. Good workers though they were and stout fellows, they did have their quirks about them. Superstition was one of them. I had run across it before. But the standby bell rang just then and I moved to the starting platform. I motioned Ngor to come along.

"How do you know he is a, a ju-ju man?" I asked.

"His bag. You see his bag, Mister? And his eyes. You see how his eyes burn? Like fires, they burn, Mister."

To tell the truth, I had paid no attention to the rather ratty little sack Conakry had brought aboard with him and I, sure as bloody hell, had seen no fires in his eyes. I was too busy looking at his marvelous arms and thinking what he could do with a shovel in the bunkers.

Still, there was an urgency, a dread in poor Ngor's voice which impressed me. Whatever it was that had his wind up, he was serious about it. He was frightened, is what he was. I was then still new on the coast, and I was of half a mind to speak to the chief about it.

We were greatly dependent upon Ngor. It was only through him that we exercised our control over the other men. He was good at his job and we had all come to have a confidence in his judgement as well. Had we not been in such a hurry to sail, and had I not been so flipping stubborn, I wouldn't have overridden him about Conakry. But the bell rang then for slow ahead and I put the matter out of my mind. Conakry reported back for his watch and I set him to work in the bunker.

It became obvious at once that Conakry had never set foot in a bunker before in his life. It was too late, of course, to do anything about that, then. But the duties of trimmer are not all that complex. His sole function is to move the coal from the bunker to the plates where the stokers can take it up for the fires. That, and hauling ashes at the end of a watch.

Early in a voyage that is all easy enough. The coal is right there to be tossed out. But as the coal is consumed, the trimmer is forced to move it for greater and greater distances, and it becomes work. Especially so in the oven-like, echoing blackness of a bunker, with only a slush lamp and the hellish glow from the fireroom door for light. There are strange sounds in a bunker, too. And the heat and the darkness and the invisible workings of a ship in the sea all make it a bad place for a man with any imagination at all.

But I had been right about Conakry's muscles. He more than made up in strength and willingness to work for whatever he lacked in experience. Actually, from the start, he did a better job than the man he replaced.

Our old ship was a glutton for coal. She was fitted with John Blair's massive engines, and a good Scotch boiler which did away with coal at a remarkable rate. Especially the cheap coal our owners, from the comfort of their Glasgow offices, felt was good enough for us. But no stoker on my watch ever had to rattle his shovel while Conakry was in the bunker. And, more than once, I saw that scarred blue-black face staring impassively out the bunker door while the stokers worked at the coal he kept heaped before them.

Even the chief noticed it, and Geordie Ross, our taciturn second, once made offer of his trimmer for mine. When I thought of it and told the chief that Ngor had said Conakry was a ju-ju man, the old man laughed and asked if I knew where he could find a few more like him.

In short, it was only Ngor, our faithful Ngor, who held to his doubts about Conakry. I did notice that the other Africans stayed well clear of the big man, but since Conakry gave every indication he was content with that state of affairs, I paid it little mind.

Until the time Ngor hit Conakry, I had as sweet-running a watch as I've ever enjoyed, either before or since.

Ngor, as a kind of petty officer, stood no watches. But he was on the gratings most all of the time, seeing that the men kept up to scratch. He carried a little hair fly whisk. He told me once it was a token of authority in his tribe. Something like a boatswain's pipe in the Navy, I suppose. At any rate there were times when, if a man did not move quickly enough to please him, Ngor would hit the man with the fly whisk. He did it lightly. Not hard at all. More as a symbolic gesture, I should say. All our regulars had become used to this habit of Ngor's and we never had any trouble of it before. But on this particular night, Conakry was moving through the fireroom on his way to the bunker. He stopped for a dipper of water and Ngor hurried him along with a flick of his little fly whisk.

I saw the thing, and I swear the blow seemed hardly enough for a man to feel at all. But feel it, Conakry most certainly did. He wheeled as though stung, and he crouched, ready to spring upon the smaller Ngor. His lips pulled back from his filed, fanglike teeth and the tribal scars stretched tight and hard across his contorted face. His eyes burned with a savage fury which brought a prickling to my skin, I can tell you that.

The second, who was going off watch, and the other stokers and trimmers there, stood as though hypnotized by Conakry's embodied hatred. The only sounds were those of the boilers and the engine and the working of the sea beyond the side plates.

Even now, I can remember the look of Conakry's face, and I have no doubt he would have killed Ngor, there and then, had not the second and I stepped between them. Neither before or since have I seen such ferocity in a human face.

"Into your bunker with you," I shouted at him.

Conakry's eyes shifted to me, then. The anger was slow in leaving his face. I half expected him to attack and tensed to meet his charge. But, in the end, he did go into the bunker. We could hear him in there, throwing the coal about furiously as though in that way he vented the rage he could vent in no other.

Would that that had been so.

Ngor, for his part, was completely taken apart. He was terror-stricken. I told him to take a turn on deck. He wanted getting hold of himself. I didn't want him there where the other men could see what a state he was in. Bad for discipline, you see. And, for the time being, I thought the whole thing would blow over and be done with. But it didn't. And it wasn't.

On the second day afterwards, Ngor failed to appear on the gratings as I came down to take the first watch. The second said he had not been down on either of the preceding dog watches, either. This was not at all like Ngor, and I felt a premonitory chill run down my back. Conakry was there, staring at me with a kind of gloating knowledge in his eyes before he stooped and disappeared into the bunker. Conakry was mixed up in this. I felt it in my bones.

The second must have felt something of the same way. "Better have a look, Third," he said. "It's not like Ngor to stop away so long."

As a step towards promoting Ngor's standing among the Africans, we had arranged separate quarters for him. We had rigged a little-used storeroom under the poop with a berth for him and a lamp of his own. That is where I found him.

He was lying, fully clothed, in his disheveled berth. His face, usually so round and shiny black, was shrunken and gray-tinged. His eyes were without luster at all. Ngor was the picture of a dying man.

"Ngor," I blurted, shocked despite myself. "What is it, man? What has got into you?"

Ngor turned his head weakly to face me, but he didn't speak and there was an air of abject hopelessness about him. He had a bucket of water there, and I took him a dipper but he wouldn't drink. I felt him, but there was no fever. He was not flushed or swollen or showing any of the classic signs of illness at all. Still, there was the very smell of death in the little room and, I confess, it put my wind up for fair. It wasn't natural for a man to go down like that, not in so brief a time.

"What is it, man," I repeated myself. I felt like an ass, but could think of nothing else to say.

Still, Ngor did not speak. But his eyes moved. They turned slowly to the foot of his berth. I saw the thing then. It was a crude, doll-like figure, made of blackened wood and bits of fur and cloth. It hung by its neck from an overhead beam, twisting and turning with the motion of the ship. And, as it turned, I saw its suffering face bore an unmistakable semblance of Ngor's.

It all came clear then. I had heard of such things along the coast, but it was my first experience. Conakry had done this out of his rage against Ngor. He had made the doll and festooned it with bits of bone and fur in a way which, to Ngor, meant certain death.

I stepped quickly, as if removing a venomous insect or serpent, and snatched down the evil figure. I ran to the door and hurled the thing as far into the sea as I could. Perhaps modern man is not so immune to such things as we might like to think. I remember, even now, a distinct sensation of horror at the very feel of the thing, and I shuddered involuntarily at being rid of it.

But, though I had done with the doll, Ngor was not. The bloody thing might well be a half mile astern, and dropping further aft with every turn of the screw, but in Ngor's mind, it was still twirling there at the end of the broken string from which I had snatched it. Nor could all my arguing change a bit of it.

By morning, Ngor was in a virtual coma. It put a pall over the entire ship. The Africans would not go near him, and all of us whites were concerned. It was the eeriness of it which put our wind up, I suppose.

"I've seen them die of it," the old chief said. "Right here on this coast. A ju-ju man makes a little dolly like that and the victim simply dies. Asked a doctor in Glasgow about it once. He said it's a kind of hypnotism, like. The wog thinks he's going to die. So, he dies. Bloody nuisance it is, too."

I couldn't have agreed more. Without Ngor, handling the other Africans would be awkward as the devil. But I didn't fully realize the spot we were on until the chief explained it.

"Ye see, Third," he said, "this Conakry fellow, if he can put Ngor down, it puts him in a good spot, ye see. The other wogs'll do whatever he says. They'll be afraid not to, seeing what he's done to Ngor."

I did see. Except for the bridge officers, we engineers, the boatswain, carpenter and steward, the ship was manned with Africans. Our Scots owners could hold down expenses that way, you see. But, in the circumstances, it meant that a bloody witch doctor with a grudge under his skin held virtual command of a British merchant vessel on the high seas.

"Aye," the chief went on. "Wi' the other wogs under his thumb, he can make us dance to his tune all right."

Remembering the hatred I had seen burning in Conakry's eyes, the thought of dancing to any tune he might call lacked appeal altogether. I accepted the chief's offer of a touch of John Crabbie's export Scotch.

"Now, ye're not to let on below, ye understand, Third," the chief admonished me. "Big thing's not to let the bugger know we're afraid of him. Now, get below to your watch. Ye'll be late."

It was one thing to assure the chief in his cabin that I would not let Conakry know I was frightened. It was an entirely different matter to stand on the gratings and feel the big negro pass by me on his way to the bunker. Despite myself, I looked at him as he went by. And he looked back. His jet eyes narrowed, and the tribal scars on his face, glistening with sweat, made a mask behind which he hid his true feelings. I imagined all kinds of things, of course, and gripped a big spanner in my hand but Conakry stooped and went on into the bunker.

"All right. All right. Hop to it," I cried to the stokers who had stopped dead still on Conakry's appearance and who stood there, staring at the bunker door as though any number of horrible things might fly out at any minute. The men did turn to, but it was a miserable watch. Nothing went right, and I could feel an instinctive crawling of my skin at thinking of Ngor willing himself to death in his little berth above decks.

I was glad indeed to see the second coming down the ladder. From his face, I could see the chief had told him what to expect and I began at once to turn over the watch to him.

"Hold on, Third," he said. "It's but four bells. It's not for relieving the watch that I'm here."

The second was right. It was not yet two o'clock. I was embarrassed at being caught showing the state of my mind.

"Then what is it you want?" I said rather bluntly.

"The chief, Third. He'd like the loan of your clock."

It was one of my several shortcomings as a seafaring man that I slept both soundly and well. I have been known to fall back into slumber, even after being called for a watch and having both feet on deck. Last trip home, I had bought a monstrous big alarm clock with a bell fit to rouse the dead. It had become something of a joke amongst us.

"My clock? What the bloody . . . ?"

"He didn't take me into his confidence like, Third," the second said. "He just asked for the loan of your clock and set me to get it. Now, does he get it or not?"

The second was not long on patience, and it was likely as not he knew no more than I about what the chief wanted with my clock, anyway.

"Take the bloody thing," I said. We were all pretty touchy then. "It's in my cabin." The second went up then, and I heard no more about alarm clocks that watch. Nor on the next, either.

Ngor, by that time, was very near death, indeed. Fear, like a tangible thing, had spread out through our native crew from Ngor's little cubicle. It was as though the ship were simply waiting for Conakry to make his next move, as though what would happen would inevitably happen, beyond all thought of stopping.

Actually, strange as it may seem, I felt absolutely no surprise when the second came into the mess and told me what Conakry had done. I was in the mess alone, and there was no question the second was in a funk. It was his watch, and he shouldn't have been out of the engine room in the first place, but even that seemed appropriate to the time, and I let it pass without comment.

"Proper kettle of fish we're in," the second groused over a mug of tea. He sat slumped over the table, as much angry as fearful, I believe now. It was not right, in his British view of the time, that a wog should have the best of a white man, and a British subject at that.

"Bundled me right up the bloody ladder, they did," the second went on. "Best I could make out, this Conakry's got them convinced the engine's possessed of evil spirits, and they won't go near the bloody thing. Bundled me out, they did, for my own good, they said.

"What does he want, Second?" I said then. "Conakry? What does he want out of it?"

The second shook his head. "Damned if I know, Third. But I got me an idea all right."

So did I. Any man who saw the hatred in Conakry's face the night Ngor whisked him could have little doubt what mercy would be shown anyone falling under his power. And there could no longer be any question about Conakry's hold over our native crew. Loyalty based on fear it may have been, but it was loyalty, nonetheless.

"Have you told the chief?" I said then.

"Aye," the second blurted disgustedly. "Aye, I told him. And you know what the bloody chief's doing, Third? He's holed up in his cabin, with that alarm clock of yours torn all to hell and gone and scattered over his desk."

"He's what?"

"You heard me. And all he said was 'Did ye pop the safeties, Second?' Now, can you picture it, man? The ship in the hands of savages, and him sitting in his cabin playing with bloody alarm clocks."

I was not so ready to give up on our chief as the second, but I had to admit what he said did sound a touch strange. And the ship was slowing noticeably as her fires cooled. That was real enough.

"Maybe you have a suggestion, Second?" I said.

"No," he said sullenly, "but I'll be damned if I'd be sitting in my cabin playing with bloody clocks." He drank of his tea. "The Captain's got guns. All ships have guns. That's all we got to do, pot Conakry. The wogs'll be just as happy as us to see him done in."

Knowing the natives, I was not so sure as the second that they would not harm us if we touched Conakry. Without Ngor, we had no way of knowing what the big black told them. But, before I could reply, the chief appeared in the mess doorway. He had something in his hands but it was covered with a hideously-colored bureau scarf he bought for his wife once in Gibraltar. She, poor lady, had the sense to refuse it, but it was a prominent fitting in the chief's cabin on board.

"Will ye come with me, Misters?" the chief said. "I may be needing the two of ye."

There is no describing the curiosity I felt for what it was the chief had in his hand, but he volunteered no news and we got up and followed him aft to the stokers' mess.

Conakry had quite taken over there. Big and arrogant, he sat at the head of the littered table while the others served him and kowtowed to him in other ways. They got rum from somewhere and I felt a sudden fear for the Steward. Our Steward was not the man to give rum to natives. Not willingly.

"Conakry," the chief called out then, in a voice grown used to being heard over the clamor of a hundred engine rooms. The other blacks drew back before the power of a white man's voice but Conakry didn't. He stood up, squaring his shoulders and lifting his chin, while all the time staring his insolence down at us. He was a magnificent physical specimen, you had to give him that. But he was drunk, as much with the knowledge of power as with the rum which made his lips shine.

"Conakry," the chief said again. "Look, Conakry." He stepped then into the mess and put what was in his hands onto the mess table opposite the big black. Conakry stared at the covered object curiously but without any obvious concern until the chief pulled away the bureau scarf and we saw what was under it.

It was a ju-ju doll, carved in a crude likeness of Conakry. Its eyes were blank and its arms reached out in the classic gesture of the blind. The other Africans recoiled as though thrown back by some sudden force emanating from the horrible little figure.

Even Conakry seemed shaken for a moment. But only for a moment. After all, hadn't he made such dolls himself? Didn't he know they were nothing more than lifeless wood and bits of cloth. And, in the way of one magician appreciating another's art, he grinned at the chief.

"Conakry," the chief cried again. He made a motion with his hand and the blind doll began to walk across the table towards Conakry, weaving slightly with the motion of the ship. Conakry stiffened. He tried mightily to stand up to this living thing. If the doll had remained motionless, he might well have brought it off. But the sight of the blind doll groping its way towards him, its blank eyes staring, its blind hands outstretched, was too much for him.

He looked at the chief as though begging him to call off his hideous little creature, but the chief stood firm. The doll's feet made scratching sounds on the table and Conakry's eyes came back to it.

Then, a most remarkable thing happened. The chief noticed it first. He caught at my sleeve and pointed. Conakry was going blind. His eyes were actually filming over and his hands, instinctively, were lifting before him. He straightened, his back to the bulkhead.

"The bugger's blind," I heard the second gasp behind me. "The bloody beggar's blind!"

Then, with a scream I will remember to my dying day, Conackry lurched forward, stumbling, falling, knocking aside all before him. Completely, hysterically blind, he felt his way to the doorway and out onto the weather deck.

We watched him go, white men and natives alike. He collided with a winch and fell. He got up and stumbled over a padeye, hitting his head against a hatch coaming. He got up again, blood streaming horribly down his face. Then, groping, he found the bulwarks and without warning of any kind, pulled himself up and over.

It was all over in less time than I've taken to tell it. I, for one, was breathing hard and not at all sure that I would not be sick. But it was over and the chief's matter of fact voice made it bearable.

"Ye'd best see to your watch, Second," he said. "And, Third, will ye have a look-in on Ngor. He'll be all right now that yon savage is nae more wi' us."

And that, indeed, is the way it was. And, as I said in the beginning, it's not a thing you'll be finding in many books on seagoing engineers.

THE RIVER

There is a peace about rivers. Especially such rivers as the Rio Flores, after it has left its turbulent mountain youth far behind and contented itself with a ponderous meandering through coastal rain forests to the sea. Here the river flows, slow, dark, and murmurous in the green shadows of great trees which lean far out from the banks to trail their branches and suspended vines in the water. There is something soothing, something reassuring and comforting in the calm and purposeful marching of the water. But there is something ominous, too, in its darkness. Something disquieting and awesome, at times.

Honk Taylor lived there on the Rio Flores, in the little town of San Gregorio. He had a well-rusted tank landing craft, a relic of Vietnam. He ran it as a kind of combined freight boat and ferry for the up-river plantations. When not on the boat itself, he lived in a tin-roofed shack built on stilts out over the river. He moored the boat to the stilts, making a kind of self-contained economic enterprise.

There was a crippled old man to serve him some-times as deckhand, and there was Jose Alcazar to sell him rum when the nights grew too long and too dark and too close on the river.

All this was Honk's life. He asked no more. He wanted no more. The people of San Gregorio accepted him for what he was, and he, them. And, God willing, it would continue like that, so far as Honk was concerned, until the day he died.

Then, one early morning, not long ago, there was a roaring of jeep engines in San Gregorio, and the squawking and squealing of chickens and pigs as a detachment of government soldiers careened through the town and disappeared in the direction of Tiburon, the next and much larger town down river.

Honk cursed and rolled up onto one elbow in his protesting old iron bed. He spread apart the plaited palm fronds which formed the walls of his shack and peered sleepily out into the street, along the blank walls of plastered houses and flimsy siding of shacks not much better than his own. San Gregorio was not a town to excite much admiration, even on the Rio Flores.

It was even less impressive as Honk looked out, since everyone had taken cover. Dust still hung in the air and the chickens milled nervously.

"Ay, Paco." Honk called. "*Que pasa?* What goes?"

A young man, thin with the thinness of youth and brown under the sagging white of his singlet, stepped from around a corner and looked up and down the street to see who had called. Seeing no one, he was puzzled. Along the street, others were stepping out from doorways, cautiously, fearfully, but it was obvious none of them had called.

"It's me," Honk called. "Over here. What's going on?" He pushed larger the hole in his wall.

The young man's face brightened as he caught sight of Honk through the parted fronds. "It is the revolution," he shouted. "It is the day. It is said that already there has been fighting." As though taking courage from the young man in the street, the townspeople rushed out from their houses and buildings and ran, shouting and laughing with excited faces, in the direction from which the soldiers had come.

Honk's face sobered and his eyes watched the running people. "What's all the excitement?" he asked Paco. "Where's everybody going?"

"They go to welcome Romero, Señor Honk," Paco said, his eyes shining. "We all go to welcome Romero." Then, after a pause, "Do you not come, too, Señor? Do you not welcome Romero, too?"

Honk smiled a too-weary smile. "No, I do not go to welcome Romero."

"But he is a hero, Señor. He is a great man. He fights for our country. It is right that we let him know we are with him, that we stand beside him."

"Okay. Okay, so he's a big hero," Honk said. "He's your big hero, not mine. Now, how about knocking off the noise and let me get some sleep."

Anger darkened Paco's face. "You joke, Señor? You make the joke, maybe?"

Honk didn't answer. He studied Paco's indignant young face, seeing in it the twin lusts of blood and patriotism. Jostled by the people rushing past him, Paco glared at Honk with all the passion of the zealot. Still without speaking, Honk let the palm fronds fall back into place and rolled over to sit up on the side of his bed.

"That's the trouble with revolutionaries," he said. "They got no sense of humor."

An old man, Old Manuel, mender of nets and deckhand on Honk's boat, squatted in a corner of the shack, fanning a crude charcoal brazier to life. The old man nodded without speaking. He looked incredibly old, dry, wrinkled, his brown skin gray with the ashes of age. His back humped up ludicrously and his legs twisted under him so that he moved, when he moved, with a horrible crab-like gait. He couldn't really do the work of his job but Honk kept him on anyway.

Honk leaned to pull on pants and shove his feet into sandals. The river side of the shack was open to the world, to the wide reach of the river at San Gregorio, and to the viscous warm breeze which dawdled over the water. Honk moved to that side of the shack, as he did every morning, to look out over the river and to drink deep of its peace. The green walls of the rain forest pressed tight on the river and leaned out over the water as though begrudging the space the river took. Sometimes the leaning trees were undermined by the current and fell into the river.

Honk liked to see the trees fall. His sympathies were all with the river. Sometimes in the dark nights, when everything was still and the rum fumes boiled in his brain, sometimes, then, Honk thought of the river as being like a man's life, and of the jungle as being like all the things which crowd in on a man's life, to press and squeeze until it is dark and narrow and running inexorably towards an end no one can see.

By reflex, Honk checked his boat, his eyes moving from mooring line to mooring line until he was certain all was right. The ugly old craft's battle paint had long since given up to rust and river mud but in Honk's eyes it was beautiful. The boat made everything simple.

When he was in his boat, there was only he and the river and the river knew what it was about. There was certainty in the steady purposefulness of moving water. The river knew where it was going and why. All the stinking, leaning, pressing, vine-choked trees in the world would not stop the river.

The lid of Old Manuel's coffee pot lifted with the pressure of steam and dropped back with a tinny tap which stirred Honk from his morning mood. He turned and washed his face in a rusty basin of river water, wiping hands and face dry on a scrap of dirty sacking. He combed his thinning hair with his fingers. The coffee pot lid tapped more insistently, rising and snapping shut on little puffs of white steam, more and more quickly, as though marking cadence for the quickening steps of some approaching disaster.

That was what came of the soldiers' dashing off in their jeeps so early in the morning. It had nothing to do with Honk. But, you could never tell in a place like San Gregorio.

"Go get something for breakfast, *viejo*," Honk said to Old Manuel. "Tell Miguel I will pay him tomorrow."

The old man nodded and pulled himself up onto his crooked legs. "Maybe, Señor Honk, if there was money, maybe there would be a bottle," he said, grinning. "In honor of Romero, maybe?"

"*Andale*," Honk snapped. "We're shoving off pretty soon. Let Romero buy his own bottle."

"I only thought . . ."

"Well, don't," Honk growled. "Now get your butt over to Miguel's. And ask about that new manila. It should have been here two weeks ago."

Without further protest Old Manuel nodded and hitched his way out the door. He stopped in the doorway only long enough to point and to say, "It is Romero. He comes now."

Through the open door, and through the shack's flimsy walls themselves, Honk could hear the shouting and singing of the people as they re-entered the town, crowding about the rebel leader and his grimy, unshaven men whose only neatness was in the oiled cleanliness of their guns. The people were singing the song Romero had taught them to sing before he went into the hills for the revolution.

The shouting and the laughter and the singing came closer, until it stopped outside Honk's shack. "Ay, Señor

Honk," a deep, commanding voice called, but Honk did not go to the door.

Romero called one more time. Upon getting no reply, he stooped and stepped through the door. Darkly handsome, broad grinning, and utterly virile in his youth, utterly conscious, too, of the picture he made, with guns strapped to him and the combat clothes of American Marines molded to his sweating body.

"*Hola*, Señor," Romero said. "You did not come to meet us?"

Honk sat at his table. "Coffee, Romero?" he said "New pot, just off the fire."

"You did not come to meet us, Señor Honk. What am I to think of that? Everyone else in town came to meet us."

"All hail the conquering hero, that it, Romero? The war's already won, and we hail the conquering hero," Honk paused. "Better take the coffee while it's still hot."

Romero's dark face flushed even darker in anger at not being taken seriously. But the anger passed. The world, that morning, was far too pleasant a place for anger. "You joke, Señor Honk," he laughed. "You make the joke. Always, you make the joke."

"Yeah. Regular clown, ain't I?"

Romero laughed again. "Yes, Señor," he said. "You are a clown." Then, more seriously, "A very foolish clown."

He glanced at Honk's boat moored to the shack's footing piles. "Last week, I asked for the use of your boat. It would have made our job much easier. But you said I was a fool. You said I could not win, no? You said the soldiers would tear me up in little pieces and leave me for the dogs. You said these things, no?"

"I said them."

"Hah." Romero gloated then. "Now, you see you were wrong, Señor. Now you see who is the fool. Already, we have met the soldiers, and they have run from in front of us like curs from the scent of the jaguar. Already . . ."

Honk made as though to interrupt, but Romero would not listen. "No, you listen, Señor. They ran before us, you hear? They jumped in their jeeps and ran."

Romero paused, as though gathering himself. Then he stabbed his finger at Honk. "And, now, Señor, I will tell you. I ask again for the boat. I will win without it, but it will be easier if we have it. We do not have to ask, Señor. We can take it. But I do not want it said that Romero asks those to fight who do not want to fight. I . . ."

Honk slammed his coffee cup onto his table. His face was red with the anger in him. His jaw pushed forward. "You <u>are</u> a fool, Romero," he said. "You're a young, loud-mouthed fool. Those soldiers are not running, you idiot. They've got tanks in Tiburon. Tanks and machine guns and mortars. All they're doing is sucking you out into the open. Get wise, for God's sake, Romero. You follow those monkeys, and you're buzzard bait."

But Romero would not hear. Secure in his young arrogance, he laughed. His blood was hot and running in him. But there was no rancor in his voice. He grinned. "We saw the soldiers run, Señor Honk," he said. "We saw that. We saw how the people of the town ran out to join us. It was a wonderful feeling, Señor Honk. I . . ."

"They ran out there because the soldiers are gone, for Christ's sake," Honk blurted. "Let the soldiers come back, and they will run to meet them just as fast."

Romero's face sobered. Anger glinted again in his eyes. "That is not so, Señor," he said. "The people love me. The people . . ."

"The people love nothing, Romero," Honk broke in, his voice bitter. "The people are <u>people</u>." Then, pleading, "Look, Romero. You are young. You're young, and you still believe a lot of things. Let me tell you . . ."

"I have no time," Romero began. "I . . ."

"You have time," Honk shouted. He pushed past Romero, slammed closed the door to the street and stood with his back to it. Neither spoke for a time. The sounds of the river flowing under the shack came to them through the floor boards.

"Well?" Romero snapped, challenging. His slung rifle slipped off his shoulder, ready to use. "Do not make me do this, Señor Honk," he said. "You have been good to me. We have been friends. Do not make me do this thing."

"Romero, listen," Honk said quietly, ignoring the gun. "The Captain of the soldiers was here last night. He knew you were coming today. He talked about it. He . . ."

"He talked with you?" Romero grabbed at Honk's shirtfront and held Honk to him. His voice was dangerously controlled. "What did the Captain want, Señor? Why did he talk to you?"

"He wanted me to talk some sense into your head, God damn it. He thought you might listen to me."

Romero hesitated for but a moment. Then he snorted. "He is afraid, Señor. The Captain talks the big fight. But he is afraid. You will see, Señor. You will see what . . ."

"He's not afraid, *hijo*," Honk said. "I know the Captain. So do you. You know that he is not afraid.

"He does not like the thought of killing someone he once counted as friend," Honk said bluntly, "But he is not afraid." The words fell heavy in a sudden silence. A jungle bird called from the trees across the river. They could hear the call clearly. And it showed in Romero's face that Honk's words had lodged. But, just then, the people in the street began to sing again the song Romero taught them to sing:
"Rise, ye sons of liberty.
Lift your arms in holy fight.
Rise, ye sons of Liberty.
Live again in Freedom's light."

The song rose and fell with the deep voices of men and, here and there, the rising, twisting wail of women's shriller notes. The air pulsed with the beat of the song. Its words came through the thin walls of the shack and spread out over the calm, uncaring water of the river. The song cast a spell over their world, a gripping, holding spell, from which Honk wrenched himself.

Someone pounded on the closed door. "Romero. Romero," excited voices called. "We are wasting time, Romero."

Romero moved to push Honk aside, but Honk stopped him with a hand on his chest. "We were friends here, *hijo*," Honk said. "You. Me. The Captain. Have you forgotten that? We drank together. Played chess together. Right there. Right there on that table. We . . ."

Romero's face softened, "Yes. Yes, we were friends, Señor Honk," he said quietly. "I have nothing against the Captain. I have nothing against you, Señor."

"Then knock off this crap," Honk cried, "stop it now, while there's still time. Go on back to the hills. If you stop now, the Captain will not follow you. He said for me to tell you that. He said that, if you stop now, it will end here. If you don't . . ."

Romero pushed Honk's restraining hand aside. He moved his head toward the sound of singing in the street. "It is too late now to talk of stopping," he said. "You hear them singing? That is my song, Señor Honk. They sing it for me."

"You owe those jackals nothing, son," Honk pleaded. "They're using you. They're not worth what you're trying to do for them."

Romero smiled then, a small wistful smile, but a smile nevertheless. "I know you are meaning to help me," he said. "I know that you mean well."

"I'm trying to save your stupid ass," Honk said then, his voice tight in his throat. "I'm trying to keep you from throwing your life away for nothing. I . . ."

"For nothing, Señor?"

Honk held himself for a time, looking into the younger man's eyes. "All right," he said at last, "so everything's not perfect in this country. It never has been. It probably never will be. But, what good's it going to do to go out and get yourself and a lot of other people killed? What good will that do?"

Again, Romero smiled, ruefully. "I don't know, Señor Honk. Maybe you are right. Who knows? But someone must fight. Someone must care enough to fight. Maybe you are right that I do not know how to fight. Maybe you are right in that. I have had small experience." He paused and met Honk's eyes with his own. "It is for experience that I came to you, Señor. It is with experience that you could have helped."

Honk snorted, but he didn't answer.

"You see? If you do not help, Señor, I must . . ."

"You haven't got a prayer, son," Honk said then, both sadness and exasperation mixed in his voice, "I'm telling you, the Captain's sucking you into a trap. And don't think he'll go easy on you because we were friends. The Captain's not that kind of a man. He . . ."

"All right. All right," Romero broke in angrily. Fists were again pounding on the door and voices calling for him. There was a taut silence between them for a moment. Then Romero said quietly, "As I said before, Señor, maybe you are right. But it is too late to talk of that now. I have a mind to see what is wrong in our country. I have a heart to care. These things have fallen to me. I have to do the best I can with them. It is that way. That is the way it is."

Honk moved to answer but Romero stopped him. "I have little time now, Señor," he said. Their eyes met and something wordless passed between them. It was as though they were saying good-bye before a long journey. As though something big and important were ending. Honk had not had a son of his own for a long time. Even then, the boy had been little more than a baby. He did not know what it would be like to lose a son who was a man, but he thought it must be like something he felt then with Romero.

"I have to know, Señor," Romero said quietly. "You will not help me?"

Honk shook his head.

"Is it because you think I am wrong, Señor? Or because you think I will fail?"

Honk did not answer at once, and the fists pounded again on his door. He turned to look out over the river, reaching as though by instinct for the comfort he had come to expect from its broad moving water. But this time, there was no comfort in it for him. This time, the river was just water. Nothing more.

"Which is it to be, Señor?" Romero pressed. "You owe me an answer. Because we were friends, you owe me this much."

Without turning to face Romero, Honk answered him, his voice low and wooden-sounding. "It's not my fight, son," he said, "I'm sorry, but it's not my fight."

Oddly, Romero seemed to relax at getting Honk's reply. He seemed to become taller. It was as though some dreaded thing had been brought into the open and could then be faced. "Ay," he said quietly. "It is not your country. As you say, it is not your fight. I had no right to ask. I am sorry I asked help of you, Señor. I am very sorry."

"Romero. For the love of God . . ."

"No." Romero moved to the door and took its crude handle in his hand. "Say no more, Señor. I have no time to listen." He paused. "But, Señor, because we were friends, I do not want you to think I hold lightly the advice you give. But there is this I want you to know. There is this I believe. Even if I am to fail. Even if I am to do that, Señor, there is worth in trying. I must believe that, Señor. I must believe there is some worth in trying."

Then, before Honk could answer, Romero turned and was gone. The crowd sounds welled up as Romero appeared among them and the sounds faded as he led his men away and the crowd followed after. Honk stepped to his door and watched them go. He watched his men fall in behind Romero. There were so pitifully few of them, and they held their guns so awkwardly, their faces alight with that special blend of fear and excitement with which untried young men face danger.

But the townspeople were properly gallant. The young women ran alongside the men, holding on to their clothes and offering cool drinks, laughing, gay red lips over the whiteness of their teeth. Small boys tagged along, mimicking with straining strides the pace of the fighters, and dogs ran, barking, out ahead.

Old Manuel pressed back against a plastered wall to let the parade pass. He clutched to his breast the bottles and bundles Honk had sent him to fetch. Romero did not even see him. Those who did brushed past him without so much as a glance.

"Come on. *Andale, viejo.* It's late. I'm hungry," Honk called.

Old Manuel scuttled, bent and unsteady, through the dust of the street and put down the things he carried on Honk's table. "The crowd," he muttered. "There were so many of them. I am old, Señor. It takes time for me . . ."

Honk ignored the Old Man's excuses and took a brown bottle from the lot on the table. He pulled the cork with his teeth and put the bottle to his lips. He drank deep and grimaced, shivering at the burning of the rum in his throat. "They're fools," he blurted, "stupid fools."

They were angry words Honk used. But there was no anger in his face. There was only a sadness. And a wetness in his eyes.

"*Si,*" the Old Man said as he worked with the breakfast, "*Es verdad,* it is true," he agreed. "Much fools. It is true, they are."

Honk drank again from the bottle. "They think they can fight tanks and airplanes with rifles and pistols — and fancy talk."

"Ay, they think that," Old Manuel said. He put the last of the breakfast on the table and pulled off his hat, holding it in front of his chest in a gesture of humility. "The breakfast," he said, "she is ready, Señor."

"Well, it's not my fight," Honk said again as he sat down and put the bottle ready to hand.

"Ay. It is not your fight," Old Manuel agreed again.

Honk ate, but he ate absently, as though the meal were of no great importance. As he ate, he drank, but the rum did no good. Sometimes he spoke. Once he said, "I've had my war, *viejo*. I've had too many wars." Another time he said, "It's crazy. All for nothing. It's . . ."

Honk's voice trailed off into nothingness. He was, for a time, helped by the rum, in an earlier time. A time of fire and explosion. Of burned ships and torn men. Of battles won and lost. And horrors he had felt free of only after finding the Rio Flores and the peace it had come to mean for him.

Old Manuel said nothing at all to anything Honk said and, finally, Honk fell silent. The shack was quiet. The sounds of playing children came through the thin walls, and the calling of women from one to another. Except for the drunken braying of Romero's song coming, from time to time, from Placido Marti's bar, it might have been any other day in San Gregorio.

Honk finished his breakfast. Then Old Manuel ate and cleaned away the clutter of the meal. "I go to make the boat ready," he said then. "You said we are sailing. Yes?"

There was enough of the rum in Honk then for it to show in his voice and in the wetness and the looseness of his lips. "No, no," he mumbled. "The, the engine needs looking at. I'll get to it in a little while." He drank again and peered closely at Old Manuel to see how he would take the lie.

The Old Man simply nodded and settled himself into his corner where he squatted with the accepting patience of the old poor.

"They run up against a tank and they won't stand a snow ball's chance in hell," Honk said abruptly.

The Old Man nodded soberly. He knew Honk was talking about Romero and his men. He watched Honk with his faded and rheumy eyes.

After that, there was another long silence in the shack.

During the silence Honk got to staring at Old Manuel's crooked legs. He gestured with his bottle towards them and he asked gently, "It is said in the town, *viejo*, that you got your legs in a revolution."

The Old Man nodded. He smiled uncertainly. "*Si*," he said. "With one named Rodriguez. It makes many years now, Señor."

Honk spat on the floor. "It is said, Old Man, that you have been a cripple ever since. That you have eaten filth and worn rags. It is said that, before I came with my boat, that you lived and slept with the dogs under the porch of the hotel."

"These things are true," the Old Man said with a quiet dignity. "I have slept with the dogs."

"You have paid well, Old Man," Honk went on. "You have paid well for your revolution. All these years. And for what? What good did your revolution do? What did you get out of it?"

The Old Man shrugged. "Good, Señor? Who is to say what is good. We fought then, as Romero fights now, for what we thought was good. But there is no way to tell what is good, Señor. There is no way for a man to know with his mind what is good. He can do only what he <u>feels</u> is good." He tapped his thin chest. "Only what he feels in here is good."

Honk snorted. He moved as though to drink again from the rum bottle, but stopped. "And do you feel, Old Man, that Romero is doing good now? Do you feel that in, in there?" He pointed to Old Manuel's chest.

The Old Man ignored the sarcasm in Honk's voice. "I have too many years," he said, "for what I feel to make any difference. With these legs, I would be of small use anyway."

"And me, Old Man," Honk pressed. "Do you feel I am doing good? Do you feel I am right in not helping Romero?

"It is not for one man to tell another what is right and what is wrong, Señor. I . . ."

Honk lurched to his feet and clutched at the Old Man's rags. "Tell me, Old Man," he shouted, "All morning, since Romero left, you've been looking at me like something washed up by the river. Now, tell me, what is it you think about me."

The Old Man held passive and unresisting in Honk's grasp. "You have no need to know what it is I feel, Señor," the Old Man said. "Already, you feel in yourself what is right and what is wrong. Already you know that."

Honk glared into the Old Man's face for a time longer. Then he released his hold and turned to look again out over the broad flatness of the river. The Old Man spoke again. "It has been a long time since you have drunk the rum the way you have drunk it this morning, Señor," he said. "It has been a long time since your face has been so full of storms, since you have, have been so rough with an old man." He paused. "It is these things which tell me you know what is right for you to do, Señor."

Honk seemed to think on the Old Man's words for a long time. Then, quietly, calmly, and without turning from the river, he began to speak. "I had a home once, Old man," he said. "In the States. I had a wife. A little boy. I left them one day. To come here. I thought I was looking for something. I thought I needed something."

The Old Man made no reply, and Honk turned to face him. He motioned to the Old Man's legs, his old and crooked legs. "Your wounds show, Old Man," he said. "People can see your wounds and know not to expect too much. But some wounds don't show, Old Man. Some wounds hide deep, and people don't know they are there. Sometimes people expect too much of men with wounds like that."

"I have seen men with wounds like that, Señor."

"Then don't expect too much of me, Old Man," Honk said, his voice tight. "Don't expect too much out of me."

"It is not I who expects, Señor," the Old Man said. "It is you who expects. You deny it, but it is you who expects. That is your wound, Señor. You still expect, you still expect much of yourself."

Honk turned away, angry. His arms were rigid down his sides and his face was drawn in tight down-trending lines. "I expect nothing of myself, Old Man. There is nothing left in me to expect."

"If that were true, Señor, there would be no need for us to talk this way. We would be on our way up the river."

"It's not my fight," Honk said. "I've had my fight. A long time ago. I had a belly-full of fight. I want no more. I, I'm neutral. I don't care anymore. I don't care what happens."

"Only the dead are neutral, Señor."

Honk looked at the Old Man's withered legs. "The dead, and the crippled, eh, Old Man?"

"I have not said that I am neutral, Señor. I have not said that."

Honk met the Old Man's eyes with his own for a time without speaking. They could hear the sounds of the street coming through the shack's thin walls. They could smell the smells of the river mud drying in the nooning sun. Yet, neither spoke, and it was Honk who, in the end, turned away once more to look out over the wide reach of river. It was Honk who spoke first.

Without looking at the Old Man, he said, "I count them both as friends, Old Man, Romero and the Captain. You are saying that I have to choose between them?"

"I do not say that."

"Maybe not. But you think it, Old Man. Don't you?"

The Old Man did not answer until Honk turned and looked directly at him. Then he said, slowly, "Yes, Señor. I think it."

"I told you, Old Man," he blurted, his voice holding a defiance. "I'm neutral. This is not my fight. I came down here to get away from fights, God damn it. It's . . ."

"You must choose, Señor," the Old Man said then. His voice had grown stronger and more firm as he talked. It was as though he had grown straighter, too, in talking so with Honk.

Honk did not reply, but his face held stubbornly defiant and he lifted the rum bottle again to his lips. "It's not my fight," he said again. "I came down here to haul bananas for you monkeys. You want to knock each others' heads off, that's fine with me. I'll be around to haul bananas for whoever's left."

The Old Man went on as though Honk had not spoken. "You must choose, Señor," he said. "Or the Captain will choose for you."

Honk stopped then and looked at the Old Man. "What's that supposed to mean?"

"If you choose to help Romero, Señor," the Old Man said, "you must do so quickly. Already, by now, there will have been the fight before Tiburon. Already, the Captain will be on his way here. And the Captain is not such a man who will ask for the use of your boat, Señor. The Captain will take your boat. He will take it with his guns, Señor."

"The Captain will have no need for my boat now, Old Man," Honk said. "If there has been a fight at Tiburon, the Captain will no longer have any need for my boat."

"He will have a need for it, Señor," the Old Man persisted. He spoke patiently, as though explaining something to a child, but his old eyes were hard and demanding. "We, both of us, know, Señor, that Romero could not have won the fight at Tiburon. We know that it is the Captain who will win the fight at Tiburon. Romero and his men — those of them who are left — will have scattered into the jungle."

Honk listened without speaking, and the Old Man went on. "There is a rendezvous, Señor," he said. "Far back in the hills. Far up the river. Those who are left will gather there."

"But I see no need the Captain could have for my boat."

"There are no roads to the country of the rendezvous. Only rough and narrow trails. The men of Romero could not be caught over such trails, Señor. But by water . . . If the Captain has the use of your boat, he could be at the rendezvous first. He could be there waiting and he could get them all, Señor. That is the need the Captain will have for your boat."

The possible truth of what the Old Man said worked its way into Honk's mind and he put down the rum bottle. He put it down on the crude table, and a suspicion grew in his eyes. "You speak with great certainty about all this, Old Man," he said. "How is it you know all this?"

Again, it seemed that the Old Man stood straighter. His eyes met Honk's and there was challenge in them. "I have not said that I am neutral, Señor," he said, proudly.

"Then you're one of them. You are one of the men of Romero."

The Old Man did not answer, but it showed in his face that he was, indeed, a rebel, and unrepentant for the fact of it.

"It wasn't me, then, that Romero came here so often to see," Honk went on. "It was you, Old Man. It was you he came to see. It was you, wasn't it, Old Man?"

The Old Man did not answer at once. When he did speak, his composure was shaken. "Yes," he admitted. "Romero came here to see me."

"You put him up to this, you started the whole damned thing."

"Yes," the Old Man said, distraught. "But it was not supposed to be like this. I told Romero to wait. I told him we were not ready. But Romero is young, Señor. He is full of the heart. He would not wait. He said that I was old and that my legs, my legs made me afraid to fight."

"And now he is dead." Honk said the words flatly, letting the words themselves place blame on the Old Man.

The Old Man looked to the floor then and his face grew heavy with the grief in him. "It may be," he said. "It may be that he is dead."

"Romero, and God knows how many others," Honk shouted suddenly. "Dead. All dead, Old Man. Ay. It's a good piece of work you've done. You and your crappy revolutions."

"Someone must fight," the Old Man said, his voice dull and old again. "Someone must care enough to fight."

"I remember the words," Honk said bitterly. "Now I know where Romero got them. What was the rest of it? 'There is a worth in trying.' That was what he said, Old man. Just before he went off to die, he said that."

"Yes, Romero would have said that," the Old Man said. Then, as Honk turned away with disgust in his face, the Old Man went on. "It is possible, Señor," he said, "that Romero is dead. And others as well. But some would have got away. Now they will all die if the Captain gets the use of your boat. There will be firing squads in the square and all of them will die."

Honk turned and looked at the Old Man. "What difference does that make to you, Old Man? You've had your fun. You've sent the silly brave young men with their straight legs off to die. What difference does a few more make? Huh, Old Man? What difference will a few more make?"

The Old Man winced under the lash of Honk's words. But he gathered himself and spoke firmly. "It may be as you say, Señor," he said, "that I killed the young men who fell this morning before Tiburon. But it is the man who gives the Captain the use of his boat who will kill those who will die tonight and tomorrow."

Honk's mouth opened for the reply which boiled up in him, but no words would come as the enormity of what the Old Man said struck home in him.

"It is not I who will kill those who stand in front of the Captain's firing squads, Señor," the Old Man went on. "It may be that Romero is not dead. It may be that he is with those who flee now through the jungle to the rendez-vous. It may be that Romero will be among those the Captain will trap there at the rendezvous."

Again, Honk did not answer at once. He held silent while his mind accepted the possible truth of what the Old Man was saying. "The Captain will not know where the rendezvous is," he said then. "He will have to look for it. It could take him days to . . ."

"There will have been prisoners taken at Tiburon," the Old Man said. "The Captain will know exactly where the rendezvous is. The Captain has ways of learning things from prisoners."

"It is only a chance that Romero got away," Honk said.

The Old Man seemed to find it hard to speak. "It is not only of Romero I think," he said. "I think of the others, too. Those who escape, if they live, will try again. That is the important thing, Señor, that there be other times to try."

The Old Man was openly pleading with Honk by that time. "If the Captain has the use of your boat, Señor, if the Captain arrives first at the rendezvous, it will be the end of the trying for a long time. Maybe forever, Señor. That is the important thing, Señor."

Despite himself, Honk was moved by the Old Man's words. Not so much by the words themselves, but by the awful urgency of his voice, by the pain riding naked under the age-dullness in his old eyes, by the courage that seemed almost indecent in so warped and ugly a body.

Honk turned away from the Old Man. He looked out over the river, and his voice was heavy. "It is of Romero I think, Old Man. It was Romero who was as a son to me. It was Romero who reminded me . . ."

"Of your own son, Señor?"

Honk took in a long breath and let it out before he replied. He nodded shortly. "Yes. Yes, he reminded me of my own boy. They would have been about the same age. Romero reminded me of him."

Honk turned quickly then and stepped to the table. He took up the rum bottle and faced the Old Man, his face stricken with grief. "It is Romero I think about, Old Man," he said. "It was Romero who was as a son to me."

The Old Man swallowed hard, as though something were stuck in his skinny old throat. His eyes were wet. "Believe me, Señor," he said, "it is in my heart to know how you feel. Believe me, Señor."

Honk snorted his disbelief. He drank deep from the rum bottle, grimacing at the fiery stuff in his throat. "How would you know, Old Man?" He motioned with his bottle to the Old Man's crippled legs. "All shot up. Living with the dogs under the hotel porch. What do you know of sons, Old Man? Except for those of other men that you send out to be killed in your stupid revolutions. Answer me, Old

Man. What do you know of what I feel? What do you know of sons?"

"I know how you feel, Señor," the Old Man said, his voice sounding strangely quiet after the violence of Honk's outburst. "I know how you feel, Señor, for Romero is my son."

At first, it was as though Honk had not heard what the Old Man said. He was moving the rum bottle again to his lips when the words took form in his mind. He stopped and looked at the Old Man, letting his eyes ask the question he could not find the words to ask.

The Old Man nodded. "Romero is my son. The Padre and the Good Sisters raised him, but he is my son. I was not always as I am now, Señor."

Slowly, Honk lowered the rum bottle, his mouth slack with surprise. "Romero is your son," he said, then. "Romero is your son, and you sent him out to be killed. You did that to your own son?"

"I did not send him, Señor," the Old Man said. "I tried to stop him. As, I suspect, you tried to stop him. The time was not yet right." The Old Man paused. "But I am proud that he went, Señor. I am proud that my son went."

For what seemed a long time, neither of them spoke. They heard the sounds of the river under the shack, and the calling of the town's mothers for their children, and the crowing of a game cock, and the cry of a jungle bird from across the river. They smelled the river mud. They felt the heat of the sun through the shack's tin roof.

During the time while neither of them spoke, Honk thought of the Old Man as he must once have been. He thought of the long years when he lived under the porch of the hotel with the town dogs. He thought of the pride which must have been in the mind of such a man at having a son like Romero. And, in thinking of that, Honk thought of his own son somewhere in Ohio. Honk was ashamed for having left his son in Ohio.

Then, without speaking, and with his face grave with the decision in him, Honk stepped to the table and took up the glass oil lamp that stood upon it. Deliberately, he smashed the lamp's glass chimney against the edge of the table and touched a match to the lamp's exposed wick. The flame leaped up, an ugly banner of red fire and black smoke.

"What is it you do, Señor?" the Old Man said.

Still without speaking, Honk carried the lamp to the river side of his shack and threw it into his moored boat so that it broke and burning oil splashed over the inside of the boat and grew and licked along its decks until the fire reached the mooring lines and burned through them. The lines fell into the water with little hisses and the boat drifted away, burning, on the current of the river.

After that, there was no need for talking. They sat down, Honk and the Old Man, to wait for the Captain. The Captain would not be pleased. There was no telling what he might do. Honk offered the Old Man a drink from his rum bottle.

THE HOMEWARD BOUNDER and other sea stories

LETTER TO A PRIEST

By the time you read this, Father, I shall have been long at sea. If at that time you decide to act upon that which I will here tell you, you may direct the authorities to expect me in Sydney towards the end of June.

I am writing to you not only because you are a priest but also because, in the time I was on your island, I came to look upon you as a friend, as well. And I fear that that which I am about to reveal will call upon your qualities as friend as much as upon those as priest.

I was alone in my small sailing vessel some six hundred miles north and east of Hawaii, six weeks out of San Francisco on what had been a slow and most frustrating passage back towards the love and comfort I had found on your island, love and comfort I had come to believe existed for me nowhere else on earth.

I was in no danger at all, of course. My boat, though small, was sound, water and provisions more than ample. I suffered only from the ills of prolonged solitude, ills I realize now must certainly have contributed to my later actions. But I turned into my berth that particular night with no premonition whatsoever of anything out of the ordinary.

Even when I was wakened during that night by a strong smell of kerosene, I thought little of it. Lone voyagers become used to wakening often to strange and frequently never explained sounds and other sensations.

My first thought was that my lamp oil had come adrift and spilled into the bilge from whence fumes had risen to break my sleep. But a quick look soon established the fact that my plastic containers were all sound and lashed in their places.

It then became apparent that the stench was coming from outside and, still somewhat bemused by sleep, I came on deck for a look about.

There was nothing at all untoward about the decks, but the smell of kerosene was indeed stronger in the open air and I noticed then that the sea about the boat was unnaturally quiet and humped, here and there, with strange dark objects which I did not at first recognize.

Heavy clouds rode low in the sky that night, choking out all light from the stars and there was but the lightest of winds so that the sea did little more than lift and fall in a dilatory way which caused the boat to roll and shift uneasily. There was only the faint luminosity of the water itself to light the somber scene.

Standing there, then, clinging to the shrouds for support, I came slowly to understand that the oil I smelled was upon the sea itself and that the dark objects I saw all about were oddments of luggage and clothing and bits of aircraft furniture.

In short, my boat had sailed herself during my sleep into the site of an aircraft accident. That was plain enough, once the thought occurred to me.

Naturally, I scouted about for a time in search of possible survivors. The oil and debris covered a surprisingly large area, a fact I took to indicate the crash had taken place some time ago. But I coursed back and forth several times on the odd chance.

The floating oil had muffled the ordinary splashing and running of the sea so that the night took on, under the lowering sky, a most sinister aspect. I did pick up some bits of wreckage with the thought they might prove useful to the authorities when I reported my find upon reaching Suva. But I do not deny that I was relieved to shape my course away from the dreary scene.

It was then I heard, or thought I heard, a faint sound of some sort. It might well have been no more than an unoiled block or an easing line somewhere in the rigging, but it served to catch my attention.

I brought the boat to and listened for a time, half decided to make still another pass through the wreck area. But I had made what I thought a thorough job of it and, in the end, brought the boat back to her former course.

But then the sound came again, and there was no doubt of it that time. Maybe because I was more alert the second time, the sound came to me as what it truly was — a human voice.

I put about at once and headed again into the floating oil, following the faint and uncertain sound of the calling voice, much as a good dog might follow the scent of birds hiding in cover. And, in the end, I came upon a man in the water.

It is uncommonly difficult to bring a helpless person from out of the sea onto a boat, and I made a job of work of it before I was done. The fellow groaned a good deal but

I made certain before I wrestled him up that he had no broken bones.

When at last I had him safe aboard, I could see no obvious injury to him at all except, of course, the wan look of those in shock and the all-covering film of jet fuel on him, a condition which, during the operation just past, came to be mine, as well.

My companionway hatch had been modified with stout boards against the danger of boarding seas. Its opening was too small to permit the bundling below of a helpless person, so I brought up blankets and made my patient as comfortable as I could on a cockpit bench before going below to put on coffee and to break out the rum bottle.

It may seem callous, Father, but I sensed an exhilaration in having human company again after my long time alone. I sorrowed, of course, for those who must obviously have been lost in the aircraft but I saw in the fellow I had just rescued a most welcome visitor, and I busied myself with a will to see him not only safe but comfortable and welcome, as well.

As I have already said, he did not appear badly hurt and in a surprisingly short time he came around to the point he was sitting up and leaning back against the cabin trunk to take his coffee and rum. He even managed a bit of a smile from time to time and he watched with me for other possible survivors as I cruised from one end to the other of the crash scene until the coming of daylight proved beyond all hope that my patient was indeed the sole survivor.

The weather continued cold and overcast, with the clouds solid at little more than mast height. Search planes would have a most difficult time of it but I kept a sharp watch in order that I might report what I had found.

My patient, once he was able, let me bundle him below and into a berth where he promptly fell into a deep sleep, which was not much to be wondered at, I suppose, considering what he had been through.

I left him there as I settled the boat on a course for Honolulu, that being the nearest land. I put the bits and pieces I had fished from the sea into some kind of order. Then, after fixing a bite of breakfast, I went on deck lest my patient be disturbed by some inadvertent sound I might make in moving about below.

As I have said, it was good to have someone else on board. Hawaii, under the best of circumstances, was six or more days away for a vessel as small as mine. Having company would speed the days. And, certainly, there was food and drink enough on board for the both of us. I came to be quite cheerful, in fact.

When, near noon, my patient wakened and pulled himself up to peer out the companionway hatch at me, I spoke to him with what must have seemed to him an astonishing warmth, for he did no more in response than to blink his still reddened eyes and stare somewhat foolishly at me.

"Feeling better?" I repeated. "You're quite all right, you know. You have nothing at all to fear now. I'll have you safe and sound ashore in Honolulu in a few days."

"Honolulu?"

"Yes, Honolulu. Closest land, you see. And it's right downwind from where we are. We'll be there before you know it."

Looking back on it now, I realize that, even then, the fellow showed remarkably little enthusiasm at the mention of getting ashore. But then I did not know what he had lost in the way of wife or friends or near relatives. Under the circumstances, I thought, it was not all that strange that he should be less than bouncy.

"I see," he said without much apparent interest. He stared off over the sea as though half-expecting to see Diamond Head rear up out of the water at any moment — although he was looking in the wrong direction for that.

"Yes," I went on. "But sailboats are a good deal slower than jet aircraft. We are going to be together for some days. In that case, we may as well know each other's names, don't you think. I'm Robert Marney."

The fellow brought his eyes back to me with what appeared to be a sizable effort. Even then, he hesitated for several moments longer before he replied. "I'm James McRae," he said at last.

"You're most welcome on board, Mr. McRae," I said. Then, out of consideration for any bereavement he may have suffered, I added, "Terribly sorry about the crash, of course."

He merely nodded and returned to his study of the sea.

"We've plenty of food and water aboard," I said in an attempt at allaying any fears he may have had about those matters, or, possibly, simply to take advantage of the chance of human conversation presented by my new companion.

"How about a radio?" McRae said then, rather abruptly, I thought. "You got a radio?"

"Just a receiver, sorry to say. We're quite primitive in that regard."

McRae then showed his first real interest in what was going on. "There's no way you can communicate with the shore then?"

"None, save for the odd passing ship. Or, under the circumstances, a search plane."

"Then, so far as anyone knows, I'm dead?"

I must say, he didn't seem all that upset by the idea, but I didn't remark upon it and he returned again to his study of the sea.

"I suppose I should thank you for saving me," McRae said, after a time, but without much emotion at all.

It seemed an odd way to put the thing. "Not necessary at all," I said.

"You're sure no one else survived?"

"Quite. You were with me. We searched the entire area. Over and over."

"Then I'm the only one?"

"I'm afraid so." I paused then, hardly knowing how to phrase what I meant to say next. "I earnestly hope you — you lost no loved ones in the accident."

"No," he said. "No, I was alone."

"It must have been bloody awful anyway."

"Yes. Yes, it was."

And that was the extent I was ever to learn from McRae concerning the actual crash. But I didn't push him any further. "How about something to eat?" I said. "Sun's well over the yardarm, to use a nautical expression."

"You do the cooking?"

"Who else?" I laughed.

"Then who sails the boat?"

I waved towards my Hasler self-steering gear. "That contrivance does quite well. What would you like, Mr. McRae. There's corned beef and tinned things of all kinds. Just, please, let's not order much in the way of green salads or fresh milk or the like. I am a bit short in those lines."

McRae ate quite well, once I got the stuff ready. Though, I must say, he was not so communicative as I might have liked, having been for so long alone. It was only on the subject of the boat itself that he showed any interest. But on that subject he seemed quite obsessed.

"Then you do the whole thing yourself?" he asked once. "The navigating and everything."

"Yes, I'm afraid so."

"Is it hard, learning how I mean? Could a man, say, pick it up from scratch?"

"I should think so. Passably anyway. Always assuming a good boat, well found," I said.

"Could I do it?"

The question came so bluntly and with such an unwonted sentiment in McRae's voice that I was instantly put on my guard. There seemed a good deal more in his question than was accounted for by the words themselves.

"You said we would be several days in making land. It would be something to do," McRae said. "Could you teach me to do it?"

There was certainly a direction in McRae's questioning I didn't fancy at all. But there was nothing I could put my finger on and I nodded. "Don't see why not. If you're all that keen for it."

So, starting that very evening, I showed McRae how to take and work up some star sights and how to use my little portable receiver to get time ticks for longitude.

There's precious little to it, you know, what with all the tables and the like we have now. And McRae was bright enough. Within a couple of days, he could fix our position almost as well as I could.

Handling the boat itself, though, that's not so quickly picked up. Still, McRae drove himself to it with a will that was all but unnatural. He was soon able to handle just about everything in the way of ordinary sailing. Assuming nothing went amiss, he would be able to cope.

He was particularly vulnerable in the matter of downwind sailing, and that was what we were into by that time. Twice, during times I had left him alone on deck, he put us into accidental jibes which, had the wind been blowing a bit harder, could have caused a spot of trouble with the rigging.

Even experienced sailors sometimes have trouble handling fore-and-aft rigged vessels downwind, though, so that was little enough to criticize in McRae.

"You think I could handle her by myself now?" he asked one evening at dinner.

I didn't reply at once. Actually, I felt confident he could handle the boat quite well for all practical purposes. He had a natural flair for the business. But some growing doubt of him caused me to hesitate. "I don't know. Why?"

"I'm sorry about the jibes," McRae said then, as though thinking that the reason for my slowness in answering.

"Happens to the best of us," I said. "Actually, I see no reason why you couldn't handle a boat at sea. Barring mishaps, that is. But you'll need a good bit more seasoning before you're right up there. You realize that?"

"Yes."

"Anyway, no reason you can't find out. We'll be raising the islands sometime tomorrow, I'd say. Why not look into getting a boat of your own if you're all that keen for it?"

"I've been thinking about that," McRae said. He chewed and swallowed. "Not about a boat, I mean, about getting to Hawaii. Is Hawaii where you were going before you picked me up?"

"No. I was for Suva, as a matter of fact."

"That's still some distance to go, then?"

"Yes. Yes, it is." Again, I was placed on my guard by something in McRae's manner. "Why do you ask?"

"I was just wondering." He paused and looked at me closely, as though for my reaction to what he said next. "I was thinking," he said, "Would you mind if we didn't stop at Hawaii?"

"What did you say?"

"If we just went right on to Suva," he said. "I have no reason to go to Hawaii, and it seems a shame to put you out of your way so much."

"It's not all that far out of the way," I said. "Besides, we're virtually there now."

"Still and all," McRae said. "I'd like to continue on with you. If you don't mind, of course. I've come to like the life, let's say. I can get a plane back to the States as well from Suva as I can from Honolulu, can't I?"

"I suppose," I said. "But what about . . . what about your friends and family back home? Won't they be worried about you?"

One of his rare displays of emotion came then as a wry smile. "Not unless they've misplaced the insurance policy," he said.

"Oh, I say. It can't be that bad, now can it?"

"Bad enough." Then, for the first and only time, McRae told me something about himself. Married. Two children, grown. Apparently not too close, any of them. Dull sort of a job somewhere in Middle America. Neither money nor initiative, I gathered, to break away. He did make it seem bleak enough.

"I know I'll have to go back," he said with a touching desolation. "It's just that going back's going to be — bad. I'm afraid I'm going to be a big disappointment to a lot of people when I show up."

McRae looked at me then. There was nothing of self pity I could see in him. Just an odd sort of loneliness. "I would be much obliged for just a few more days like this," he said. "Then I'll go back."

I do recall an uneasiness about the business. Something was not quite right about the whole thing but the way he put it I found it hard to refuse and, in the end, I agreed. It would save me a few days. So we altered course and trimmed sails for Suva.

Until some three days out of Suva, McRae was a changed man. Bright, cheerful, helpful with the cooking and washing up. And still keen as ever on the seamanship and navigation thing. Actually, he made it one of the most pleasant times I'd ever known at sea. I forgot some of my misgivings about him.

But, as our landfall neared, he became again morose and distracted, more even than before. His actions seemed to take on a more deliberate purpose, it seemed to me, and I began to see in him some vague kind of a threat to me. I realize now this might have been no more than my imagination, but it was real enough then.

It does help, too, to illustrate my state of mind when, one night, we were caught up by a screeching black squall and the main boom preventer guy parted. Under the circumstances, it meant a nasty bit of deck work, what with the line having to be rigged through a block right out at the end of the boom, and the seas so rough as they were.

It is all part of the sailing life, though, and I turned to. I, of course, did the bulk of the work but McRae was there to do whatever he could to help. He held the line, for instance, ready to hand it to me when I might be ready.

I had hauled the boom in tight and was standing brace-legged on the little platform abaft the cockpit, ready to take the line and pass it through its block. A particularly nasty sea took the boat just then and laid her right over. My balance was tenuous at best and the rush of water, I am afraid, did the rest. At any rate, over I went.

Such things happen, of course, in a frenzy of violent action and I could not be certain at all of how I had come to fall. Nor could I recall the reflex action which must have led to my grabbing onto the trailing logline as I went over. I know now only that I found myself being dragged, pell-mell, through a wet black torrent at what seemed a terrifying rate of speed.

Though the line to which I clung so desperately could have been no more than twenty or thirty feet long, I could not see the boat. The entire world had become a black chaos of tumbling water in which the only solid substance left was that slim and sea-slimed line disappearing somewhere ahead of me.

I tried to pull myself, hand over hand, along the line but it was impossible so long as the squall lasted and I ended by taking a turn around my wrist and simply letting myself be dragged through the sea, breathing as best I could.

Fortunately, such squalls are usually as brief as they are violent and are apt to be followed by quite serene conditions. And so it was that time.

The wind settled back and the boat straightened, slowing to a pace which let me drag myself back up to her.

I remember clearly I did not cry out for help, but pulled myself up by means of the Hasler gear fittings on the stern. Even under those conditions of calm, though, I could not haul myself fully into the safety of the cockpit. Every ounce of my strength had been used up. I could do no more, fall back into the sea though I might.

McRae stood in the cockpit, staring at me as though I were some frightful apparition. I shall remember to my dying day the expression on his face, his eyes wide and fixed on me. So far as I could see, he had not done one damned thing to slow the boat and help me in any way.

I realize now that it could have been no more than the paralysis of panic. After all, he was but a novice sailor and the squall a terrifying thing but, at the time, I chose to think not. For, during those terrible minutes when I had been dragged so violently behind the plunging boat, it had come into my mind that I had not fallen, but that I had been pushed.

It seemed that I lay sprawled, half in and half out of the boat, for a very long time before McRae reached and dragged me fully into the cockpit, where I lay as though dead.

"I . . . I thought you were gone," McRae stammered. "I couldn't see you. I . . ."

"I dare say," I said. But I didn't voice what had come to be a hard conviction in my mind.

McRae had fully regained his strength by that time, and he was a large man. More than a match for me physically. Any counterattack I might plan against him would have to come about by stealth or artifice rather than by main force.

This hard conviction of which I write was that McRae was out to do me in, in order that he might continue on in my boat and remain dead in whatever world he had come from.

It was the only thing which explained all that had happened: his reluctance to land in Hawaii, his keenness to learn navigation and single-handed sailing. And now, now that he considered himself fit and competent to handle the boat alone, and we were coming up on our Fijian landfall, he had seen his chance and chucked me right out of the bloody boat. It all fit, and I came to believe it completely.

But I must say, though, that once I was back aboard, McRae was the soul of solicitude. He helped me below and gave me rum and hot coffee while I stripped off my sodden clothes and bundled myself into a warm berth. But I put all that down to his sly cunning. He was merely trying to lull me into carelessness against his next attempt at doing me in.

I must say, as well, that McRae gave no indication that he suspected anything of what was going through my mind. He was most abjectly apologetic for having done so little to help when I went over the side. He said, over and over again, that he couldn't see me and had not known what to do.

And I, for my part, let him think all was forgiven. He would be easier to cope with if he were unsuspecting. But we were nearing our landfall — McRae knew our position as well as I did — and I was convinced he would make his next move soon.

I therefore concluded that I must act before he did. And, slowly, a plan took form in my mind.

We had not yet rerigged the parted preventer which had caused all the trouble in the first place. The wind had come round into the northwest, an unusual quarter in that part of the world, and there had been no need for a preventer. Still, it should be rerigged, and it offered me the chance I sought.

There's really nothing to the job in good weather. It calls simply for passing a line through a block at the end of the boom, but it does involve leaning quite far out over the water.

"Perhaps you should do it this time," I said, trying to make a joke of it, though I must admit my mouth was dry at the thought of what I meant to do. "Perhaps you can do it without falling out of the bloody boat."

McRae did not hesitate in the least. I realize now he suspected nothing. I handed him the line and, while I held the sheet taut, he leaned out over the water, straining to reach the block dangling there.

Then, quite mercilessly, I kicked his feet from under him and he fell into the sea.

This is what I had to tell you, Father. I could quite easily have put about and pulled McRae from the water, but I didn't. I quite deliberately killed the man whose life I had so recently saved.

And all out of a delusion that he, poor devil, intended me harm.

So, there it is. I realize now, that had I but held my silence, no one would ever have known any of this. McRae was presumed dead in the aircraft accident. He would never have been missed in any event.

I must conclude then that my motive is the selfish one of wishing to ease my own guilt by having at least the knowledge of it shared with someone else.

At any rate, that's the lot. I leave myself in your hands. I am most heartily sorry for what I have done but if the police meet me in Sydney, I shall understand. I absolve you of the confidentiality of the confessional, and I apologize for the shabby way in which I am repaying all the kindnesses you showed me when I was on your island.

Should I not be met by the police, I shall assume some measure of forgiveness on your part and will make my way with all speed to your lovely island in hopes of finding again the peace and love I found there in such abundance before.

FOR WANT OF WIND

At first, there was little cause for alarm. Ships making up the west coast of Chile may reasonably expect to see a few days of calm. The *Sailing Directions* speak of it. And, if the truth be told, a bit of calm does not go badly. Not after reaching the warm sun of the Pacific. Not after two months of Cape Horn gales.

Still, there's something about a becalmed ship which makes a sailing man uneasy. Especially so off the Chilean coast where currents are willful and the swell an awesome thing at times. Captain Agnar Gunnarson felt a chill of apprehension as he went below that night.

Two months, and more, it had taken him to work his way around Cape Stiff. Two months of successive gales, each more vindictive than the last. Two months in which the wailing in the rigging never ceased and furled sails froze in their gaskets. Two months in which men forgot what it was to be dry or warm or secure in their minds. Two months in which each living hour might be their last.

But, oddly, once he had his westing and turned north, it was as though the sea gods relented and sought to make amends. For days on end, the old *Argyle* plunged along before a whistling southwester, her sheets tight as iron bars, her sails fat with the unfailing wind.

It was sailing the like of which few men are given to know, and Captain Gunnarson violated his own time-proven practice and allowed himself to think that he might yet make up for the catastrophe which had been his slow rounding of the Cape.

It was nearing the end of the time when sailing vessels could earn their keep, and Captain Gunnarson knew what the extension of time and the cost of lost gear and sails would do to whatever profit would come of landing his cargo of Scottish coal in Valparaiso. He knew, too, that the lost time would put him in port too late to claim the return cargo the agent had promised.

But, with the wind they had after rounding the Horn, there was still a chance. Even after allowing for the three topsails which exploded from their boltropes in the same screaming squall, even counting in the replacement of the splintered spanker boom and gaff, if the wind held, he might still come out with enough gain to induce the owners to keep the *Argyle* in commission for another voyage.

Captain Gunnarson had said as much to old Fergus MacDonald, mate, after a week of near ideal passage-making. "We hold this wind in to Vallipo," he said, "it can still be a paying passage out."

MacDonald spat accurately and with remarkable force to leeward. "Ye'll pay for this wind, Cap'n," he growled. "A man don't get wind like this without he pays for it. Ye can mark my words on it."

"Ah, and you're a dour one, Mister Mate," Captain Gunnarson laughed, unable to accept such thoughts. Not while his ship was sailing as she was then. Not with Valparaiso less than three days away, if the wind held. "Best ye see to yon rigging, Mister Mate," he said pleasantly. "And I'll be wanting a list of your requirements once we land."

But, dour though he might be, Fergus MacDonald proved an able prophet for that very night the old *Argyle's* great sails went slack as the wind failed her so suddenly her canvas was taken all aback and she slid to a stop in the sea, her chain sheets clanking faintly, her freeing ports setting up a dolorous tolling as she fell into the trough of a heavy swell and set to rolling.

There was no mistaking the satisfaction in the old mate's face as he greeted Captain Gunnarson's almost immediate appearance on deck.

"Aye, and it's now we'll be paying for all that fine wind we had, Cap'n," MacDonald said.

"It will pass, Mister Mate," Captain Gunnarson said easily. "There will be wind again, Mister Mate."

"I've seen weeks on this coast, Cap'n, when there wasn't enough wind to douse a candle, I have."

"There'll be wind again," the captain said again, but there was already a seed of doubt in his mind. The fair wind really had been too good to last. The implacable fates which were closing in on the *Argyle*, and all like her, were not so easily to be turned away.

Captain Gunnarson looked aloft and around. The flat and lifeless sails hung like mis-shapened black cut-outs against a spangled sky, moving at all only in response to the ship's sullen roll. The sea itself was bland and unfeeling, lifting in silken swells with never a ripple upon them, so smooth the stars shown in reflection on the water.

The crew gathered amidships, the watch below as well, as though sensing some dire misfortune. They had been sky-larking that afternoon, burstingly full of what they would soon see and do in the noisome resorts of Valparaiso; but now they stood uneasily, glancing from time to time to the poop, where the captain and Mister MacDonald stood. It was as though they blamed the captain for what had happened. And, all the time, the iron freeing ports opened on the low side and closed on the high side with a mournful, muted clanging.

"Secure those damned ports, Mister Evans," the captain shouted then to the young second who had just come on deck. It was unlike the captain either to raise his voice or to use foul language, and the second set to with a will. "Have ye never been becalmed before?" the captain's voice followed after him.

That had been the beginning of it. The captain had gone again to his cabin and recalculated, again and again, the doleful numbers which meant no profit unless he made port in good time. And, without profits, the *Argyle*, and he with her, would be taken nrom the seas, she, and he with her, had sailed for so long. But, unless the wind blew, there was little he could do, and, thus placing his trust in his own quaint concept of a God marked by a special compassion for old sailing men, he turned in.

The next day, the mountains of Chile lifted their white tops over the eastern horizon. The crew shouted and backslapped each other. Some had been to Valparaiso and recognized certain of the peaks. But there was no joy in Captain Gunnarson's eyes.

There had been no peaks in sight when the *Argyle* went dead in the water. And she had not moved through the water since. The huge swells, though they moved purposefully from one horizon to the other, served only to lift the ship and to let her down in the same water.

Still, if there were peaks where no peaks had been before, it was obvious the ship had moved over the ground. And moved closer to the land. The only answer could be that the ship was caught in the grasp of that great ocean river which sweeps up from Antarctica and courses along the west coast of South America with a sometimes fearsome power.

"Keep the hands at it, Mister Mate," Captain Gunnarson ordered as he and MacDonald lunched together that day. "We'll want to leave as little as possible for the dockyard navvies. Right?"

"Aye," MacDonald said. "If we get to dockyard." The two old friends had sailed together for a long time and spoke together with more frankness than is common between master and mate sometimes.

But the lack of wind was wearing on Captain Gunnarson's mind, and he spoke probably more sharply than he intended. "Meaning what, Mister Mate?" he said.

"Meaning yon mountains, Cap'n." MacDonald spoke through a mouth full of mashed potatoes and motioned with his fork to a scuttle through which Chile's mountains, blue with distance, appeared and disappeared with the heavy roll of the ship. "They're a sight closer than they was in the last watch, Cap'n. And me that's one of the world's worst navigators, can see it."

The second had the watch on deck. Captain Gunnarson and his old mate were alone. And, for a moment, the captain let his concern show. "By my reckoning, Mac," he said quietly, "we're making a steady three knots."

"And for the beach?"

"Aye, and for the beach."

The two old men's eyes met then for a time while neither of them spoke. They could hear the sounds of the ship as she rolled, sailing ship sounds they both had heard for many years together. And, it may be, that each thought the same thing: they were too old ever to switch over to steam. And, it may be, as well, that they then, without ever a word's being said on it, joined forces to save the *Argyle*.

"We're still some thirty miles off," Captain Gunnarson said then. "As we come closer, it may be the current will weaken. Or veer off."

"Aye," MacDonald said. "It may be."

"But, chances are, the swell will increase. That has been my experience."

"Aye. And mine."

"After your meal, I'd be much obliged, Mac, if ye'd see to the anchor gear. Nothing to be gained by not being ready. It would have to be done for making port in any event."

"Aye, Cap'n."

And, with no more being said on the matter, the two old men calmly finished their noon meal. Both had grown up in sail. And, though they were capable of fast action, they were not the kind to act hastily when it was not called for.

Thirty miles at three knots meant ten hours. The anchors could be made ready in less than one, if it came to that.

So, after their meal, Fergus MacDonald turned his watch to on a deliberate overhaul of the anchors and their gear. This caused no concern to the crew since it was a normal part of making the ship ready for arrival, even if a bit early.

Captain Gunnarson, for his part, took the poop, running his eyes over the heaving sea where no breath of wind stirred. The bright skies they had come so quickly to take for granted were gone then, and the mountains, too, in a gray pall which pressed down almost as low as the mastheads. It was a gray and depressing world in which the *Argyle* wallowed, and the swells grew steadily higher. But that might be no more than his imagination making them seem so, he thought.

But, for all of that afternoon, the *Argyle* moved undeniably closer to the land. And, though the white peaks of the Andes could no longer be seen because of the clouds, coastal hills could. And the swells were bigger.

Captain Gunnarson went below and opened the *Sailing Directions*. "Cabo Carranza," he read, "...a low sloping point. The cape should be given a wide berth as the coast has not been examined and is frequently obscured by haze."

With his recent fair wind in mind, Captain Gunnarson had laid his course so as to give Cabo Carranza a four mile offing. That would have been more than enough, had the wind of the time held, and it was the most direct route to Valparaiso. But, of course, the wind had not held and a glance at his working chart showed the captain that his ship would not clear the cape on her present course. Not if the current held and the wind did not blow.

He looked for possible anchorages where he might ride while waiting for a wind. "Rada Curanipe," he read in the *Sailing Directions*. "Vessels may take anchorage in sixteen to nineteen fathoms, and . . . vessels should always be prepared to put to sea, as the holding ground is not good."

On her present hapless course, it appeared likely the *Argyle* would fetch up in or near the Curanipe roadstead. Captain Gunnarson studied the area on his chart. Nothing remarkable showed. He read again the *Sailing Direction* admonition: "vessels should be prepared to put to sea."

But the *Directions* had no suggestion as to how a sailing ship was expected to put to sea when there was no wind. Captain Gunnarson muttered an oath and slammed the book closed. He reached for pipe and tobacco, but stopped in mid-reach as a commotion sounded on deck.

"It's a tug, Captain," Fergus MacDonald reported as the captain arrived on deck. And the normally dour little mate found it in him to grin as he stumped aft to join Gunnarson on the poop, where, together, they stood and watched the approach of a tall-stacked South American tug under an enormous plume of black smoke.

The crew became boisterous at the sight of the tug and talked once more about the expected delights of Valparaiso's famous waterfront cantinas.

"Lucky thing, that," Fergus MacDonald said. "Somebody must have reported us from the beach."

"Lucky thing, Mister Mate?" Captain Gunnarson said sourly.

"Aye, Cap'n," MacDonald said, surprised. "With yon tug, we'll have no need of wind, I'm thinking."

"Aye, Mister Mate," Captain Gunnarson replied. "But have ye given no thought to the need for a towing fee?" And Gunnarson moved away.

MacDonald stared after his captain with consternation in his face. Those of the crew who had been close enough to hear the exchange stirred ominously. It was asking a good deal of men who had just made a hard Cape Horn passage to expect them to pass up a tow. Especially so when on a ship helplessly drifting on shore.

Captain Gunnarson knew all that. He had been to sea longer than any of them. But he knew, too, the fees charged by Valparaiso tugs when they came upon becalmed ships off dangerous beaches. And he knew how thin their Scots owners shaved their freights to get the cargo in the first place. He knew there was no allowance for tug fees.

Still, there was the beach drawing steadily nearer. They could see the sand by that time and, here and there, a black rock or two with surf exploding white over them. And the hissing swells growing greater with every passing series. If only the bloody wind would blow!

The tug by then was close aboard. She sounded her jaunty little whistle and her captain called across to find if a tow was wanted.

"No. No tow!" Captain Gunnarson called, turning away as though not even wanting to see the ugly little boat.

The tug captain was obviously taken aback. "Bad current here, Captain," he called. "Many ship go on beach here. Better you take tow."

"No tow," Gunnarson shouted stubbornly. He felt his mates' disapproval behind him. He knew they wanted him to take the tow. Behind a tug, Valparaiso was only hours away. But it was Gunnarson who was captain and who must think of making the *Argyle* pay her way if they were not all to be put on the beach. "No tow!" he shouted again.

An angry growl rose from the crew gathered below the poop. "See to your anchors, Mister Mate," Gunnarson called then. "And get a man in the chains. Once we cross the twenty fathom curve, let go the port anchor."

"But, Cap'n . . ."

"Do you hear me, Mister Mate?" Gunnarson roared.

MacDonald moved as though to answer angrily, but he stopped short of a break with his captain and old friend. That wouldn't do. Not in front of the men, it wouldn't. "Aye, Cap'n," he muttered. "Port anchor it is."

Gunnarson went then to the taffrail, standing alone, watching the beach move inexorably out to meet him. The *Argyle* rolled more heavily than ever, but she was snugged down aloft and made little fuss about it. The silence had an air of unreality about it.

"I'll wait, Captain," the tug man called across the water. "Maybe you change your mind pretty soon."

"Wait and be damned," Gunnarson muttered under his breath. He studiously avoided looking at the persistent Chilean tugman.

Presently, the man in the chains began his chant of soundings, and soon after that, MacDonald asked permission to let go the port anchor, as ordered.

"Let go, Mister Mate," Gunnarson called. He walked forward to see what effect the hook would have.

The swells by that time were racing green hills of water moving out of the southwest. The larger of them were developing hissing frostings of foam as they threatened to break.

"Let go!" MacDonald shouted, and the boatswain swung his sledge. The port anchor plummeted into the water, followed by a long rumble of chain in the hawse. A red mist of rust dust rose over the forecastle head and hung there in the still air.

"Let her run," MacDonald ordered, watching the marked shots race out the hawse. Then, "That's good. Hold her there."

At first, the anchor seemed to have no effect at all. But, as the slack worked out of the chain, the old *Argyle*'s bow began to come up. The swells, taking her on the beam as they had, canted her far over with each onset, causing her to slide down their forward slopes. But, with the tightening of the anchor chain, she began to skew about. Her bows came up to meet the swells, and she presented her stern to the menacing shore.

For a time, the ship appeared to ride steady. But Captain Gunnarson was skeptical. He moved to where he could put a foot on the chain. Through his boot, he could feel the ominous twitching of a dragging anchor.

"Give her another twenty fathoms, Mister Mate," he called.

"That will bring her on the stop, Cap'n."

"Then bring her on the stop, if you please."

MacDonald did as he was told, easing out the chain until only the well-rusted bitter end shot showed on deck. And still the ship dragged.

"Bloody poor holding ground, Cap'n," MacDonald growled.

Gunnarson glanced to where the tug lay off, waiting like some filthy carrion-eating bird. "Stand by your starboard anchor, Mister Mate! Let go on my signal."

Captain Gunnarson then went aft and used the helm to give the ship as great a shear as he could in order to clear the port anchor before letting go the starboard. Then he signaled Mister MacDonald and the *Argyle* shivered as her second anchor went down.

Still, the ship continued to drag. As each huge swell charged into her, she would rear and pull back like a fractious horse against its halter. Then, as the swell passed, she would sag forward, gathering ground for her next rearing plunge against her chains. With each mighty surge, she dragged her anchors nearer to the waiting beach.

When she fetched up on the starboard anchor as well as the port, and when the strain was equalized between the two chains, she did seem to hold her own for a time. Captain Gunnarson took cross bearings which did not change sometimes for thirty minutes at a time.

"Looks like she may be holding at last, Mister Mate," Captain Gunnarson said cautiously.

"Aye," the old mate said. "Aye, seems like."

"If this swell gets no bigger, we . . ."

"Aye. If it gets no bigger." MacDonald spat over the side. "But, if it does get bigger, Cap'n, yon tug'll be hard put to get a line aboard of us afore we're in the breakers. Ye realize that, Cap'n?"

"I realize it, Mister Mate."

"And ye'll still have no tow, then?"

"That's right, Mister Mate," Captain Gunnarson said angrily.

"I've a mind to save this vessel, if you please, sir. And it's not saving her I'll be doing by running up towing bills the owners are in no position to be paying."

"Aye, Cap'n. And ye'll not be saving her by letting her go in yon breakers."

"I have no intention of letting her go in yon breakers, Mister Mate." Anger, born of his great frustration tightened the captain's face but he kept his voice in bounds, with an effort.

"Then I'm supposing ye have a nice wind ye can break out and sail us off?" Mister MacDonald said. "Or maybe something to make anchors hold in foul ground? Or maybe, something to settle this bloody swell."

"Enough!" Captain Gunnarson snapped, with iron in his voice. But he realized his old mate was trying to help, was trying to make him face the inevitable. In a softer voice, he went on: "Do ye not think, Fergus, that I would do aught I could to save this vessel? Do ye not think that, man? Do ye not see that forcing her sale to the ship break-ers would be her loss, just as much as having her strike? Do ye not see that, Fergus?"

For a time the old mate did not reply. He felt little of his captain's romantic affection for the *Argyle*, but he understood it. He had sailed a pretty little barque once in his youth for which he had felt such an affection. He respected what the captain felt for his ship. "Aye, Cap'n," he muttered. "I can see it. If ye say so."

"Anyway, she seems to be holding now," the captain said then. "With luck, we may still be able to save her."

"Aye. With luck, maybe," Mister MacDonald said. But his face made it clear he felt no such thing. He was still of the opinion the *Argyle* had used up her luck in her fabu-lous run up from the Horn.

The captain bent then to check his bearings, and MacDonald knew, with no need for being told, that they had changed. He knew it from a visible stiffening of his captain's body.

And, as though in corroboration, a massive swell lifted the ship and threw her back against her chains. There was a sound of shifting gear below and a great spreading of white water from under her plunging bows. For a time, she drifted without hindrance before the anchors again took hold and brought her bows up to meet the merciless seas.

Then, more and more quickly, the swells pushed home their attacks. Again and again, the ship's bows fell off sickeningly, only to be pulled back by the faltering anchors and to fall off again.

Captain Gunnarson's face was white under its weather tan. He looked up at his empty sails, a pleading expression on his face, and he had, for a little while, the look of a praying man. He could hear behind him the hungry growling of the surf.

And, for that final time, it was as though Captain Gunnarson were again sailing the *Argyle* through all the years in which they had been ship and master together. Storms, there had been, and terror, at times. Peace, too, and great satisfactions; and through it all, growing steadily stronger between them, that feeling which men sometimes do find for a ship. It is a sad thing when it must end.

The captain remembered, too, in those brief final minutes, the owners' office in Glasgow when they had told him the *Argyle* was no longer a paying proposition. It was the captain who had, through old connections, come up with the cargo of coal for Valparaiso. It was he who had talked the owners into giving him and the *Argyle* this one last chance.

In what was like a spasm of pain in a living thing, the ship reared and twisted away from a towering swell with white froth at its top. Captain Gunnarson staggered to hold his balance. "Mister Mate!" he called.

MacDonald, who had been keeping a respectful distance in the face of his captain's travail, leaped forward. "Aye, Cap'n."

"Signal the tug, Mister Mate," he said, striving mightily to keep from his voice the defeat he felt. It was as though he were already facing his owners across the big mahogany table in Glasgow, reporting a towing fee which would more than offset the profit from carrying a cargo of coal halfway round the world.

"Signal the tug, Mister Mate. Tell him we will take a tow." One more time the captain looked high into his futile towers of canvas aloft. "And, Fergus, will ye see to passing the line. I'll be below if ye need me."

THE HOMEWARD-BOUNDER and other sea stories

NOT FOR NAUGHT

I realize now that I shall die here on board my boat. There no longer is any pain but, after six full days without food, there is an unmistakable weakness in my arms and an ominous slowing of all my movements. Unless, as now seems unlikely, a ship should pass by, there can be little doubt as to what is to become of me.

Therefore, before it is too late, I should like to make an account of what has happened. Perhaps my boat will be found before she founders and my experience may prove helpful to others who attempt long passages alone. There may be, in what happened to me, a warning which will help others to avoid the same hazard.

It was being alone for so long that did it. I know that now. At the time, however, I confess an utter inability to handle the problem in any rational way.

I was, of course, aware of the bizarre effects being alone for prolonged periods may sometimes have upon men's minds. Accounts of long single-handed voyages abound in such things. Captain Slocum's piratical apparition, for one. But there is no way for a man really to know the thing without having gone through it himself.

I had always considered myself a well-balanced sort. With the exception of an inexplicable compulsion for lone voyaging, I was perhaps as psychologically sound as one can be. When I took departure off the Farallon Islands for what was to be a passage to the Marquesas, I had utterly no premonition of what was to come.

The first weeks, as a matter of fact, were idyllic. After working free of the coastal fogs, I found a fresh northwesterly which held steady for days at a time, slacking only a bit at night to make for easier self-steering as I slept. Nor was the sea at all unpleasant. It kept to decent bounds and grew steadily warmer as I passed southwards.

It was not until I entered the doldrums, actually, that there was any indication of trouble to come. Perhaps it was because my famous wind, to that time, had kept both my hands and mind occupied. Oh, of course, I did the usual talking to myself and was not above berating obstinate bits of gear. But, actually, I was enjoying myself immensely. There's nothing quite like it, you know, being alone that way, with a living wind and a lively sea and a vessel seemingly keen for the romp.

But that all ended one day. Quite abruptly, it was. A line of dark squalls appeared over the southern horizon and my beautiful wind turned fitful almost at once, shying away from the somber clouds as a flighty horse might shy away from the smoke of a fire. My boat stood up straight for the first time in weeks and seemed to feel her way before the failing breeze.

At the same time, the air grew oppressively heavy and warm and wet. The sea itself lost its dash and grew sullen under a gray ceiling of clouds. The dancing waves to which I had for so long become accustomed became no more than a listless lift and fall of swell out of the northwest. And, in the end, my little boat drifted to a stop, her sails slatting idly as though they had no heart even for that.

But even then, aside from a momentary sense of foreboding, I felt no real distress. There were things to be done. Bits and pieces of work which I had neglected because I had not wanted to lose any part of my lovely wind just past. So, I dropped the sails to stop their endless slatting and set about putting things right about the boat.

I remember whistling as I worked — not being a superstitious man. It was still a lark. A man has to expect a certain amount of calm. Especially when transitting the doldrums. I determined to make the best of it, to get done what wanted doing and catch up on my sleep. So, as I say, I was not doing badly to that point.

But, in a thirty-footer at sea, there is a limit to the amount of work which actually wants doing. And sleep, too, becomes tiresome after a bit. Especially when one's berth is a moist oven of a place. So that, at the end of three or four days when the wind still had not come, I found myself growing a bit testy. A nasty rash under my arms failed completely to help.

There is something about a calm, in the first place, which sets a sailing man back. He really has no assurance, you know, that the bloody wind will ever blow again. There begins to grow in his mind the thought that he just might spend the rest of his days in that small circle of the ocean's water in which his vessel drifts.

Especially is this feeling discomforting in the doldrums. There, the air itself is depressing and lacking the power to refresh. Even the rain, coming down in buckets as it does in noisy black squalls, is tepid and dispiriting. The sky has no brightness and the sea, faithful to its partner sky, becomes bleak and lifeless, stirring only apathetically to low swells passing beneath its filmy surface. There are no birds. No life at all. I do not recall seeing so much as the fin of a shark during the whole time. Nor is there any sound, save only the drumming of rain fingers on the decks.

And, for three weeks or more, I was there. Which meant I had been eight or nine weeks in all at sea, without sight or sound of another human being. I became desperately depressed, as a first symptom. I could not read. Food became tasteless. And I stalked my little deck like a madman, naked, usually, crying down maledictions of the worst kind upon that cursed part of the sea.

I alternated these periods of violent anger with spells of sullen sulking during which I buried myself in a corner of my berth and curled up in a fetal position. (You will see I am being as clinical as possible in order that this account shall be of maximum value to those who may chance to read it.) Nor would I stir myself for hours at a time, even though the cabin was a hellish place to be, a place in which every object dripped obscenely warm water and gray mold appeared to grow before my eyes.

Oddly, I seemed never to associate any of it all with what I had read of other voyagers' experiences in such circumstances. It was as though my powers of reasoning were utterly gone. I do recall that I did not even bother with my noon sights. The bloody boat was not moving. What was the point of figuring where she lay?

I speak of these things in order that others may know what the first stages of the affliction are like, so they may recognize those signs while there is yet, perhaps, time to counter them.

But I truly believe that, after what happened next, no power on earth could have saved me.

I had just finished a turn about the decks, crying, as was my habit at the time, great curses upon the stolid columns of rain squalls which circled about me. They were like squat supports for the heavy sky above, and I and my little ship were ensnared there, as though for all time, in a vast and gloomy hall. I even imagined at times that my demented ranting evoked echoes, as they would have in a proper room. I exhausted myself in shouting out my senseless rage, and stumbled for the companionway, intent upon getting below where I, at least, need not see the bloody lot.

And that is when I first saw him.

He was seated on my settee, at my table. A great, gross brute of a man he was. Dressed in well-sweated khaki trousers and a singlet which had long since given way to the sodden thrust of his massive hairy stomach. Beady eyes he had, glinting black and all but lost in deep folds of flesh. His mouth opened and closed like that of a fish as he breathed the hot, wet air. He looked up at me, not in an unfriendly manner at all, his wet lips moving in a kind of smile. It was as though he were waiting for me, as host, to make the first move.

The odd thing, as I recall it, was that I was not at all surprised to find the fellow there. You would think I would have been. There was no indication at all as to where he might have landed from. He was not wet, for one thing; he could not have come up from out of the sea. And my boat had precious little room for stowing away anything so large and noisome as my visitor. Still, I accepted the fellow's presence as being wholly natural.

There can be no doubt, of course, that I was utterly out of it by that time. The bloody great sea with its unending heat and silence and lifeless air had done its work for fair. I set about making my visitor at home in every way I found possible.

Actually, he was a passably good sort. I remember we had some rattling good conversations. It seemed the fellow was up on everything in which I had felt an interest. Which now, of course, seems no more than was to be expected since he was wholly a creature of my own imagining. Still, it was good to have company after so long alone, and I was, quite frankly, delighted with him at first. I could understand how Captain Slocum had come to develop an affection for his imagined pirate.

In that way, for several days, I entertained my strange guest. In time, I became used to his coarse appearance and his manners, which were no better. I had never seen so boorish a fellow. Especially in the matter of eating.

In the end, that is what put me off him. There was simply no end to the man's appetite. I cooked mountains of food for him and poured for him my hoarded beer and rum. Still, nothing was ever enough. He became nasty if I slowed my efforts and berated me vilely for being mean with my provisions. I can tell you that such behavior did not rest well with me, not even as a necessary cost of human company.

We had violent quarrels. I had, at first, been fearful of him, he was such a bloody big man. But he showed no inclination to violence, and we contented ourselves with shouting the most awful insults at the very tops of our voices, until one or the other of us would have enough and go on deck.

Now, there's an odd thing, too. I never saw the fellow on deck. We would be going at each other, hammer and tongs, until he, feigning injured righteousness, would heave his bulk up and through the companionway hatch. I frequently, not having had enough, would go right after him, but he would be nowhere to be seen. I had no idea in the world where he might be off to, but he most certainly was no longer on board. And, in my condition at the time, I saw nothing strange in the matter at all.

In a vessel the size of mine, there's little enough room for stores. I had tinned things in the bilges and dried provisions of all sorts tucked away here and there under berths and in whatever crannies could be found. Still, there was more than enough for me. I had been liberal in that regard. I had assured apprehensive friends before my sailing that it might be I should drown, but I most certainly would not starve.

But that, of course, was before my gluttonous companion had invited himself on board. At the rate that man ate, no store of provisions could last for very long and with still no sign of wind in that accursed sea, I became concerned.

I began to reduce the size of my guest's portions, pleading caution in the face of impending starvation for us both. But he would not listen to reason. He stormed and ranted about the little cabin with a violence which impressed me to the point I gave him what he wanted. I may as well face it, I could not bear the thought of his becoming really angry and leaving me again alone.

But each time I pulled fresh tins from the bilges or drew new supplies from out a cupboard, I felt a fear which, in the course of days, became desperation. I simply could not afford to continue feeding the fellow at his going rate, not certainly and hope to have anything left for either of us. Still, I could not make him listen.

I knew very well, of course, that if it should come to physical violence, I would have no chance against him. Nor did I really want to strike him down by stealth or treachery. It was not, in fact, that I did not like the fellow. He was just bloody well eating us both into starvation. It became clear to me that something most certainly wanted doing.

And, at last, I hit upon a plan. I would hide the food. I would tell him it was all gone. I had warned him it would come to that. If he couldn't see anything to eat, he bloody well wouldn't eat. I could sneak things out from time to time to keep us going.

I remember feeling a kind of crafty elation at the lovely simplicity of the idea. And, straightaway, I put the plan into effect.

I provoked a particularly violent argument with the fellow. I all but rubbed my hands together in my sly glee at the readiness with which he rose to the bait and took himself off, in the end, out the companionway hatch. Simple sort, he was, I remember thinking. Not really in it with someone like myself.

Immediately he was out of sight, I set about moving every crumb, grain and drop of stores I could lay my hands on from the main cabin bilges and storage spaces to the forward cabin. Boxes, tins, bottles, plastic containers — I carried them all forward and crammed them wherever they would fit. Then I closed the stout door on them, and there was nothing visible anywhere in the main cabin capable of being eaten.

I remember then cackling with insane laughter at having outsmarted my man so easily. I had worked myself into sweating exhaustion, but I had never felt so triumphant before in my life. Despite all my companion had eaten in the days past, there still was plenty left, now that it could be consumed at a more sensible rate.

Actually, I was limp with both fatigue and emotional release by the time the job was done. And I remember feeling a decided depression at the sudden thought my companion might not return. Suppose he had decided not to come back at all. Really, he was a rather sensitive type, in his coarse way, and I had no wish to hurt his feelings. If only he wouldn't eat so bloody much.

But I needn't have feared. He came back, all right. He let himself heavily down the companionway ladder, turning sideways in the awkward way he had, and blowing horribly with the exertion any movement caused him. He let himself drop onto the settee with an abandon which caused its boards to complain.

I explained to him that we would have to conserve our stores. We had no idea how long the calm would last. We were thousands of miles from nearest land. I used every argument I could conceive. I even lifted the floor-boards and showed him the then empty bilges. I threw open the cupboard doors and showed him the empty shelves. But all of it was utterly useless. The fellow was adamant.

In the end, I did as he wanted. I went into the forward cabin and came back with arms full of food which I cooked for him while he maintained a constant grumbling invective against me. I can tell you, there was little good between us at that time. While he ate, I withdrew into my berth.

Clearly, my triumph had been short lived. In my demented state at the time, I was helpless in the fellow's hands. There he sat, eating as though starved for a fortnight, and making a bloody lot of noise about it, too. As I nursed my knees to my chest, I realized drastic measures were called for.

Very well, then, I remember thinking, if that's the way things were to be. My mind worked with all the brilliant clarity of the truly insane. Since I was so patently under the fellow's control, I must take the remaining food not only beyond his reach, but beyond mine as well. At least temporarily. I clearly remember adding that last, and being pleased with myself for being so foresighted.

So I once more provoked the fellow into leaving the cabin. Then, moving with a sly haste, I set about doing what wanted doing.

I once more put all our stores into the forward cabin, after first dogging down the heavy forward hatch in a way which made it impossible to open from on deck.

I then took my saw to the spinnaker pole and, after measuring carefully, cut it into a series of lengths which would just reach, in a horizontal line, from the door to various solid projections in the cabin itself.

My first thought had been to barricade myself there in the forward cabin with the food until the greedy fellow gave up and went away. But, there again, you see, I had no real wish to be done with him. I simply wanted to preserve my dwindling stores from his ravenous appetite which, as I saw it then, would be the death of us both.

But I knew, in my befuddled state, that if the food remained where I could possibly get at it, the fellow would again have his way. The answer, then, must be that the food be placed beyond my reach as well. But how?

My boat was a stout vessel, built to North Sea standard, but my hungry visitor was a powerful man. Half measures would not do. So, in the end, I took the lengths of spinnaker pole I had cut. Cleverly, I placed them and fixed bits of sail twine to their after ends and passed the twine over the top of the door between the two cabins.

By placing the stout timbers just so, and by arranging the sail twine just so, I could close the door in such a way that the timbers would drop into place and provide a force-proof jamb.

I remember sweating in concentration over the job. The boat's motion made it a hard piece of work, at best. Several times, everything seemed ready to fall into place, only to be spoiled by a sudden lurch of the sea. It was hot, frustrating, maddeningly obstinate work, but I was driven by a maniacal purpose and, in the end, it did work.

Not even breathing, as I recall it now, I maintained just the right tension on the sail twine as I eased the door to. Then, as I slacked off the twine, I felt the lengths of spinnaker pole fall into place, one by one. For a moment, I stood watching the door, as though waiting to make certain it was indeed closed to stay.

Then, wildly, crazily, I laughed and threw myself against the door. There was utterly no give in it. I was hurled back. Bruised and panting, I again felt that passionate surge of triumph I experienced before in believing I had bested my strange guest.

But there was yet more to do. No door, however strong, could stand up to a man with tools such as I had in my kit. So, once more, I set about doing what wanted doing. Starting at the forward bulkhead of the main cabin, I methodically worked my way aft, stripping my boat of everything which could conceivably be used to batter, pry, cut, or break wood.

My box of carpenters' tools I dragged on deck and heaved over the side, cackling gleefully as I did so. Even the winch handles and gear shift lever — all over the side. The anchors might well be used as battering rams — over the side with them!

There was no escaping the mad thoroughness of my work. No single thing capable of smashing open that door was overlooked. If it were to be broken through, it would be broken through by man alone.

So, there I was, standing naked in the cockpit, ranting insanely and waving my arms about in that gloomy world of gray water and black sky in which I had been trapped so long, daring my gluttonous visitor to come back and raid my precious provisions again. We'd bloody well see who was master of my own boat.

I don't know now how long I carried on in that way. I do remember I was hoarse for days afterwards. And I remember the sense of utter desolation which replaced my elation when my visitor failed to reappear. I had never felt so alone. I remember crying then and pleading piteously for him to come back.

But he never did.

Now, I realize he was never here at all. The food I cooked in such abundance was either eaten by myself or thrown over the side in the cleanup. But the jammed door to the forward cabin is real enough, and the food which could have sustained me, as you who may find my body can see. You can see where I scratched at it and beat upon it with my fists. It is my blood you see staining the wood. But I could not open it. In my madness, I did my work well. And I shall very much regret if my boat is never found at all and all of this shall prove to have been for naught.

THE HOMEWARD BOUNDER and other sea stories

THE *CALEUCHE*

My father was a poor fisherman of Chiloe. It happened one day that a great storm was driving his boat onto the dreaded rocks of the Farallones de Carelmapu. When it seemed there was no way at all for him to survive, he prayed and promised his only son, me, to the service of God and the Holy Mother Church if he should be spared. And God spared my father.

That is how I came to be a priest and came to stand one day in the black elegance of my new dignity as an ordained servant of God on the beach of Carelmapu waiting for my father to come in his boat and fetch me to our old home just outside Ancud on Isla Chiloe. There was a ferry across the Canal de Chacao, but my father wanted to meet me in his boat. He would thus be better able to display me to his friends.

I was then a young man and full of my importance before the simple villagers who gathered about me, staring from a respectful distance, but not daring to speak to one so exalted until bidden to do so. I remembered some of the older of them as friends of my father, but I had long since forgotten their names. It would be beneath the dignity of a priest, in any case, to speak with them without reason. I stood apart with my rich new leather bags and waited alone for my father to come.

I could see his boat far out in the Canal de Chacao making heavy weather of it in what was but a moderate wind, but one which blew against the strong currents of the Canal to make a violent sea for such a small boat. When a boy, I had many times seen my father come that way out of the sea, and I felt a great warmth as I watched him approach.

It was not easy for a poor fisherman to make of his son a priest in the Holy Mother Church. Especially so for a poor fisherman of Chiloe where life is harder even than on the mainland of Chile.

Isla Chiloe remained under Spanish rule for several years after mainland Chile gained her independence. Even now, mainland Chilenos are apt to look down upon us Chilotes as backward and ignorant people. I met the problem many times in the seminary at Santiago and had consciously worked to remedy my native accent lest I be recognized as coming from Chiloe.

It is a hard land, the Isla Chiloe. High enough in the Southern Latitudes to bear the brunt of great storms which come out of the Southern Ocean, it is swept often by the winds and seas of God's wrath. Its dark growth of Southern beech rain forest is peopled with blinding mists and unexplained happenings which have led over the years to the growth of legends and myths which I, with my holy power as priest, hoped to banish, for the greater glory of God and His Holy Church. They were pagan beliefs and the work of

Satan, things a Godly man could not in good conscience abide.

The *Caleuche*, for instance. This was a legend of sailors and fishermen who believed in the blasphemous thing with all their hearts when I was a boy, and I suspected they still did that day I waited on the beach for my father. I determined, even then, to make it my first order of business upon reaching my first parish on Chiloe to have done with the *Caleuche*, once and for all, in the interests of the poor benighted souls of Chiloe's seamen. It was my holy duty. It was something I could do in repayment for the sacrifices my father had made in order that I should become a priest.

Father O'Rourke in Ancud had helped, I knew, but the money needed to make a priest of a boy from Chiloe was far beyond the power of a poor fisherman to earn. I knew my father must have done many hard things in order to keep his promise to God. And I knew that his friends among the other poor fishermen of Chiloe had helped, too. The least I could do for them from the heights of my new eminence was to lift from them the blight of the heathenish *Caleuche*.

The *Caleuche* was a phantom ship of ancient design, square-rigged and bluff in the bows. Her sails were in tatters and she was fitted with a tall aftercastle, after the manner of her time. Still she sailed dead into the teeth of the gales which always blew when she was seen. She was much like the legend of the Flying Dutchman in other parts of the world. But in Chiloe she was the *Caleuche*, and the ignorant seamen of that isolated island believed that sight of her, glowing with unearthly fire in the darkness of the storm, was portent of certain doom in the wild island waters they sailed — unless they were protected by charms made and sold by charlatan *brujos* on the island.

I felt a flush of righteous anger simply in thinking about how these wretches had for so many years robbed the benighted seamen of the island of money which could better be put to the service of God and the Holy Mother Church. Well, I would put a stop to the dirty business.

My father's boat was then close in to the beach, and I forgot my stirred anger in the joy of seeing him again after so long. I praised God for His mercy in preserving my father to see his son in the habit of a priest. But I was dismayed at the toll the sea and his years of hard labor had taken on my father. Even at a distance I could see how bent he was and the whiteness of his hair under his worn old canvas hat. While I was away in Santiago becoming a priest, my father had become an old man.

He ran his boat right onto the sand, letting run the sheets and, leaping over the side in his awkward old-man way, ran and fell to his knees at my feet. He swept off his hat and sought to kiss my hand. At least, I had the decency to stop his doing that and pulled him to his feet that I might embrace him.

"Father," he cried in a cracked voice I had all but forgotten. "Your blessing, Father," he cried. "Your blessing on a sinner." And again he dropped to his knees before me.

I realized then that it was what he most wanted, and I blessed him in the names of the Father and the Son and the Holy Ghost. My own voice was cracked then, too, I fear and I felt such a surge of love for my father that tears came to my eyes.

He rose, then, and stood before me in his rags, his sea-tired eyes moving over my face. His scarred and line-cut hands felt the rich cloth of my habit and moved up my arms as though he could not bring himself to believe that I was truly there. "Welcome, Father," he said at last. "Welcome home."

"I am not 'Father' to you," I said quietly lest the others hear. "To you, I am still Paco. To you, I am always Paco."

But I could never keep him from calling me, his own son, Father. His eyes filled and spilled over onto his weathered cheeks and his face wrinkled in the thousand creases of a fisherman's smile. He turned then to the small crowd gathered about us in respectful silence.

"*Hola, amigos,*" he cried in his old-fashioned way. "Behold, my son, the priest. He comes back to bring us closer to God. He is my only son and I gave him to God."

Everyone on either side of the Canal de Chacao and the northern part of Isla Chiloe knew the story, I am certain. But my father told it again to the people on the beach and they murmured in amazement at how it had come to pass. When he was through, my father asked me if I would bless the people and I did. They knelt in the sand all about me and bowed their heads in a pure devotion seldom seen now in more refined places.

I was moved, despite my learned urbanity, and gave the blessing with all my heart. Praying God to watch over these simple people and to help them in their hard pursuit of life. It was the kind of thing which made all my studying, and my father's hard work, seem worthwhile.

It was time then for us to go. It was ten miles and more across the rough Canal de Chacao to our little village outside of Ancud, waters which become so violent that large ships are warned of the danger in the sailors' publications. But my father knew the waters well, and we set out without fear.

His exulting friends, the villagers of Carelmapu, took us up and carried us through the sand and shallow water to the boat, keeping us dry, though they became soaked. Others brought my new leather bags and covered them with old sails that they might not be wet with spray on the passage.

It was a glad occasion and my father glowed with the happiness of his great hope achieved. The villagers shoved us off and we sheeted in the sails, gaff main and jib, to put out into the Canal. It was a good feeling to be again with my father in his boat. It was the same stout craft I had known as a boy. Heavy, well-fitted and well-fastened wood,

worn then by the long years of its service. All hard edges
had long since been smoothed by the pressure of its work.
The tiller, though it had never known varnish, was bright
and polished near its end by nothing more than the rubbing
of my father's hands.

For a time neither of us spoke, savoring in silence
the pleasure of the boat's easy movement and our being
together again. The village of Carelmapu shrank and drew
together behind us in the form towns show the sea, and we
moved steadily towards the blue hills flanking Bahia de
Ancud across the Canal. When we did speak, it was of my
mother, the gentle woman I remembered but faintly, who
had the iron strength to stand with my father in his deter-
mination to make of me a priest. She died shortly after I
went away to the seminary and there had been no money
for me to come home for the funeral.

"Was she sick long, father?" I asked. "Did she suffer?"

"It was bad," my father said. "But the Good God has
His reasons and it helped her to know where you were."

"I would have come if I could, father," I said then,
even though that was not entirely true. The priests at the
seminary had offered to pay my way home but there was an
important examination coming and I did not want to miss it.
May God forgive me. "I will pray for her," I said.

We talked of other things then. Of Father O'Rourke
and old friends of my father and their children with whom
I had grown up. I was kept so busy with my studies as a
boy that I had no close friends but I remembered some of
them and wanted to hear what became of them. All, of
course, had become fishermen or simple craftsmen like their
fathers. I was the only one who went away.

Landmarks of Ancud were prominent by that time.
The cathedral a half mile southward of Punta San Antonio,
a church with a red roof a quarter mile southwestward of
Punta Piedras, and a statue of the Virgin on the slope of a
hill south-southwestward of Punta Piedras, as well as an

isolated house two hundred yards southeastward of Punta San Antonio were all as I remembered them.

The city of Ancud itself sprawls down the western slopes of Peninsula Huechuen, in a small valley surrounded by wooded hills on the eastern shores of Bahia Ancud. It is divided into two parts. The higher part stands seventy to eighty feet above the sea. It is here that the main plaza is and the cathedral and government buildings, as well as the homes of the better classes.

A lower part contains the shops, warehouses, customhouse, and clutter of the town's commercial life. There are ferry landings and some piers with hand cranes, all of which were then in need of repair. Ancud, humble though it was, was the metropolis of Isla Chiloe. Its cathedral would be goal of my life, for I was ambitious then to rise in the service of God.

My father pointed out the changes which had come about in Ancud while I was away, but we did not land there. We veered off and came to shore some distance away on a pebble beach before a disheveled huddle of fishermens' hovels and a scattering of poor boats pulled up above the tide line or moored offshore.

This is where we lived when I was a boy. I could see my father's hut, no worse nor much better than any of the others. Made of driftwood and beach stones, it stood low to the ground and was seemingly too fragile to withstand the storms I remembered lashing it about. Poor though it was, it wakened in me new memories of my boyhood and my dead mother who had so softened the world for me then and I felt a lump grow in my heart.

My father blew his battered brass foghorn and shouted from the boat as we closed the beach. Echoing shouts came back from the huts and people streamed from them in glad welcome to us. Children danced in hardly-to-be-contained excitement, and even the grown men and women ran to the water's edge with broad smiles on their faces. We were home.

Here, too, as in Carelmapu, we were lifted bodily from the grounded boat and landed dryshod well above the waterline. There was a great babble of welcome which stilled only when I stood before them and the peoples' exuberance was quelled by their awe of me, one of their sons who had become a man of God. They fell silent then, and my father had me bless them as he had me bless the villagers of Carelmapu.

The joy could not thus be contained for long, though. Old Jorge Ortiz whom I remembered from before had his violin. Others brought guitars. There was a much-dented trumpet and a home-made drum. Music was struck up, and the people sang in glad fiesta. Fires were lighted, food was brought, and fat bottles of cheap wine were handed round. Children darted about in shrieking play. Elders sat apart or came shyly to give me their names and ask if I remembered them. My father gloried in it all, knowing that it was he who had made it possible for me to be a priest, and basking in the mingled adoration and envy and reflected warmth. He forced glasses of wine into my hands. Most of the people drank direct from the bottles, but that would never do for a man of God.

It had taken us longer than I realized to cross the Canal de Chacao. The sun was low and soon the beach was dark, with the licking light of the fires and the wan glow of lamps in the huts the only light. But still the people celebrated my return. I grew tired. There was no one with whom I could talk intelligently. The food was coarse and the wine less than good. My earlier sentimental appreciation for my home village and its people waned and I told my father that I was going to retire to pray.

I could tell that he was disappointed but my father made my excuses to the people. He explained that men of God had obligations not known to ordinary men, and the people accepted my going with a murmuring of good nights and prayers for God to go with me. But the party went on with little lessening.

Inside the crude dwelling, I lay on the bed which had been mine as a child, across the room from where my father and mother slept. The only other furnishings were a rough driftwood table and three chairs, with a rudimentary cupboard by the cook fire and some pegs for clothes to be hung. The floor was God's earth, with a reed mat or two. I was glad that when I got to my own church, a decent house would be provided.

At any rate, I did sleep. Sometime during the night the party ended and the fires died down. My father found his own bed without waking me, and the next day we went in to Ancud to see Father O'Rourke and the bishop who would assign me to a church.

I remember as a boy thinking the cathedral in Ancud must have been the grandest building in the world, but after seeing the great churches in Santiago, it seemed poor indeed. Still, Father O'Rourke's greeting could not have been warmer had we met in Saint Peter's itself.

Father O'Rourke had grown old, too. His hair was all but white, and his always-pink face was dusted here and there with ash-like patches. His robes hung on him as though from a pole. The cancer which would kill him was already showing its marks.

But he drew me to him with a strength which was surprising in one who seemed so frail. He could not have been kinder and he laughed and teased my father about what had become of me. He recalled how I had left, a skinny little boy with big black eyes and here I stood, a tall and handsome man of God. My father blushed and hung his head in embarrassed pride.

And when I was brought into the presence of the bishop, Father O'Rourke regaled the great man with outlandish stories of my virtue and devotion to God and His

Church. The bishop allowed both me and my father to kiss his ring then greeted me with amused good humor.

"Father O'Rourke has told me of you, Father," the bishop said, smiling. "I had expected someone more monumental. A halo, perhaps."

It was then my turn to be embarrassed, but the bishop laughed and asked if I would like to celebrate Mass in the cathedral on Sunday. I knew Father O'Rourke must have arranged that, but I was too overwhelmed to more than nod my head and again kiss the bishop's ring.

That Sunday, when it came, was the most glorious day of my life. Father O'Rourke helped me serve the Mass, and people from miles around came to see Chiloe's own priest preside.

My father was there, of course, along with all the people of his village, all dressed in their poor best and openly awed by the splendor of the building and the richness of my robes.

After that, I could imagine no greater triumph possible. I stayed that night with Father O'Rourke in his quarters, and the next day he took me, along with the bishop, to see my new church. It was in Quetalmahue, a small village on the southern shore of Punta Aucan about three miles west of Punta Arena.

It was not a grand church, but it would be close enough to Ancud and its cathedral for the bishop to keep me in his eye for advancement in keeping with my talents. And I would be near to Father O'Rourke for his guidance and counseling in the ways of the church. It was a good enough church for a first posting, and I set about at once to make a name for myself in the service of God.

Once I was settled in at my decent little house, I thought immediately of my vow to eradicate the superstitious belief in the *Caleuche*. That would be my first concern. I would even seek invitations to speak to other churches. I would stop at nothing until the cursed legend was discredited throughout Isla Chiloe.

I had talked with Father O'Rourke the night I spent in his residence following my saying the Mass in the cathedral. It troubled me that Father O'Rourke was not more supportive of my fervor in dispelling superstition on Chiloe, but I did not long let that deter me. Oh, I knew then what God wanted.

At any rate, I took the occasion of my first sermon to preach against the *Caleuche*. My father had seen to it that all the village fishermen were there. It was not often that a son of the island became a priest and spoke to them in their own humble church.

They listened respectfully, along with their wives, as I flayed them for their blasphemous belief in superstition. Their faith and trust belonged with God. Their salvation amid the hazards of the sea and its storms was the Holy Cross, not some satanic fetish of wood and leather and polished stones hung about their necks. The money they paid the *brujos* for these worthless trinkets was better spent by the Church in its good works for them all.

In my young ardor, I was merciless with them. And, soon, they were hanging their heads and making furtive glances from one to another. I could see some of the wives clutching their husbands' arms in the terror I stirred. The fear of the *Caleuche* with which they had so long lived was then joined with fear of the anger of God which I called down upon them.

I talked for a long time that day and when I was through, I watched with a great satisfaction as the people filed from the church in silent awe of what I said. The glad joy which had marked my return to the village became a solemn air of despair at having become entangled between their genuine fear and Love of God and their dread for the deadly *Caleuche*. But I, in my raw innocence, took that to be a measure of my success in freeing my people of heresy.

I had my father to dinner that night in the modest but comfortable house provided for me by the Church. There was good wine, and food well-prepared by my housekeeper. But, try as I might, I could not lighten my father's mood. He could not bring himself to be critical of his son, the priest. But neither could he bring himself to enjoy the comforts his sacrifices had earned for me. He was clearly ill-at-ease, and when I brought up again the subject of the *Caleuche*, he became more so.

When I asked him what his fellow fishermen's reaction had been to my sermon, he was evasive and non-committal and changed the subject to something else. This was troubling, but it did not occur to me that he, my own father, might also believe in the *Caleuche*. Surely, he would know better and I laid his mood to the excitement of my return and the weariness of old men. We drank the good wine and talked of other things.

The next day he took me to pray at my mother's grave and we were again father and son as we had been so many years before. I wept at my mother's grave and prayed God with all my heart to reward her with the peace and serenity so often denied her on earth. My father comforted me and we were very close, one to the other. Even the villagers, my parishioners, sensed my sorrow and made touching little gestures of condolence. All would have been well with me, had it not been for the *Caleuche*.

For, after my first sermon in my church, the sermon in which I had so fiercely assailed them for believing in their cursed superstition, the fishermen would not come again. Of them all, only my father came, and old Esteban who was crippled with age and no longer went out to fish. Even the wives came in smaller numbers and watched me apprehensively as though fearing new threats of damnation and doom from me if their men did not repent and mend their ways. Their children looked upon me with large and fearful eyes.

The fishermen continued to look upon me with respect when we passed in the village. They doffed their caps and murmured their wishes that God might go with me but they did not pause for a word and they kept their eyes from mine. The village became a cold and reproachful place. And when I walked along the beach where their boats were drawn up on the sand, I could see the men still wore about their necks on leather thongs the crude charms against the *Caleuche* made for them by island *brujos*.

Being young and arrogant and, oh, so sure of my own righteousness, I let my frustration turn to anger and spoke ever more violently from my pulpit, invoking the power of God and the Church against those who flouted their holy authority.

I even went again to Father O'Rourke and sought his counsel as to what I should do. And again he cautioned me to patience and a greater charity. I could not understand his reticence.

The *Caleuche* was an evil superstition, nothing more. Was it not the duty of the Church and her servants to fight such things? Did I not have a holy obligation to strive against ignorance?

Still, Father O'Rourke would not support me and turned aside my fervid indignation with laughing good humor, advising me to bide my time and to strengthen my own faith in God's omniscience and His penchant for moving in strange ways. He gave me wine and suggested I stay the night that we might discuss more fully my first days in my own church.

He poured us good wine in fine glasses, but I would not stay. I was disappointed in Father O'Rourke. I expected better of him. I forgot that, but for him, I would not have been a priest in the first place. I seethed with an anger difficult to hide; but I am certain now he recognized it.

But I would not so easily give up my fight against darkness. The sullen resentment of the village fishermen continued against me. And they continued to wear about their necks their blasphemous talismans. I turned then to the only ally I had, my father.

I knew that my father had always enjoyed a marked respect among the fisherman. I saw it when I was a boy. They often sought his advice and counsel, and followed his example in matters of fishing and weather and the like. So I went to him for help in convincing the other fishermen of the error of their ways.

I waited in my father's hut for him to return from fishing. It had been a bad day for him. He caught few fish, and he was tired and wet, yet still he brightened when he saw me at his table.

"Ay, Father," he said, "What brings you to our house?"

The question was an earned reproach for I came infrequently to his home in those days. The comforts of my provided house and the excellence of the meals prepared by my housekeeper were too enticing to be given up for the poor accommodation of my father's house. And the lack of breadth and depth in his knowledge of the world made for poor conversation.

"It is the matter of the *Caleuche*," I said, coming abruptly to the point. "The fishermen will not give up their cursed charms which are abomination in the eyes of God. They risk their immortal souls for this nonsense. They do not listen to me."

My father stood without moving, just inside the low door of his hut. Water draining from his wet clothes made a black puddle at his feet. He seemed to shrink before me, and there was a pleading in his eyes. "What . . . What would you have me do, Father?" he murmured.

"I would have you talk to them," I said harshly. "They will listen to you. For the sake of their souls, talk to them, father."

He did not want to do it. I could see that. Even in my young blindness, I could see that, but I would not relent. Playing upon his love for me and the great pride that was his for having made of me a priest, I persisted, implying that his own soul was at risk if he did not do as God wanted. And, God forgive me, I even threatend him with the loss of my love if he failed me.

In the end, he did agree and I left his hut with a greater optimism than I had known in days. I knew the other fishermen loved my father and were likely to do what he said. It was uncomfortably humbling for me to realize that he had more influence over the fishermen than I, a priest, but I laid it to their ignorance and commended myself for my wit in using the tools at hand to gain God's way.

But the next Sunday the fishermen again did not come to my church. After the Mass, I stormed out into the village street and saw, one after the other, that the fishermen still wore their awful bits of magic about their necks. Thry turned away from me in what I took to be shame for their stubborness. They would not meet my eyes and they made no reply to my shouted recriminations and warnings. They simply turned away and went into their poor houses.

More angry than ever, I sought out my father. Since it was Sunday, I knew he would not be fishing. I found him in his hut, praying on his knees before the little shrine he had made there of sea shells and driftwood in honor of my mother. Her faded picture was there and candles against the gloom.

The candles flickered as I opened the door and my father turned to see who had come. "You did not talk to them," I charged without preliminary. "They are still wearing the evil things. They still do not come to hear God's word."

He got to his feet. I should have helped him but I didn't. "I talked to them, Paco," he said. It was the first time since my return that he had used my boyhood nickname, but I didn't notice. "I talked to them, Paco," he said again, "but they do not listen."

Enraged, I let my disappointment in him show, and he cringed before me. He could not bear the thought of displeasing me. Even more than his fear of God, I think his fear of displeasing me devastated him. He fell to his knees before me and clutched at my hands, tears wetting his seaworn face.

But I would not relent. I stared over his bent head to the shrine he had built to my mother. My heart was bleak. My own father had failed me in my service to God and I felt a great emptiness in me.

Then an even greater dread came over me, an awful suspicion. I tore my father's hands away and pulled open his coat and the shirt under it. And there I found, suspended from a leather thong, what had become in my eyes one of the world's great evils. It was one of the damned talismans against the *Caleuche*.

Shocked, I let fall his coat and shirt and stumbled out the door of his hut. I needed the light of day. How could I hope to prevail in God's holy work when my own father joined with the forces of evil against me. I could hear my father crying after me, but I would not listen and hurried back to my church where I knelt in fervent prayer.

I never spoke with my father again. I made no attempt to see him, and he stayed clear of me except for Mass when he sat at the back of the church and kept his head down. I no longer spoke out against the *Caleuche*, but the villagers kept their coldness towards me. Even my goodhearted housekeeper spoke to me only when necessary. I was very much alone.

It is a climatic oddity that in the Isla Chiloe changes in the weather are foretold by unusual refractions and other phenomena. On days of calm winds and high temperatures the rocks and islands and houses seem to vibrate and take on odd forms at times, separating into sections or being lifted up or disappearing altogether. Distant objects are seen with great clarity. In a little while cumulus clouds will gather in the north and the sky will darken until hidden in complete nimbus. The snow-topped peaks of Monte Melimoyu, Cerros Yanteles, and Volcan Corcovado on the mainland become lost in dense clouds which spread and lower over the valleys and the sea.

All these things are well known to the fishermen of Chiloe who see them as sure precursors of bad weather, the kind of weather in which the *Caleuche* is likely to be seen. Fishermen at such times haul their nets and run for shelter, often arriving only briefly before the outriding squalls of great storms.

The beach before the village becomes at such times a scene of great activity. Boats are drawn up beyond reach of the sea and loose gear is secured against the wind. Birds wheel in anxious flight before the squalls and the first huge drops of rain fall. And all this in the deepening gloom of racing clouds.

Despite my recent despair, I was still pastor to these people and I went to the beach to be of what help I could. The people crossed themselves as I went by, but were too distracted by the coming peril to do more. I helped pull boats high on the sand and helped secure masts and sails. And even as we worked, I could see the cursed *Caleuche* charms about the fishermen's necks.

It seemed that all but a few boats had made safe haven. Of those not in, the chances were good they had reached shelter at other villages. I prayed that was so, for one of the missing boats was that of my father.

Old Esteban, he who no longer fished, took it upon himself to telephone the other villages, but none of them had seen my father. The only reported sighting of his boat had it proceeding on out to sea, even as the others fled before the storm.

A sudden fear took hold of me. The sea off the beach had become a torment of black water and white crests, all joined in cloud and rain. Without proper coat or hat, I became soaked, but I did not feel the wet. I looked out into the storm with growing dread, unable to draw myself away from the terrible scene.

In the end, old Esteban came and, with his wife, led me to my father's hut. There they struck a light and set it on the table. And I saw there the small object of wood and leather, polished smooth from rubbing against my father's chest for all those years he was working himself into old age that I might become a priest.

Even now, all these years since, I can recall the awful realization which came over me. Guilt and remorse and and a sobbing need for forgiveness swept over me. I sent old Esteban away and sat alone in my father's hut while the storm beat at it and blown water stained the floor black before the door.

I remembered as a boy sitting in that hut on such nights and listening to my father and his fishermen friends telling their tales of the *Caleuche* and the disaster which inevitably followed its sighting if the man were not protected by charms and talismans. And, dumbly, I fingered my father's own protection against the *Caleuche*, protection he had left ashore in order to please me.

And I knew, even then, my father was dead, that I would never see him again.

I do not know how long I sat thus alone. But sometime during the night Father O'Rourke came. The villagers had sent for him. We prayed together and he came to tell me much I had not known before. My father had not only been a believer in the *Caleuche*, he was a *brujo* who made and sold charms against its threat. The money which was used to make me a priest had come from the sale of the sacreligious things. Father O'Rourke comforted me as best he could and tried to convince me that God does indeed work in strange and wondrous ways. And, in the end, I think he did.

I am still a priest of Chiloe. I never attained the cathedral of my young ambition. But I have learned much of the workings of God, I think. Father O'Rourke is now long dead and I am an old man. But the villagers have come to love me and I am content. I now wear my father's old amulet over my habit and God understands, though the Church in Santiago does not, and I know that I shall never be a bishop and that I shall die here in Chiloe.

SAN JOAQUIN

There had always been for Hank Marten a special charm about California's San Joaquin River, where it first meets the push and suck of Pacific tides and wanders almost pensively through a quiet world of reeds and tules and waterside trees before surrendering, at last, to the sea. Especially so at night when the hard heat of the day is softened and the winds become no more than the gentle breathing of a sleeping world and there is no sound other than the occasional splashing of a fish or the murmuring of current about an anchor line.

At times like those, a troubled man can sit alone in a cockpit and let the silent evidence of the stars remind him that, in the end, all will be well and that human sorrow, too, does pass.

Always before, Hank had been able to go to the San Joaquin following some hurt, much as a wounded wild animal will run to water, and find there a solace that was both healing and certain.

He went there, for instance, after a Saturday night automobile accident ended the laughing life of Nancy, his nineteen-year-old daughter. Twenty-three, she would have been, now. And, after some days, he found himself able to accept what, in the beginning, was impossible to accept.

Hank went there too, when Nancy's mother, Mary Lou, decided that twenty-five years of marriage was enough. The San Joaquin, that time, too, had helped him live.

But this time, after more than a week, even the San Joaquin did not help ease the sodden ache which began with Mary Lou's call telling him that their only other child, Johnny, would not be coming home from Vietnam. Not alive, anyway.

After the funeral, and after doing all for Mary Lou that she would let him do, he went, as though driven by some feral instinct, to the *McChree*. He bent on the sails and turned her towards the San Joaquin and that special place on the San Joaquin where his little family for so long had spent their summer breaks.

It was a small, lagoon-like bit of water off False River. Johnny found it one time while on a dinghy voyage of discovery. The Dunk Hole, he called it. He had trouble pronouncing G's when he was little.

The entry was just large enough to accept the *McChree's* broad beam, and the channel jogged hard right just inside so that boats transitting False River could pass without knowing of the place. When Hank anchored, he pulled in close under the waterside trees, with the thought that his tall mast might be hidden in their branches and not be seen to betray the hideaway.

That is where Hank went because of Johnny's not coming home. He put out a stern anchor and passed a bow line around a tree on shore, which is the San Joaquin way of mooring. He rigged the awning and did all the other chores of settling in, making them last because he dreaded the idleness which must come when everything was done.

Hank and Johnny spent the boy's last leave here in the Dunk Hole. Surely, a healthy boy of nineteen must have had more exciting things to do with his last days at home than to come there with his middle-aging father, but he insisted not. He and Hank were much alike and Johnny knew how hard the divorce had been for Hank.

Hank looked about him, once everything was secured. For one wrenching moment it seemed that Johnny must simply be away in the dinghy, which the kids had named *Paddy* in keeping with the Irish name of the family boat. Surely, soon he would hear the thock and squeak of oarlocks and hear Johnny call some laughing something over his shoulder as he drew close.

But, no. *Paddy* nuzzled under the *McChree*'s quarter as usual, nor was there any call. Hank was alone. But he remembered with a stabbing clarity that last time there with Johnny.

"It won't be so bad in the Coast Guard, Dad," Johnny tried to explain. "It won't be like being in the Army or Navy. The Coast Guard tries to save lives, not take them."

They talked about that a long time, Hank and Johnny, before he enlisted in the Coast Guard. Johnny had been a gentle boy, much like his mother in that way. "I don't want to have to kill anybody, Dad."

"Not many people do, Johnny."

"Then why do they? Why do we have wars?"

Hank couldn't answer that, of course, but he did talk with Johnny about it. And not only that one time. Hank remembered the boy's solemn young face when, at last, he decided to join the Coast Guard rather than wait to be drafted into the Army. He remembered how relieved Johnny was in the belief that, in the Coast Guard, he would not be called upon to fight.

Then, almost at once, following basic training, he was sent to Vietnam.

There were letters, of course. Short letters, for the most part, but all like folded portraits which opened in Hank's eager hands to show him in familiar expressions and turns of phrase that Johnny lived and remembered him.

"We don't do much, Dad," Johnny wrote. "Patrolling most of the time along the coast and stopping junks to search them for contraband.

"We haven't found anything yet. I hope we never do. The people look so pitiful. We come up alongside them in our big powerful cutter and they look up at us with their eyes full of fear, begging us not to hurt them.

"It's got to end, Dad. I don't know what is right or wrong anymore, but I <u>feel</u> wrong in being out here. I think so often of you and Mom and Nancy and all of us back there in the Dunk Hole. I hope someday . . ."

Hank still had that letter. It was the last he ever got from Johnny. It was below, in a drawer under the chart table. He kept it there. All the others were in his apartment in the city, but he kept that one on the boat. He remembered, now with a greater poignancy than before, the chill of foreboding he felt upon first reading it.

Maybe, he thought, that is why the San Joaquin was slow in working its usual magic for him. Maybe, if he threw the letter away, he would be all right. He even went below once with the intent of throwing it over the side but he could not bring himself to do that. It was too much a part of Johnny. Too much of the little he had left of his son. In the end, he put it back in its drawer.

So, he spent the days which followed waiting for the comfort he hoped would come. Sometimes he caught himself watching the entrance to the Dunk Hole, as though comfort would come as a visible thing, making ripples in the still water like a boat or a swimming animal.

But, most times, Hank read. The *McChree* always had a good store of books. The Martens had been a reading family. There is a comfort, of sorts, in books and he was able sometimes to lose himself that way.

But it was a short-lived comfort and Hank, more and more, hugged his grief to his breast, as the ancients are said to have held wild foxes to their chests, letting the little beasts tear at their flesh. He knew it was not a healthy thing to do, that danger lay that way, but there was little he could do about it.

Sometimes Hank came to feel that Johnny was alive and with him. The whiskey did that. He did drink far too much. Just as he had when Nancy was killed and when Mary Lou left him. But he drank deliberately. There was a purpose in it. He was not an alcoholic. Not normally. Not yet.

When he was drunk, Hank <u>knew</u> Johnny was there. Sometimes even Nancy and Mary Lou came. He talked with them and they were together again there in the *McChree*.

He would cry out in great bursts of laughter at the jokes they played upon each other. He nodded soberly at the profound thoughts they explored in long after-dinner conversations in the cockpit. For a little while, things were as they always had been.

But it was all delusion. He would sober up and be alone again. That hurt. More and more, he simply stayed drunk. Before, when he had suffered through the loss of Nancy and Mary Lou, Johnny had been there to help the alcohol. This time, with Johnny no longer there, the alcohol could not do the job alone. But it was the only ease Hank could find, even briefly.

Later, he knew that he must have been very drunk when Eddie came. He remembered he was in the cockpit. He had not bothered to fix an evening meal. The last bottle of whiskey on board was nearly empty. He remembered being concerned about that.

He remembered when he first heard the outboard motor out in False River. He remembered more clearly when the motor stopped. Fishermen frequently went through that stretch of False River but they seldom stopped. Then, after a time, Hank heard the sound of rowing.

He had seen Johnny come so many times in just that way. The wooden thunk and groan of the oarlocks and, as the boat drew nearer, the chuckle of bow wave and small splash of the oars. It was all part of the delusion born of drink, but this time the sounds did not go away as they had before.

"Mister Marten?"

Hank could not answer at first. His bleared eyes brimmed over and he stood up in the cockpit, clutching at the boom with its furled sail for support.

"Mister Marten? Is that you, sir?"

It was a young man's voice and Hank was instantly on guard. "Yes," he blurted thickly. "I'm Marten. Who are you? What do you want?"

"My name is Eddie French, sir. I want to talk with you." He was resting on his oars, but the heavy rental skiff drifted closer. It looked like one of Korth's.

Drunkenly suspicious, and not at all sure that this was not another of his hallucinations, Hank resented the intrusion. "How did you find this place?" he demanded. "Who told you where I was?"

"Johnny, sir," the young man in the boat said. "Johnny told me about it. Mrs. Marten told me how to get here."

"Johnny? Mary Lou?" Hank's fuddled brain would not register the names clearly. He had heard them so often through the past days, but then they had come from his own tongue. This time they came in a strange voice. This time the figure which spoke them did not fade away as he stared at it.

"May I come aboard, sir?"

Hank nodded but, he made no offer to help. Eddie French pulled the skiff alongside and streamed it to the current so it wouldn't bang against the *McChree*. He had been around boats. He secured the painter and turned to Hank. "I hope you don't mind my coming," he said.

The boy's voice was hesitant and his face was haunted in the starlight, a fact which was clear to Hank even in the state he was in. He was larger than Johnny had been, Hank could see that when he stood, but there was a stabbing similarity in the two faces: the one alive before him and the other but remembered. Maybe, he thought, it is because they were both so young.

"No. No, I don't mind," Hank mumbled. He was still confused, but he was moved by the boy's sadness.

"I don't want to intrude. If you . . ."

"You said you wanted to talk with me?"

"Yes. Yes, I do."

"About what?"

Eddie's face broke then. Hank thought he would cry. He looked away to spare the boy embarrassment. The water was dark in the shadow of trees. There was no wind. A night bird flew low overhead and was gone.

"Johnny," the boy said. "I want to tell you about Johnny."

"You knew Johnny?"

"We were shipmates. We used to go ashore together. We used to talk together. He told me about you. He . . ."

"Then you're Eddie French!" The name finally registered in Hank's fuddled mind. He took hold of the boy's shoulders in almost a frenzy of emotion.

"Yes, sir. I am. I . . ."

Hank held Eddie at arm's length, "Johnny mentioned you in his letters. You must have been good friends."

Hank sat down and pulled Eddie down with him. Neither of them spoke for a time, as though they both were at a loss for words. Hank noticed the whiskey bottle on the bridge deck and pushed it out of sight behind him though, God knows, the boy would have to be noseless not to have smelled whiskey on Hank's breath.

"Have you eaten yet, Eddie?"

"No sir. But I'm not hungry . . ."

"Nonsense," Hank stopped him. "I haven't eaten either. I'll hack open a couple of cans of chili or something. Come on, give me a hand."

Hank did not notice that he had lost his own sadness in responding to the boy's. For the first time since learning of Johnny's death, he thought of something beyond himself and his own sorrow. In finding another's sadness, he had lost some of his own.

As they moved about in preparing the meal, Eddie's mood softened, as well. They came to an easier exchange. The soft glow of cabin lamplight on varnished wood and the warm smell of the alcohol stove made a comforting atmosphere. They were soon talking much as old friends might talk, but neither of them mentioned Johnny during that time.

It was only after dinner that they did. It was late by the time the simple washing up was done. Hank had some Courvoisieur on board, and cigars, but Eddie choked on the brandy and coughed violently with the cigar.

"Here, give it to me," Hank laughed. "No use in making yourself sick just to be polite."

"I'm sorry, sir. It's just that I never learned to drink or smoke." Then, as though embarrassed, Eddie went on. "Neither one of us did. Johnny, I mean. The others used to kid us about it. Johnny didn't smoke or drink. You knew that, didn't you, Mister Marten?"

And there was Johnny between them again. Eddie was alive and with Hank. Johnny was dead. He would never be with Hank again. Hank felt a sudden fierce resentment for this boy's being alive. Eddie sensed the hostility and drew back.

But the feeling passed. "Yes. Yes, I knew that," Hank said, keeping his voice level. He paused. The boat shifted to a whim of the current. "You said you wanted to talk to me, Eddie," Hank prompted. "Was it something specific?"

"Yes, sir." Eddie steeled himself with a clearly visible effort. "I want to tell you about Johnny, Mister Marten."

"What about Johnny?" Hank kept his voice as gentle as he could, but he was moved by the look on the boy's face.

Eddie stared at Hank with an air of utter dejection. "I killed him, sir," he blurted.

Hank didn't say anything but the warm night was suddenly cold.

"I did, sir," Eddie cried. "I killed him. He would be here. He would be alive, if it hadn't been for me."

"Maybe you had better tell me about it," Hank said tightly.

After a long, tense pause, Eddie began to talk. "I, er, we were on patrol. We stopped a sampan. It was in shallow water. We put over the inflatable, we carried one just for that reason." The boy's voice was tight. The words came out in quick, ugly little knots of sound.

"Johnny and I were told off for the boarding party. Mister Borden was in charge. We put over. There were two Vietnamese in the sampan. They looked like fisher-men. They didn't look any different from all the others we stopped. Nothing had ever happened before."

Eddie stopped then. He wouldn't look at Hank any more. He was silent for what seemed a long time. Hank waited without speaking. His throat was too tight for him to speak. He was beginning to sense something momen-tous and horrifying in what Eddie was saying.

"There was some canvas in the bottom of the sam-pan," Eddie finally continued. "Mister Borden told Johnny to see what was under it. I was watching Johnny, sir. I should have been watching the Vietnamese. That's what I was supposed to be doing."

Eddie's voice shrilled then, almost hysterically. "It was my fault," he cried. "I should have been watching the Vietnamese. I had a gun. I could have stopped them."

"Stopped them from what?" Hank said. But already he could feel a chill rising in him.

"One of them had a knife," Eddie went on. "If I had been watching him, I could have kept him from killing Johnny!"

Eddie did lose control of himself then and sank in a shuddering heap on the cockpit bench. Hank stood up. He looked down at the sobbing boy. For a savage moment he hated him. His arms tensed as though to pick him up and throw him physically clear of the boat. God in Heaven! Johnny's death could have been prevented. Johnny might, at that very moment have been alive, if . . ."

Great, gushing waves of self-pity washed over Hank. He damned God and His senseless world and all the senseless humans in it for what had happened to him. For the agony and suffering he had been put to.

All the hurt which had come before: Nancy, Mary Lou. Now, Johnny himself, all of it focused in one scalding bath of pain for having learned that Johnny's death could have been prevented.

Blindly, almost instinctively, Hank reached for the whiskey bottle he had shoved under the cushion. But even the burning of whiskey in his ravaged throat could no longer hold the pain at bay. He threw the bottle away and lurched forward to stand, clutching the forestay, to let the soft river wind make cold the tears on his face.

Hank never knew how long he stood so. He later knew only that some time during that night the anger passed. He knew he didn't pray; he was not the type, but sometime before dawn he came to realize the suffering Eddie French must have endured, torment so intense it had driven him to seek out the very father of the man for whose death he felt responsible, knowing what that father's reaction must be. It would be a powerful thing to make a man do something like that.

And Hank realized then, for the first time, how much Mary Lou must have suffered from Johnny's death. She and Johnny had been closer, in some ways, even than Hank and Johnny had been. It must have been hell for her. Hank cursed himself for having forgotten Mary Lou and stumbled aft to look down again upon the silent boy in the cockpit.

Hank bent and touched him. "It's all right, Eddie," he said. "It's all right."

And, suddenly, Hank realized it <u>was</u> all right. He slipped down on the bench beside Eddie, and acceptance came at last to him. In coming to recognize Eddie's torment, Hank came to accept his own. He knew it wasn't Eddie's fault. No more than it was the fault of the faraway Vietnamese, who were themselves, in all likelihood, dead as well, and remembered only in the grieving hearts of parents of their own.

It wasn't anybody's fault. Hank tried to tell Eddie that. He tried to ease Eddie's hurt and, in doing so, eased his own.

Eddie began to sob again. Hank let him. He put his hand on the boy's shoulder. Slowly, the night wore on until, finally, Eddie slept. His head rested on Hank's leg. The leg grew stiff but Hank did not move for fear of waking the boy.

Hank looked up through the black tracery of overhanging tree branches to where the brighter stars burned through gathering dawn mists. And, again, he thought of Mary Lou.

Mary Lou had told Eddie French where to find him. She knew where Hank would be, even though he, in his blind anguish of self-pity, had not bothered to tell her. Mary Lou had remembered.

And, if she remembered that, it was possible she might remember still more. She might remember all the good things there had been with them. She might . . . Tomorrow, he would call her. There might still be time for them.

Thinking this, Hank looked down at the sleeping boy for a long time. Then he looked out of the boat and watched a swimming muskrat draw a long silvery Vee across the dark waters of the San Joaquin.

THE CONTRIBUTION

It rained that morning. A hard, splashing, straight-up and-down tropical downpour that drummed on the tin roof of the piershed and collected in shining dimpled pools on the paving of the pier itself. The ship's decks gleamed wet and streaming where she lay moored. The jungle back of the rusted corrugated iron roofs of the town steamed in the rain. The stench of copra and rotted wood seemed even heavier than usual in the sodden air.

Captain Erling Larsen cursed the rain and shouted from the bridge wing. His khaki shirt was wet and foul-smelling. It clung to him, clammy cold, despite the warmth of the rain. "Mister Clarence!"

"Yes, sir?" The ship's first officer stepped out from under the starboard shelter deck and squinted up through the rain.

189

"Get your tarps over the hatches, Mister Clarence," Larsen ordered. "We've got to get out of here. We'll batten down underway."

"We're not finished, Captain. Another hundred bags will see us done. Can't . . . ?"

"You heard me, Mister Clarence. Get tarps over the hatches and stand by to handle lines."

Clarence mumbled something which didn't carry as far as the bridge, but he ducked back out of the rain and in moments half-naked deckhands ran out and lowered heavy tarpaulins over the open hatches.

"Rig in your booms, Mister Shelton," the captain called then to another officer standing in the small shelter offered by the forecastle break. "Secure your winches and tackle. We're getting underway. Chop, chop!"

Shelton waved acknowledgment of the order and Larsen fished in his shirt pocket for cigarettes. The tobacco was damp and he had trouble getting it lit. He cursed and lighted another match.

"What's up, Captain?" Mister Clarence pulled himself up the bridge ladder and joined Larsen in the shelter of the starboard wing. "We could top off in thirty minutes, once this rain knocks off."

"We don't have thirty minutes, Mister Clarence," Larsen said. "The Navy's ordered us to clear the area as fast as we can. The rebels are expected here any time now. Things'll be simpler if we're not around. Cigarette?"

Clarence dried his fingers on his shirt tail and took the offered smoke. He nodded over the side. "What about them, Captain?"

The captain frowned but he didn't look at the people huddled in the shelter of the piershed overhangs or squatting in the rain, looking up at the ship. Their sodden bundles and baskets lay strewn about them, some still lashed to carrying poles.

The captain drew deep on his cigarette. He seemed angered to be reminded of the people on the pier. He resented their silent, patient staring. He resented it as a man resents the soundless begging of a hungry dog who sits and watches him eat. "I don't know," the captain said. As though against his will, he looked at the people on the pier. "Why don't they get out of the God-damned rain?" he blurted angrily. "Why do they keep looking up here?"

"I guess they think we're the last shot they got at getting away," Mister Clarence said. "From the looks of them, I'd say they don't have much more run left in them."

"Well, that's their pidgen," the captain muttered.

"Hard to tell what'll happen to them," Mister Clarence said. "Poor buggers. You hear some pretty hairy stories about how the rebels treat the ones they catch."

"They'll get by."

"Yeah." Mister Clarence flipped his cigarette over the side. "I guess maybe you're right, Captain. Everything seems to work out — one way or the other. I remember when the Japs came in out here during the War. That wasn't very pretty. I remember . . ."

The captain ground out his own cigarette then, and in a sudden, half-vicious gesture, threw it out into the rain. "I was here, too, Mister Clarence," he said. "You'd better see to your hatches."

"I was down in Java. We had just . . ."

"I said you had better see to your hatches, Mister Clarence," the captain said again, his voice hard. "And tell the boatswain to get in the accommodation ladder. Those people down there may panic when they see us getting underway. There's no use in asking for trouble."

"Yes, sir," the mate said. He stood for a moment longer looking down at the miserable refugees on the streaming dock, his expression a blend of pity and regret. "We could carry a lot of them, Captain," he said quietly. "We

191

could carry them on deck for no longer than it would take to . . ."

"Mister Clarence!"

"Yes, sir. I was just thinking. It . . ."

"Well, don't." The captain paused, and he, too, looked down at the huddled people and their pitiful belongings. His voice became softer, almost gentle. "There's nothing we can do, Mister Clarence. Nothing at all."

"We could take part of them. We . . ."

Anger showed then in the captain's face, but he held it back. "The insurgents have patrol vessels in the area, Mister Clarence," he said. "They have airplanes. If we take these people on board, Mister Clarence, if we help them to escape, we would be giving the rebels all the excuse they'd need. They'd attack us in a minute, Mister Clarence."

"But, Captain . . ."

"That's enough, Mister Clarence!" the captain said. "I've seen a bomb hit on a crowded ship. It makes a frightful mess, Mister Clarence. I've no wish to see it again."

The mate didn't answer at once. He had the junior's natural reluctance to argue with his senior, but he was also deeply moved by the plight of the helpless people along-side. "It's a chance we'd be taking," he admitted. "But, if we leave them here, they won't even have a chance. They won't even have that much."

"They will adjust, Mister Clarence," the captain said, his voice wooden. "They will get along, somehow. They always do. The people lived, even under the Japanese in the war."

Mister Clarence seemed still to want to plead for the refugees, but the captain cut him short. "You have your orders, Mister Clarence. Carry them out, if you please. Report to me when the ship is ready to get underway."

"Yes, sir." The mate turned to go, then stopped, pointing, with a wry smile, to a white man making his way towards the ship. "Here comes your rummy, Captain. I guess he decided to come with us, after all."

The captain frowned, looking to where the mate pointed. The man on the dock was small and slightly built, dressed in a soiled rain-drenched white shirt and khaki trousers. He picked his way gingerly through the squatting refugees. He had trouble keeping his balance and, sometimes, would touch a dripping head or shoulder to keep from falling.

"Soused again," the captain said, his voice grimly amused. "Well, let him aboard, if that's what he wants." He turned to go. "I'll be in my cabin, Mister Clarence."

The cabin seemed wonderfully welcoming to the captain, even if a little stuffy. The pounding of rain on the piershed roof, while still clearly audible, was muted to a hum and there was the comfortably familiar rush of blowers and pulse of pumps that is a ship. The sounds of the winches was there, too, and the sounds of the booms swinging in and of the men tugging the heavy hatch covers in place. These things were home to the captain and hearing them, he could forget the people on the dock alongside. Soon, he would be underway and back to the clean simplicity of the sea and its problems. Thinking these things, the captain stripped off his wet shirt and pulled a dry, crisply pressed one from a drawer.

"I say, you wouldn't have another of those, would you, Captain?"

The captain turned, irritation showing in his face. "This is my cabin, Phipps," he said.

"Yes. Yes, I dare say it is." Phipps was the man on the dock. At closer range, he seemed even more nondescript, even more dissolute, with only a certain steadiness about his eyes to say that here was, in fact, a man. His hair, long and untrimmed and startlingly black, hung in dripping spears on his forehead as water spread in a growing stain about his feet. His thin body shivered as though with a sudden chill. The captain tossed him the dry shirt.

"I'm obliged to you, Captain," Phipps said amiably. "Funny how cold a warm rain can make a chap." He busied himself with stripping off his old shirt and putting on the dry one which proved to be a good enough fit.

"Here," the captain said, relenting. "Maybe this will help." He held out a glass of whiskey.

Phipps looked up and saw the glass. His eyes brightened. His tongue licked along his lips in an open show of anticipated pleasure. "You do have a soul, Captain," he said. "You do, indeed." He took the glass and drained it at once.

"I see you decided to come with us, after all," the captain said. "Good thing you came when you did; we're shoving off. Got new orders."

"You're leaving? Right away?"

"As fast as we can. How about you, coming or not?"

Phipps tried to drink again and grimaced at the empty glass. His eyes met and held on the captain's. He twitched his head toward the dock outside. "What about them, Captain?"

"I don't know. They're no concern of mine. My job's to get this ship clear before it's seized."

"And that's all, is it?"

Quick anger showed in the captain's face. "You're damned right, it is. Now, we went over this last night, Phipps. Clarence has been chewing on me this morning. I don't want to hear any more about it."

Phipps' eyes moved to the brown bottle on the captain's chest of drawers. "I can't help wishing you might reconsider, Captain," he said without taking his eyes from the bottle. "You have no idea what the insurgents will do with those people out there, Captain. No idea at all."

The captain finished buttoning his dry shirt. He glanced at his watch. "You still have time to get off before we sail."

"Get off, Captain?"

"Yes, get off," the captain said, his voice hard. "I told you last night I would take you out of here. I told you that. And I told you I wouldn't take the others. Now, if you don't shut up about it, I'd just as soon leave you here, too. You listening?"

"I'm listening," Phipps said. He got up from the chair he had taken unasked and helped himself to the captain's whiskey, also unasked. He poured and sat down again before he spoke. "Tell me, Captain," he said, "Why do you make an exception of me? Why do you take me and not the others? Is it because I am a white man? Is that it? Does that make my life more valuable than those of the others?"

The captain frowned and turned away. "It's a practical matter, Phipps," he said. "You're not a native of this country. Those people on the dock are. Nobody gives a damn about you. But if I haul the others out of here, I'm taking sides. I'm interfering in the internal affairs of the country. It would leave me open to attack and the loss of my ship."

"The people on the dock stand to lose a good deal more than a ship, Captain," Phipps said solemnly.

"The people on the dock don't have a ship." The captain turned his anger on Phipps. "Neither do you, for that matter. It's easy for you to put on that holier-than-thou face and . . ."

"A man's life is worth more than a ship, Captain. Any man's life."

"Not more than my ship," the captain blurted. He, too, reached for the whiskey bottle and a glass. He poured too quickly and spilled some. He drank the drink in one gulp. With the bottle still in his hand, he wiped his lips dry.

"Any man's life, Captain," Phipps said again softly. Then, as apparent aside, "Is your ship worth more than <u>your</u> life, Captain?"

The captain drank again from his empty glass, "Yes, God damn it. Under certain circumstances, it is."

"Certain circumstances, Captain?"

The captain turned away. "You wouldn't understand, Phipps," he said.

Phipps reached and took the bottle from the captain's hand. "I guess I wouldn't, Captain." He drank again. "I guess I wouldn't at that. However, this is doing nothing for the people on the dock. We can't just leave them out there to be chopped down by the first rebel patrol to come along, now can we?"

"And why not?" the captain said. "This is their country. They'll be better off here than anywhere else that will have them. They'll get along."

"You keep saying that, Captain."

"I keep saying it because it's the truth, God damn it. Okay, so some of them get shot. Most of them won't. They'll learn to keep their mouths shut; after a while things won't seem so bad. They'll get used to it. It will . . ."

"You really mean that, Captain?"

"Why not?" the captain shrugged. "Oh, sure, I'd be a big hero if I took these people aboard and dumped them off somewhere. But, what then? Would they be any better off in some Hong Kong slum? Would they have any more to eat? Any more freedom? Would they, Phipps?"

"They'd have a chance, Captain."

"Sure, a chance to rot and starve in some sweat shop. They'd have a chance to be cheated and robbed and worked to death so some fat bastard could get rich off of them." The captain paused then, and his voice softened. "Sometimes, Phipps, the hard thing is the best in the long run. Sometimes, we . . ."

"They don't have to go to Hong Kong, Captain. There are other places."

"Like where? The Philippines? Indonesia? Australia? You know damned good and well, Phipps, that if I get these people on board this vessel, God alone knows where or when I could unload them. You know that, Phipps, so make up your mind, you going with us, or not?"

"You may be right, Captain," Phipps said pensively.

"You know I'm right." The captain turned away and looked out a port. The rain still pounded on the piershed roof, raining as though it would never stop. "You know I'm right, Phipps," he said again. He said it as though he wanted Phipps to say he agreed.

"I said you <u>might</u> be right, Captain. I don't think you are, but I'm willing to concede that you might be. I've been wrong before, on occasion."

"Meaning what?"

"Meaning that all the things you've just said may be true. It <u>might</u> happen the way you say. I don't know. All I do know is what <u>will</u> happen to these people if you leave them here. I do know what will happen to them in that case."

"I still . . ."

"Look, Captain!" There was pleading in Phipps' face. "These people out there are not the ones who will 'get along', as you say. The ones who will 'get along' are back in their own villages now, cooking rice for the rebels and pointing out the right roads to them. The ones out there on the dock are the ones who will resist, Captain. They are the ones who will fight back. They are the ones who will die, Captain."

The captain was moved by Phipps' words. It showed in his face. But he frowned and stared out into the rain, hearing and feeling the hum and throb of motors and blowers which are the signs of life in a ship, even when it is at a dock. His ship was important to the captain. It was all he had to show for more than forty years of living. It was his ship he thought of. "You are asking me to risk my ship," he said tiredly, without turning away from the port.

"I am asking you to save more than two hundred living human beings, Captain."

The captain turned and faced Phipps. There was sudden dislike in his eyes, something almost like hate for this man who threatened his ship. "It's easy for you, isn't it, Phipps? It's easy to ask someone else to give up everything he has. Well, what are you prepared to give up? What's your ante?"

Then, as though thinking of a wholly new thought. "What's your angle in this anyway, Phipps? What difference does it make to you what happens to these people?"

Phipps didn't answer at once. He held his empty glass between his hands and lowered his head. "They've been good to me, Captain," he said slowly. "I've lived here with them since the War, you know. They've been very good to me."

"You're British, aren't you?"

"Yes. Yes, but my family were all killed in the bombing. I didn't — I never went back home. Didn't seem much point in it. I've made my life here. I . . ."

"Yes. I see what you mean," the captain said. "I've seen the kind of lives white men make for themselves out here."

His pride stung, Phipps sat erect in his chair. "I'm afraid you don't see, Captain," he said. "I'm afraid you don't see at all. Maybe, at one time, that might have been the reason I want to help them. Make it simply an act of gratitude for all they've done for me. But it's more than that now, Captain. A great deal more."

"Meaning?"

"Meaning that a man has a frightful lot of time to think, out here. You know, ships are sometimes months apart and between ships, there is nothing. Thinking can be a most uncomfortable thing under conditions like those, Captain. Lying in bed at night, for instance, with the rain drumming on the roof and the night smells and the darkness everywhere. You have no idea how dark these villages get at night, Captain."

"Get to the point, Phipps."

"The point is, Captain, that it's not enough for a man just to stay alive. He must do more than that. He owes more than that. He . . ."

"He owes what, for Christ's sake? You . . ."

"A man owes it to himself, Captain," Phipps interrupted. He owes it to himself to do what he can to help."

The captain again did not answer at once. He glanced at his watch. "You figure you owe it to yourself to help these people, that it, Phipps? It would be good for your soul? That why you're in here pestering me?"

"In a way, in a way, I guess you're right again, Captain." Phipps smiled then, wryly, and looked at the captain. "I figure you owe it to yourself, too, Captain."

"Well, you figure wrong, Phipps. I don't owe anybody anything. How you figure I got to be master of a vessel like this? Somebody took me by the hand and led me into this cabin? Showed me what to do? How to talk? How to take a star sight?" He snorted. "Well, nobody did that, Phipps. Nobody ever helped me. Not one lousy soul, and I'm not throwing away everything I've sweated and slaved to get. Not for some fuzzy-headed idea that makes no sense in the first place."

"You're wrong, Captain. You're terribly wrong . . ."

"I'm not wrong!" the captain shouted then. He looked at Phipps with scorn in his eyes. "How would you know what I'm talking about, you rum-rotted bum? Why didn't you go back to England, Phipps? Why didn't you go back and face life, build something, make something out of yourself?"

The captain paused, trying to control himself. "You're weak, Phipps," he went on more quietly. "You're like all weak men, you want somebody else to do your working and fighting for you. You want to sit back and tell the other guys how to do it. Well, it's not working, Phipps. Not this time. Not with me."

Phipps grinned weakly from his chair, trying to cover his hurt. "I don't argue with you, Captain, about my worth. You seem to have worked it out quite accurately. I am, doubtless, all you say I am. However . . ." He paused. "However, it remains, it is I who is trying to save those people out on the dock. I flatter myself that that is a sign of — well, of strength, if you like. It is at least the sign of a good heart." Phipps grinned again his sickly little grin.

The captain snorted. "Good heart? It's a sign of a soft head, Phipps. How strong do you have to be to risk somebody else's ship? How good-hearted do you have to be to ask somebody else to stick his neck in a noose?"

"Captain, I merely . . ."

"No, you wait a minute, Phipps. You're in here asking me to risk my ship over some harebrained idea you got about saving those people outside. What's your share in it? I asked you a while ago, what is your ante? What are you putting up?"

Phipps looked away, a deep sadness in his face. "I have to admit, Captain, I have very little to put up, as you say." He emptied his pockets and smiled ruefully at the thin spread of coins and pen knife in his palm. "I assure you that if I had a ship, I would do as I am asking you to do. But since I do not have a ship, again as you have pointed out, I have only what I have in my hand to offer."

The captain laughed, shortly and without humor. "Fifty-fifty, huh, Phipps? You give what you got; I give what I got. That right?"

Phipps didn't answer. There was the beginning of defeat in his face. He thrust his meager fortune back into his pocket and ran his tongue along his lips. He looked at the whiskey bottle but he neither asked nor reached for it.

The captain finished his own drink and replaced the bottle on the chest of drawers. "Okay, Phipps," he said with an air of putting an end to the thing. "You've made your pitch; you've got your answer. You going with us, or not?"

Phipps looked up but before he could speak, a clamor arose from the dock alongside and a shot slapped hard and flat over the rain and ship sounds.

The captain stood as though frozen for an instant, questions burning in his eyes. He turned and broke for the door. Phipps did not leave his chair.

The captain burst out into the passageway aft of his cabin and ran to the head of the ladder leading down to the main deck. He stopped there, his face tight at what he saw.

Mister Clarence, the first mate, was just putting foot to the bottom rung of the ladder, starting up. Behind him, a stocky man in wet cotton and a floppy hat held a machine gun ready. Two more men stood just to this man's rear. They, too, held ready guns.

"They — they want to see you, Captain," Mister Clarence said. He was clearly frightened.

"The shot, Mister Clarence," the captain said. "What was that?"

"One of the people on the dock tried to stop them. They killed him."

The man behind the mate poked him with the muzzle of his gun and said something in his own language. The only distinguishable word was 'captain'. Mister Clarence wet his lips with his tongue and looked up at the captain. "Please, sir," he said. "He wants to see you."

The captain nodded coldly. "All right. Bring him up," he said. He led the way back to his cabin where Phipps still sat. Phipps had helped himself to more whiskey and sprawled in the captain's own chair, glass between his hands.

The rebel leader followed the captain into the cabin, searching it with his eyes for any possible threat. He fixed on Phipps. The other two rebels remained outside in the passageway, their guns ready. Mister Clarence saw his chance and was gone.

"Well, what do you want?" the captain said shortly but the man obviously knew no English.

"Perhaps I can be of some service to you, Captain," Phipps said, getting to his feet. "I speak the language rather well."

"Find out what he wants and get rid of him," the captain said. "I want to get the hell out of here."

Phipps spoke with the rebel. He spoke briefly, listened, then spoke again. He seemed to be explaining something, as though to a small child. But the rebel remained adamant. He clutched his gun even tighter. Whatever it was he wanted, he was not giving it up. Not to Phipps.

"He says the ship is not to leave," Phipps said to the captain. "His is but a small patrol, and he says you are to stay here until he can check with someone of greater authority."

"You tell this bugger, Phipps, that this is an American vessel, properly cleared and ready to sail," the captain said, anger tight in his voice. "You tell him that, Phipps, and you tell him I'm going to sail whether he likes it or not."

Phipps smiled. "I'm afraid I've made those points already, Captain, but the chap remains a bit stubborn. He says he cannot allow you to sail. He says that he will use whatever force is necessary to see that you do not. And, I dare say, he means it."

The captain's face flushed, but he held his voice level. "Find out how many of them there are."

"As I understand it," Phipps said, "there is just this fellow, the two out in the passageway, and two on the dock. Five altogether. You see, this is not a very important town. They don't seem to have expected to find a ship here."

"Another thirty minutes, and they wouldn't have," the captain said bitterly.

Phipps grinned. "A bit of spilt milk, wouldn't you say, Captain? But, I say, this does change things about a bit, doesn't it?"

"Meaning?"

"Meaning that you're pretty much in the same boat with the people on the dock, don't you see? They're not leaving now. Neither are you."

"I'll leave," the captain said, his voice hard. "This may hold us up a few minutes, but I'll leave. Make no mistake about that."

"I wouldn't count on that, Captain," Phipps said. "I wouldn't count on it at all."

"What are you driving at?"

"I'm simply telling you, Captain, that you stand a very good chance of never sailing from this port. From what this chap tells me, the rebels would love very much to get their hands on a ship like this. He expects some sizeable recognition for his initiative in getting it for them. I dare say, they will be able to find a good use for it, indeed."

"They can't do that," the captain blurted. "This is an American ship."

"So was the *Pueblo,* as I recall," Phipps said evenly. "It was your own reasoning but a few minutes ago that your taking the refugees on board would give the rebels an excuse to seize your ship. Isn't that so, Captain?"

"But I didn't take them on board. I . . ."

"You know that, Captain," Phipps said. "And I know it. But the world doesn't know it. The world will know only what the rebels choose to tell it. They are quite likely to say that they captured an American ship in the act of loading bandits, enemies of the revolution."

"But . . ."

"After all, Captain, they did find you here, lying at a dock, with steam up and lines singled up, ready to cast off. And with a large number of people standing by on the dock, ready to board."

"I wasn't going to load them, God damn it, Phipps. I told you that. I've been telling you that for the last half hour."

Phipps smiled easily and nodded toward the rebel soldier. "You needn't convince me, Captain," he said. "There's the chap you must convince. And, I dare say, it may prove a sticky job."

The captain cursed under his breath. He pulled a cigarette from a pack on the chest of drawers and lighted it, frowning in concentration. He drew deep of the tobacco smoke and blew it out. "Feeling pretty proud of yourself, aren't you, Phipps?"

"I confess I do detect a certain amount of poetic justice in the situation, Captain," Phipps said. "But, the fact remains, this development does little to help the people on the dock. As you may recall, that was my purpose."

The captain went then to an open port and called down to the main deck forward. "How much longer before we can cast off?"

"Ready now, sir," the answer came.

"Captain, I would not advise your trying to sail with these chaps on board," Phipps broke in. "They can make a frightful mess with those guns of theirs."

"I have no intention, Phipps, of sitting here and letting some slope-head tell me what I can and can't do on my own ship." He paused and glanced at the rebel soldier. "Sooner or later, they'll get careless. We can rush them. We . . ."

"Someone will get hurt, Captain."

"I suppose you have a better idea."

"A thought has occurred to me," Phipps said. The rebel soldier growled something then and Phipps calmed him with a placating word or two. "There is, perhaps, one way in which we can extricate you and your ship, Captain."

"What is it?"

"It involves the people on the dock, Captain," Phipps said. "I want that understood from the start. I will be party to nothing which doesn't include the rescue of those people out there."

Anger and frustration alternated in the captain's face, but he controlled both feelings. He was prepared to promise anything which offered him a chance to get again to sea. "All right. All right," he said. "If it can be worked."

Phipps grinned at the captain. "Very good, Captain," he said. "I wouldn't ask lightly anything which might prove an inconvenience to you. Not for the world."

The captain flushed. "Knock off the sarcasm. What's your pitch?"

Phipps sobered. He glanced at the rebel soldier. "This chap's primary concern, it seems, is that the ship be held here until the arrival of his superiors. Right?"

The captain nodded. "So you say."

"Very well, then. Suppose we find some way in which we can assure him that the ship will not sail yet, at the same time, permit himself and his men to enjoy the, admittedly limited, but nevertheless adequate, amenities of the town. He's bound to be tired and hungry after the events of recent days."

"Meaning?"

"Meaning that, if I can get all but one or two of our little friends away from the ship, you may be able to disarm the remaining guards, pack the refugees aboard, and get clear before your actions are discovered. In this rain, you would be quite invisible when only a few cables from the dock. Wouldn't you say so, Captain?"

The captain nodded, still not committing himself.

"Very well, then. Shall I proceed?" Phipps said.

The captain drew deep of his cigarette and ground it out in an ashtray. He nodded toward the rebel soldier. "This looks like one suspicious monkey," he said. "How you going to con him?"

"The rebels are quite adept in the use of hostages," Phipps said. "I will simply propose to our friend here that he be accompanied by the ship's captain when he retires ashore to refresh himself and prepare the way for his superiors' arrival. It is most unlikely that the ship will sail without its commanding officer. I shall be most persuasive, Captain, I assure you. I'll give him some business about your having to clear with your agent ashore. In any event, he's not likely to know much about the ins and outs of shipping. He . . ."

"Did I hear you right, Phipps?"

"I presume so. I spoke quite distinctly, I thought." Phipps paused and smiled, although the skin about the corners of his mouth was tight. "Do you detect any flaws in my plan, Captain?"

The captain swore. "I detect one hell of a flaw in it," he rasped. "Are you trying to say you want me to act as hostage with this monkey and that while I'm gone, you'll take off with the ship? That what you're driving at?"

Phipps laughed. "Of course not, Captain," he said. "I said nothing of the sort."

"But you said . . ."

"I said merely that I would tell this chap that the ship's captain would accompany him as hostage and guarantor of the ship's not sailing. Now that's quite different from what you just said."

"But I am captain of this vessel. I . . ."

Phipps stopped him with an upheld hand. He stood and stepped casually to a bulkhead hook and lifted the captain's cap from it. "Not at all, Captain," he said. He smiled and tilted the cap to a rakish angle on his head. "As a matter of fact, I am master of this vessel."

Meaning struck then in the captain's mind. He wet his lips with his tongue and glanced at the rebel soldier. "You're crazy, Phipps," he said. "You realize what they'll do to you when they find out?" The captain's mouth felt dry. His stomach tightened.

"I have some idea," he said. "Nevertheless, unless you have a better thought, I suggest we proceed at once. This chap is getting a bit impatient, I am afraid. And there's no telling, really, when his superiors will arrive, is there?"

"You can't be serious, Phipps?" the captain said.

"Oh, but I am," Phipps said. "I see no other course which offers any hope of success whatever. Now, shall we proceed? Delay simply adds risk to risk." Then, before the captain could reply, he turned and spoke to the rebel soldier in his own language.

The captain could see the suspicion in the rebel's face. He saw the narrowing of his eyes and the tightening of his fingers about his gun. Then he saw how things changed as Phipps talked. He saw the man relax and lower his gun. He saw him leave the cabin with Phipps. He saw it, but it seemed unreal nevertheless, as though it were something which would go away if he could but close his eyes.

Phipps stopped at the door and turned to look back at the captain. "You asked me, Captain," he said, "what I was prepared to give up in order to help those people out there on the dock. You dwelt at great length upon the magnitude of the sacrifice I was asking of you — the possible loss of your ship, no less." He paused and smiled sadly. "I do trust that this thing I do will bring our contributions more nearly in balance."

"I was joking, Phipps," the captain said. "For Christ's sake, I never thought you would . . . It never occurred to me that you might . . ."

"A great many things did not occur to you, Captain."

The captain found it hard to answer. He tried twice before he could form the words. Even then, all he could find to say was, "I'm sorry, Phipps. I really am. I'm — well, I'm sorry that . . ."

"It's all right, Captain," Phipps said. "Under different circumstances I should have been no more than the village drunk, I am afraid. This will, perhaps . . ." He paused. "I suggest you act quickly, Captain. As soon as my companions and I are out of sight. I shall buy you as much time as I can, but things are apt to be unpredictable. I should not like to think that my contribution, small though it may be, might be wasted."

The captain nodded, unable to speak, and Phipps was gone. He and four of the rebel soldiers walked in the rain around the end of the piershed and disappeared in the direction of the town. Phipps, of course, saw nothing of what followed, but his plan worked precisely as he had outlined it.

It was a simple matter for the captain to stroll past the one remaining guard and to bring a fid down hard on his head. After that, it was only a matter of hustling the refugees on board and cutting the mooring lines with fire axes. It was done in minutes. Then slowly, silently, the vessel moved away from the dock and faded into the rain. There was no sound from the beach, no sign that anyone had seen her go. The rain drummed on the roof of the piershed, just as it had all day.

In a
Leather-bound Diary

This evening, as I always do when the Bay begins to smoke with gray night mists and there is a moan of wind in the sky, I remember Wilson Lambert with a special poignancy. For it was on such a night as this that I saw him for the last time.

The trees are bare at this time of the year and from my window here I can see the shore and the little pier and the mooring where my *Mavourneen* once rode. And it is almost as though I were standing there again and watching her sails slowly merge with the offshore murk, and hearing Wilson's call hanging in the wind.

It is no longer fashionable, I know, to speak of men as being doomed; but there was something of doom about Wilson Lambert. There always had been. I grew up with him here on the shore. I sailed with him and hunted and fished with him. And, all the time, there was that lurking air of doom about him. I can think of no other word for it.

When Wilson went away to sea during the war I hoped he wouldn't come back to our little town. He would have been better off had he settled someplace where he and his family were not known. But he did come back, and he moved into the old Lambert house out on the point with his grandmother.

Old Lady Carver — she was Wilson's maternal grandmother — was even then feeble with age. Someone had to take care of her and the ties of family had always been strong in the Lamberts. Certainly, Wilson had little other reason to stay out there with the embittered old woman. The whole town knew her feelings for him, and for his father before him. Still, Wilson did stay with her and cared for her as best she would let him.

It was a big, dark, hulking house, the Lambert house, with high thin windows and lightning rods and slim brick chimneys, with a dusting of sea salt showing a wan gray over it all. There was a morbid, depressing air about the place even when the sun danced on the water and gull wings flashed white in a cloudless sky.

It was no place for a young man. And Wilson was still young, then. He needed more than he was ever apt to find in that old house on the point. That was why I was so pleased when Ann Masters came to our town. She was strange here. She didn't know about Wilson. And she was the kind of woman who loves a man strongly.

Wilson did become different with Ann. Lighter, somehow, and able even to laugh at times, and to lose the shadows in his eyes.

Yes, they were happy that summer. At least they had that much. There were times when we were all together in the *Mavourneen* when I all but forgot the diary. I think Wilson did, too.

But now I know that neither of us ever really forgot it. We pushed it, sometimes, into the backs of our minds but always, always it was there. We knew it was there, and we knew that it would never go completely away. That is what I meant about Wilson's being doomed.

When he came over here to my house, this house, near the end of that summer, I could tell from his face that the diary was again with him. His face was as troubled as the southwest sky, and his eyes as dark as the squall clouds building there.

"It looks like wind, Wilson," I said. "You sure you want to . . . ?"

"You don't have to go," he said shortly. "I'd like the use of your boat, that's all."

From another man, the words would have been an affront, but Wilson and I were friends. I had known him long enough to sense in him the dark needs which sometimes drove him to do things he would later regret. I knew most of all his need for wind and water and a tiller in his hands when the diary was too much with him.

"I'll go," I said simply. We left it at that while we rowed out in the dinghy and made the *Mavourneen* ready. She was a beautiful thing, the *Mavourneen*. As beautiful as her name. But strong, too, and made stronger by the care both Wilson and I lavished on her. As I glanced again at the squalls moving across the Bay towards us, I had no fears for the *Mavourneen*. I knew every fitting in her, and every rib and plank.

Wilson nodded curtly from the cockpit as I looked aft to let him know I was ready forward. On his nod, I ran up the main and set the downhaul taut. I dropped the mooring. The *Mavourneen* sagged off before the wind, feeling for her footing. I set the jib. She heeled deeply, then caught herself and stood up to the wind.

Wilson was handling her roughly. The breath of the approaching squall was erratic. It blew in hard, hammering gusts, first from one quarter then another. The *Mavourneen* had little chance to find herself, and Wilson was not helping her.

By the time I had the halyards secured and had come aft, the squalls were upon us. The *Mavourneen* staggered under the initial blows. Her sails clamored momentarily, but Wilson had no mercy. He held her down and made her fight her way free. And fight her way free, she did.

It was suddenly dark almost as night. The sky filled with the rush of wind and the rumble and crack of thunder. The Bay ran white with tormented water, and spray arced in pretty aerodynamic curves over the weather bow to rattle in the sails and shock us both with cold hard volleys. The lee rail was lost in a smother of white from the shrouds aft, and the quarter wave licked higher than the gunwale itself.

I looked at Wilson. His face was wet with spray, his eyes fixed on the leading edges of the sails. There was a terrible expression on his face. There was pain in the expression. And despair. And loss. And sadness. And — yes — doom and the knowledge of doom.

In the flashing of lightning, I could see the tortured lines dig themselves deeper into his face. In the intervening darkness, I could sense the essential loneliness of his trouble and I felt helpless, knowing that I could help him most only by staying away until the storm winds and the wash of the sea cleansed him of his devils and gave him the strength to stand again and fight back. So, I huddled in the lee of the cabin trunk and waited.

The wind, though it was blowing harder than ever, had settled down. It became a steady force which the *Mavourneen* found herself able to harness to her own purpose. She flew as I had never known her to fly before. The seas had not had time to build high enough to trip her, and she slashed through the Bay chop as though she knew what she was doing for Wilson.

And, slowly, the *Mavourneen*'s spell did its work. Wilson's face softened. His eyes lost their terrible fixation. He let himself see the dramatic violence which is sometimes a summer squall on our Bay. His hand relented on the tiller. He became one with the *Mavourneen*. Rather than driving her, he <u>sailed</u> her, as though feeling in his own flesh the force of wind and the clash of water. Together, they turned the wild power of wind and water back upon themselves and made profit of them so that, within a few minutes, we sailed out again into bright sunshine and the storm was no more than a dark muttering moving off to the northeast, though the waters were left strangely disturbed.

For the first time, Wilson looked at me. He shifted to a more comfortable position. "Thanks," he said quietly. "Thanks, Jim."

I knew, of course, that some particular thing must have triggered the mood in Wilson which had sent us careering off through the storm, but I had learned long before that it did little good to question him at such times.

We got the sails down and the *Mavourneen* snugged in just as the evening chill moved in from the sea. We went below then. In the warm, wood-glowing cabin, by the light of oil lamps, we had some rum, and I put together some cold meat and cheese, and some ruddy wine Ann had left on board. And there Wilson told me what had set him off.

"I broke it off with Ann today, Jim," he said.

I had suspected something like that. There had been other girls. And there had always been the diary.

"Same old reason?" I said.

"Same old reason," he nodded. He finished his wine, and we rowed ashore. I didn't see him again for some time. There wasn't any use in trying to argue with him at those times. I had tried before.

But I did see Ann. She came to my house the very next day after our stormy sail. I made her a drink, and we sat on the terrace. "All right, Jim," she said directly. "Tell me about it."

"About what?" I stalled.

"Wilson," she said simply. "He said you would tell me." For the first time, I could see a weakening in her control. "I don't care what he's done, Jim," she said. "I don't care what's happened in the past. I . . ."

I finished my own drink with a swallow. I thought of Wilson's grandmother in that lonely old house out on the point. I thought of the book which might, even then, be clutched in her bony old hands, and the evil glitter in her eyes. "It's not the past Wilson's worried about, Ann," I said as gently as I could.

"What?"

I got up then from the lounge and spread my hands in a gesture of exasperated frustration. "I know it sounds crazy," I said. "Here, with the sun shining and everything, it does sound crazy. But, believe me, Wilson is serious about it. And so is that crazy old woman out there on the point."

"Serious about what?" Ann cried. "What on earth are you talking about?"

"About the diary, damn it. Didn't Wilson ever tell you about his father's diary?" I gave up then. "Oh, hell," I said. "All right. Here it is. Straight. You want another drink?"

She shook her head.

"Wilson's parents were killed, Ann. In a sailing accident, right out there off the point. A steamer ran them down in the fog. Wilson's grandmother had always felt her daughter — Wilson's mother — had married beneath her. She hated Wilson's father and she blamed him for killing her daughter. When they both were killed, the old woman took Wilson and raised him. In a way, she . . ."

"But what does all that have to do with Wilson and me?" Ann said.

"The old woman found a diary Wilson's father kept, Ann. She read it, and she noticed that everything that ever happened to Wilson's father has happened to Wilson. In exactly the same way, at precisely the same stages in their lives. Wilson's life has been a carbon copy of his father's, Ann."

"But . . ."

"Please, Ann," I protested. I wanted to get it over with.

"Wilson's father had pneumonia at age six; Wilson had pneumonia at age six. Wilson's father was bitten by a snake at a boys' camp; Wilson was bitten by a snake at a boys' camp. On precisely the same finger. Wilson's father went to World War I and was wounded in his left forearm; Wilson went to war and was wounded on the left forearm. Wilson's father . . ."

"But, Jim . . ."

"The point is, Ann," I persisted, "every single significant thing that happened to Wilson's father has happened to Wilson. In exactly the same way, at exactly the same stage of their lives."

"You mean . . . ?"

"That's exactly what I mean."

"But I still don't see what that has to do with Wilson and me."

"Ann, listen," I said. "Wilson's father was thirty-one years old the day he sailed out past that point with his wife. Wilson will be thirty-one next week."

Ann put down her glass and looked out over the Bay for a time without speaking. Then she turned back to me and, with a strange little smile, she said: "You're not serious."

"Deadly."

"But it's insane. It's — it's medieval, for God's sake." She laughed, but the laughter choked off short. "This is the twentieth century, Jim. You can't expect me to . . ."

"I told you it was crazy," I said. "You asked me what was bothering Wilson, and I told you."

Ann laughed again, this time more easily. "Well, if that's all it is," she said, "I'll just go to him and . . ."

I held up my hand to stop her. "I said it sounds crazy here, Ann, in the bright light of day. But at night, out there on the point when the wind moans and the fog comes rolling in, it doesn't sound so crazy. Besides, all those things — coincidences, if you like — they did happen. It's all written down in that diary the old woman has. It's been pounded into Wilson ever since he was old enough to hear. You can't expect just to snap your fingers and have it all go away."

I would not have talked so long had Ann not been looking at me the way she did. She was looking at me as though I were something distasteful. Disgusting. "You actually believe it," she said at last. "You actually do think there's something to it, don't you?"

Her manner stung because, really, I was not all that sure about the matter. And I knew a good many people there along the shore who felt the same way about it that I did.

"It's not a question of what I think, Ann," I said. "It's a question of what Wilson thinks. I can tell you right now he thinks there's something to it. I can tell you something else, too, Wilson is not going to make anyone he loves part of a life he thinks is doomed."

Ann stood there then for a time without speaking, looking at me as though I had failed her in some vital way. In the end, she walked past me and out through the house as though I had ceased to exist.

I saw neither of them after that for several days. I missed them badly. The place seemed empty without them. Even the *Mavourneen* seemed to mope at her mooring. I could not go aboard at all without the hurting memory of what it had been like when they were there: Wilson sprawled on the port bunk, propped against the forward bulkhead, while Ann busied herself with salads and sandwiches and their talk and laughter filled the boat.

But there seemed little enough I could do about it and I simply assumed, when I did not hear from them, that they had gone their own ways and that the whole affair was ended, just as so many other such affairs had ended for Wilson. So, perhaps you can imagine my surprise one afternoon when I got a call from Ann.

"Can you invite us sailing this evening, Jim?" she asked at once. "Wilson and me."

"Today?" It was a stupid reply, but she had taken me completely by surprise. What she asked was the last thing in the world I expected to hear that day.

"Yes. This afternoon. Right now." Ann paused then. "And, Jim, don't tell Wilson I'm coming. Please, Jim."

"Ann, are you quite sure you want to do this?" I said. "Start it all over again and everything?"

"Yes. Yes, I'm sure." She paused again. "Just trust me, Jim," she said. "Everything is going to be all right."

"All right," I gave in at last. "I don't know whether Wilson will come or not, but I'll ask him."

Ann hung up without replying. I didn't know what the hell to do. I was quite certain Wilson would not come if he knew Ann would be along. And I didn't want to be placed in the position of deceiving him. I knew how he felt about Ann, and it took a certain amount of nobility for him to give her up as he had — for the reason he had. I admired him for it in a way, I guess, and I didn't want to make things any harder for him than they were.

Still, there had been something in Ann's voice which allowed me no rest. I made myself a drink. I stared out to sea. I studied the jackstraw pattern pine needles made on the terrace stones. I turned on the stereo. I turned it off. Finally, I drove over and invited Wilson for a sail. Surprisingly, he accepted. I hadn't expected he would.

We were at the pier, getting into the dinghy, when we heard Ann's car. I had begun to think she had changed her mind about the whole thing. She ran around the corner of the house, her eyes searching for and finding Wilson. She stopped short then. She had a leather-bound book in her hand.

Wilson's face lighted for a moment. But only for a moment. He muttered a curse at me and moved as though to make off.

Ann stepped in his way. "Don't blame Jim," she said. "I made him do it. It was the only way. You wouldn't talk to me. You wouldn't listen. You wouldn't let me . . ."

"I wouldn't let you because there's nothing to — to let," Wilson said angrily. "For God's sake, Ann, do we have to do this? Can't we just let it die? Do we have to torture ourselves?"

Ann ran to him then, her face drawn in a strange expression of mingled joy and pain and fear — and dread. She held the leather-bound book before Wilson's eyes. She laughed crazily. There were tears on her face.

"Look at it, Wilson," she cried. "Here it is. It's your father's famous diary. See, there's his name on it."

Wilson actually paled. "Where did you get that?" he demanded. He snatched at the book, but Ann drew it back.

"I stole it," she said defiantly. "I went out there to talk to your grandmother and when she wasn't looking, I stole it. I snitched it right out from under her nose."

Wilson turned then and looked at me, distraught. His look pleaded with me to help him, to do something.

"You think your whole life's written in this book, don't you, Wilson?" Ann went on.

"Give it to me, Ann." Wilson choked out the words. "For God's sake, don't read that. I . . ."

Ann looked at Wilson for a time, smiling gently. Then she moved to him and gave him the book. "There's nothing to read, Wilson," she said softly. "There's nothing in it. There's never been anything in it. The pages are blank."

Wilson did not understand at once. Then, as understanding did come to him, he looked at the book and opened it and let the vacant pages fan past his thumb. "What are you trying to say, Ann?" he said wonderingly.

"There's never been anything written in the book, darling," she said. "There's nothing to be afraid of. The pages . . ."

"But grandmother said . . ."

"She hated your father very much, Wilson. She couldn't hurt him anymore, so she hurt you. She hurt you by making you think your life . . ."

Wilson's face moved in a tremulous, still skeptical smile. "Then everything she said, everything she . . ."

"None of it was true," Ann said. "None of it ever happened. She told people it was written in the diary like that, but it wasn't. No one ever saw the diary. You never saw it, did you?"

"No," Wilson admitted. "No, I never saw it, but . . ."

"Neither did anyone else," Ann said. "Everyone just assumed the old woman was telling the truth. You just accepted it. Everyone did."

Wilson opened the book and again let the blank pages run through his fingers, his face slowly lighting with the full realization of his release. He smiled then, a sudden, fierce, violent smile, and he held Ann to him, pressing her close.

Ann's face, as I saw it over Wilson's shoulder was suddenly white and drawn. It was only when Wilson held her off to look into her face that she smiled again and laughed.

I banged an oar on the pier and jokingly called for them to break it up. They drew apart then, Wilson with a broad grin on his face and lipstick looking silly on his mouth. "We going sailing or not?" I demanded.

Wilson laughed as I had never heard him laugh before in my life. He took Ann's hands in both of his. "How about it, Ann?" he said. "How about taking the *Mavourneen* out past the point and blowing some of the dust off?"

"The fog," Ann said. And, again, I felt a kind of apprehension in her. "It looks as though it may get worse."

But Wilson would not be denied. He held up the old diary and smiled. "There's nothing to be afraid of," he said. Then, more soberly, "Is there?" Ann laughed and shook her head. And, in the end, she agreed to go with him.

"You don't mind, do you, Jim?" Wilson said to me, and I realized I had just been invited to remain ashore. I laughed and handed Wilson the dinghy painter and got back onto the pier, shoving them off as I did so. I took the old diary to keep for him.

From the terrace of my house, I watched them row out to the *Mavourneen* and get her underway. The fog indeed was forming that evening — much as it is forming tonight — and the horns were beginning to call. When the *Mavourneen's* sails slowly faded beyond the point, I felt old and left out. But I felt good, too, for Ann and Wilson. We were all friends. It was good to think we were back together again. I resented it when the telephone rang.

The call was from Bill Potter who runs our little town's only book store and who does custom bookbinding as a hobby. "Jim, I've been trying to reach Ann. Is she there?" Bill said.

"She just left," I said. "She'll be back later. Can I give her a message for you?"

"Yes, if you will. Ann brought in an old diary the other day and had me rebind it with new pages. I wasn't in when she picked it up today. I guess she forgot to pick up the old pages. Just tell her she can pick them up any time she . . ."

Suddenly, I remembered what I had seen in Ann's face when Wilson held her in his arms and she looked at me over his shoulder. I felt a cold fear growing in me. "Listen, Bill," I said. "Is anything written on the old pages?"

"Yeah. Why?"

"Do you have them there? Read me the last entry."

"Hell, Jim. This is a diary. It's private. I can't . . ."

"Just read it, Bill," I said. "I'll explain later. Read it!" I guess I put enough in my voice to convince him, for, after a pause, I heard the turning of pages and Bill read:

We are very happy this night. The fog is coming in, but we will sail tonight. We will sail and sail and sail until we know that we are not dreaming. We will sail out beyond the point and . . .

Bill was still reading as I gently replaced the telephone on its holder. I wandered blindly out onto the terrace where wisps of fog already were feeling their way inland through the trees. To seaward nothing showed. I could hear the horns and, somewhere beyond the point, a steamer's whistle. I remembered Ann's eyes and the way she had stood for a moment, her hand lifted in good-bye, and Wilson's call in the wind.

I picked up the old leather-bound diary then from the terrace table and fanned its pages past my thumb. They were all new and stiff. I had not noticed that before.

THE HOMEWARD BOUNDER and other sea stories

To Show the Flag

I t may not be as pronounced as it once was, I suppose, but there is still a noticeable strain sometimes between officers of the Royal Navy and those of the British Merchant Navy. One of my oddest experiences in the RN came about, as a matter of fact, because of that unfortunate truth.

I was then but a young sub-lieutenant in one of His Majesty's cruisers in the Med . . . and a good number of years ago that was, I can tell you. Our CO was an unusually stiff specimen of a starchy breed whose opinion of Merchant Navy officers was less charitable even than those of other RN men of the time. "Not gentlemen. Not gentlemen at all," he was apt to harumph of Merchant Navy officers, pulling his impressive moustaches.

It was sheer bad luck that our ship drew the assignment it did in the first place. We'd had some engine down time in Alex which kept us in port when the rest of our lot sailed on exercises off Malta with forces from Gibraltar. We were the only suitable vessel in port when the signal came, so the job was ours.

It was equally a matter of luck, I suppose, that Captain Jock Adair, Merchant Navy, was available at the same time. His tramp was laid up for one reason or another and the Admiral Commanding thought it prudent for us to make use of him.

The job was to show the flag a bit in the Arab countries beyond Suez. The world's navies were coming to appreciate the benefits of oil fuel over coal just then and it was suspected there was a good deal of the stuff under the Arabian sands. The Lords of the Admiralty thought it would be well if we buttered up the Arab a bit, I suppose, just to be on his good side, you see.

Some of our Army chaps of the time had some rather eccentric types who got on well with the Arab but the senior service, I am afraid, knew bloody naught about him. I suspect their Lordships were shrewd enough to know that, too, and that is why they required our CO to take old Adair along.

You see, Adair had sailed the Arab coasts for twenty years or more. In the way of the old tramps out of the Clyde ports, a good many of his crew were Arabs, not counting officers, of course. Most often those old time tramp masters served as their own agents in dealing with port authorities, such as they were, and I can think of no better way, come to think of it, for a man to learn a coast. I reckon their Lordships figured much the same way and sent Adair with us to furnish valuable local knowledge. Although it made sense to my humble sub's mind, it fell well short of pleasing our CO. He needed no bloody Merchant Navy clod to show him anything, much less how to get along with a mess of wogs. Our CO shared the unfortunate tendency of Englishmen of the time of calling all natives of lands east and south of Italy wogs. Sometimes they included the Italians as well, for that matter. It promised to be a frosty period on the bridge.

Nevertheless, in the Navy, orders are orders. Our CO did question his instructions but he got no more for his pains than even more direct orders not only to embark Captain Adair but to give heed to his counsel and to render him the honors due a RN captain. This in the interest of impressing the Arab, I suppose. But it did absolutely nothing to improve our captain's frame of mind.

I first became directly involved when, as the most junior officer in the mess, I was told off to fetch Captain Adair from the beach in Alex. The Officer of the Deck, Freddie Borden, as I remember, called away the gig for me and I thought nothing of that at all. It was customary for us to use the gig when bringing off guests, especially so guests of any importance. Our CO, however, found a good deal to think of it.

He heard the pipe and came storming out on deck with fire in his eyes. Since I was at the accommodation ladder, ready to embark in his bloody boat, I caught the full force of his disagreement.

I no longer remember his precise words, of course, but his meaning was clear. The officers' motorboat was good enough for a bloody Merchant Navy captain. He'd not have his gig used for so lowly a purpose. And, if I prized my chances of advancement in His Majesty's senior service, I would bloody well remember that.

Well, there was nothing for it but for me to fall back upon the junior officer's only safe haven. I replied, "Aye, aye, sir" with all the conviction I could muster and dismissed the gig, while asking the OD to call away the officers' shore boat for me.

This petty little incident not only served to illustrate the CO's regard for Merchant Navy types, it also established me, early on, as suspect in the CO's eyes out of mere association alone. Where, before, I had probably been no more than an empty uniform to him, now I had become the puling idiot who had wanted to profane his gig by hauling a Merchant Navy officer in it.

At any rate, I was glad enough to be clear of the ship in any kind of a boat at all and came upon the Fleet Landing in Alex with my ears still well aglow from the ragging the Old Man had served me. The boat's crew, in the way of ratings, already knew about my awful lapse and I imagined all kinds of hidden derision going on behind my back. That did little to mend my mood but there was bloody naught to be done about it, and I stepped ashore with all the dignity I could find at hand.

I had been given no description at all of Captain Adair, but there was no chance in the world of mistaking the old ship's master. Even in the searing heat of a Gyppo noontime, he was dressed in a square black suit of heavy wool, with an equally square hard hat set on his head and heavy bulb-toed boots on his feet. A well-weathered leather kit bag sat on the ground beside him, and he regarded the ordered bustle of Navy business all about him with a kind of mingled wonder and contempt.

The lack of good-feeling between Navy and Merchant Navy was not all one-sided, you see.

Anyway, I came to him and saluted smartly. "Captain Adair?"

"Aye," the old man growled.

"Sub-Lieutenant Markham," I said. "I'm come to fetch you off. Are you ready, sir?"

He nodded and I commandeered a passing rating to load his kit in the boat. But he bristled and took up his bag himself. "I'm no bloody Navy Nancy," he said. "I'm man enough to carry my own gear."

Well, that was good enough for me. I did a little bristling of my own. I was then still young and quite proud of my single gold stripe. After all, I was sworn to lay down my life for King and country. That was a good touch or two above hauling bloody freight around the world. I began to think that maybe our CO had reason for his view of Merchant Navy types.

But that was all well above the level of any practical concern on my part. My job was to get the old bugger on board. Still, I could not help an inward grin or two at the thought of how this crusty old curmudgeon and our CO were going to hit it off.

I need not have been in doubt. We came alongside smartly, and old Adair climbed the ladder, spry enough, still carrying his own kit bag. Not deigning to salute the colors, or anything else for that matter, he looked at the ranged side boys as though they might be infected with some loathesome contagious disease and confronted our CO with absolutely no give in his manner.

To tell the truth, I was somewhat surprised to find the side boys and the CO present at all. I could only assume that the CO, on reflection, had decided that it is in the interests of a Naval officer's career to do what their Lordships required in the way of such things.

But had he expected to soften up old Adair by any show of Naval courtesy, he was sadly mistaken.

"You got a line adrift over your starboard quarter," the tramp skipper growled. "Foul your bloody screw, it will, the minute you go ahead."

Our CO flushed a pretty red and drew back his hand which old Adair had not bothered to take, in any event. We were off to a grand start.

Since I had fetched Captain Adair on board, I suppose, I was told off to show him to his quarters for the voyage. The CO had given Adair his own cabin; he would live in his sea cabin for the duration. I suspect this was as much to be free of Adair as it was out of any concern for his comfort.

At any rate, I saw the old man settled in, then hurried off. Stations for Getting Underway already had been called.

For some time after that I was busy with the largely unnecessary rigmarole the Navy goes through in getting a ship to sea. I thought no more about Adair until we were clear and settled down to steaming watches. It was all pretty much routine, but green young officers are well advised to pay close attention to their duties, no matter how common.

The word, of course, had already passed among my brother officers about my adventures of the morning, and they were agog with curiosity about Adair. Some of them had seen the confrontation between him and our CO on the quarterdeck and were looking forward with open delight to future developments. Naval service can be boring to a degree and diversion is to be welcomed and savored to the full whenever offered.

Being young and new on board, I would have loved to enhance my standing with accounts, lurid as possible, about Adair's coming on board, but I actually knew no more than I have already told and had to fall back upon a mysterious silence, leaving the delicious implication that I knew a great deal but that needs of the service prevented my telling all I would like.

This served only briefly, however, in lifting my status for in mid-afternoon we were all called to the wardroom to hear Adair for ourselves and everyone could see for himself the monster in question.

Our CO presided in person, but it can't be said that he enjoyed the business. Nor that he exuded much charm towards our guest. For one thing, he dwelt far too long on the fact that Adair was on board at their Lordships' direction, implying broadly that Adair wouldn't be on board short of anything less than that. With sarcasm dripping from his every word, our CO pointed out that Naval vessels sometimes were required to take civilian pilots when entering strange harbors though they were seldom needed at all.

The Navy's officers were quite capable, you see, of handling any job given them without help from civilians.

"Nevertheless, their Lordships feel <u>Mister</u> Adair may be of some assistance to us, and I am confident all of you, as Naval officers and gentlemen, will render to him all the courtesies and privileges due him as master of a British tramp steamer."

I never saw such a left-handed lot of blather in my life.

Nor was I surprised, upon looking to old Adair, to see that he was reacting every bit as might be expected. The CO went on with a resumé of our mission, then introduced Adair and turned over the meeting to him.

The eastern Med is a well-warmed sea unsoftened in those days by anything like air conditioning, but old Adair still wore his black. His only concession was the removal of his hat, a move which revealed a startling two-tone colour scheme of a countenance — weathered leather below his eyebrows, and fish-belly white above. He was bald, but for a white fringe about his ears, and he had small black eyes which peered out from under black brows like suspicious little animals caught, through no fault of their own, in the midst of low and contemptible associates.

Truculent was the word for him as he set out to tell us about the Arab and what it was we were likely to meet in his country. But, after a time, he warmed to his subject and made as though genuinely wanting to help. After all, it was bound to be flattering for an obscure tramp skipper to be called upon to come to the aid of the almighty <u>Navy,</u> and to have the officers of that haughty service hanging on his words.

"First off," he began, "is the bloody country itself. Naught but sand and rock for the most part, all heated well past boiling a white man's brain. The sea itself's like a hot bath drawn for the Devil's pleasure, brimming with snakes and sharks and crawling with bloody pirates, though that's not likely to be a concern for you lot, what with your guns and all. The ports and towns, what there are of them, are not much more than stacked rocks and mud bricks. Finding them's no problem, you can smell them for miles at sea. Simply steam upwind and you're there.

"As for the Arab himself, best thing to remember is he's a touchy fellow. Muslim, you know, and the odd infidel is well in season if caught alone ashore. Best thing's to stay on the bloody ship. Even there, you got to keep an eye peeled or he'll steal the bloody paint off your bloody side plates. And touchy's not the word for how he feels about his females. But you've got bloody naught to fear about that, you won't see any. Liquor's out, too. Best not even to offer it."

Old Adair had us in his palm by that time, and not only the junior officers, either. He spoke with obvious authority, and I came to feel a good deal more respect for him than I had felt on the landing in Alex. It was a hard country he described and it wanted good men to survive in it as he had for so long.

He went on for a good long time and when he was through, there were questions and answers. You could see the old man was impressed by the respect we showed him, and he responded with a human warmth I had not even suspected in him before.

Which is not to say he backed off from his rough facade to any great degree.

After that first day, however, I saw very little of Adair. I suppose the more senior officers were in contact with him as we drew near to our assigned area of operations, but I had no need to see him, come to that. I never once, for instance, saw him on the bridge and the CO's steward, a cheeky Yorkshire man, told me Adair seldom left his cabin.

The Arab waters are exceedingly warm, as I already have mentioned, and I should think he would want to come out from time to time for a breath of air, if nothing else. But

I suppose he was used to the heat, having been out there so long and all. Then, too, after that first rather friendly meeting in the wardroom, our RN chaps turned rather sour on Adair, I am afraid. Like underlings everywhere, I suppose, they took their cue from our CO. And our CO was utterly unappreciative of his Merchant Navy guest. It would do a junior officer no good in his eyes to be seen in cordial intercourse with old Adair and, like chaps everywhere, our officers were quick to pick up on that.

In any event, it was all straight steaming until we reached the Arab ports. There was little need for Adair's counsel, and we proceeded normally. In fact, our first two port calls went off smoothly. Adair gave us a briefing on each of them and things went glowingly. Even our CO came to soften a bit when he saw how well things worked when Adair's advice was followed.

The whole drill turned into just another piece of work, and we became a bit slack, I am afraid. It was damned uncomfortable, for one thing. The country was everything, and more, that Adair had told us it would be. Air conditioning did not exist then, even as a word, and our steel ship, burning tons of coal every day as she was, and baking in the sun as well, became a bloody awful torture chamber. We all marvelled, I think, at Adair for, hot as it was, he never once doffed his black suit and those bulb-toed black boots laced up over his ankles.

Still, all things pass, and we held ourselves to it for King and country, as the saying goes.

Our first spot of trouble didn't come, in fact, until what must have been our third or fourth stop. The town, dry, dun, and dusty in the awful sun, seemed no worse than any others we had seen, but Adair warned us that the Sheik or Emir or whatever he was, who ran the show was worth watching. Turned out, he was younger than any of the other blokes along that stretch of coast and uncommonly ambitious to add to his mangy realm.

231

At any rate, our CO turned out the guard and band and manned the rail for this character. I didn't see how he could have done anything more. Still, the fellow came aboard of us with a face you could have used to curdle milk. Touchy wasn't the word for him. Even Adair was hard put to sweeten him up. That he had brought with him a piratical-looking lot which appeared every bit as displeased as their boss, didn't help a great deal. They were loaded down with rifles and cartridge bandoliers and those big curved daggers the Arab is so fond of.

I had frequently been impatient with our CO. You couldn't say that he did much to make life pleasant for his junior officers, but I had to feel sorry for him for having to entertain this chap from the beach.

There were some sore moments, as you might expect, but we came out of it fairly well until it came on time to sail. When he learned where we were bound, our guest announced that he, too, was on his way to that place. He also said that since we had been so good to him, he would let us carry him there in our nice comfortable ship.

I saw our CO's face change colour, but the Arab chap was watching him closely and the CO could not react in his customary vigorous manner. I could swear there was a cruelly satisfied glisten in old Adair's eyes as he watched our CO's distress but he said nothing.

Our orders hadn't said anything, as I recall, about our taking any native potentates to sea with us. But they had been explicit about our doing whatever needed doing to please the buggers. Besides, it was but a day or two along the way. We could manage, somehow.

Anyway, we did take the sheik aboard, and his whole retinue. It was as murderous a looking lot as I had ever seen; dark-faced men in voluminous robes which blew in the sea wind, and every mother's son of them armed to the teeth. They eyed us with every evidence of satisfaction for the excellent targets we would make, given the chance.

But that's not all. They brought a varied lot of goats and sheep with them. I had not known it before, but the Muslim, like the Jew before him, it turned out, has peculiar ideas about what it is he eats. His animals, for example, must be killed and prepared according to ritual. The Navy's stores of perfectly good meat were not to be trusted at all you see, for God knows, pardon the expression, how or by whom it had been slaughtered.

At any rate, this odorous herd of bleating animals was hoisted aboard from shore boats and ensconced in an improvised pen on the foredeck. The poor blokes responsible for keeping that part of the ship clean did what they could, but it still was a bloody mess to make of one of His Majesty's warships, and we all longed for the time when we could put the lot ashore, sheik and all.

All in all, though, it went rather well. Oh, there was some petty business of deliberately pointing the wrong way to Mecca when it came on time to pray and the like, but for the most part things did go well. A lively trade in souvenirs in fact developed between the sheik's retainers who, some of them, actually showed signs of friendly intent towards us.

I think now it would all have ended well, had there not been an intervening port call. Even the sheik himself warmed somewhat to us and did what he could to repay our hospitality, that being a strong part of the Arab's culture, you see. He handed about such gifts as he had and had his guard give us a demonstration of their skill with rifles. Bottles were thrown over the side and the dusky marksmen made short work of them, to our decently muted amazement. Floating bottles are difficult targets, and the sheik's men could have had few chances to shoot from a moving ship.

But there <u>was</u> an intervening port. The home quarters, it developed, of our sheik's prime enemy. We were duty-bound to put in there, of course, but old Adair warned us of reefs and shoals in plenty if we did. Our CO tried to put a brave face on it, but even he could not cover his concern entirely.

At any rate, in we went with our resident sheik gloating from an elaborate Tent of State he had erected on the quarterdeck. You could just see his pleasure in arriving in his rival's bailiwick in such style. It gave him a leg up, I suppose, on the locals, and it was clear he meant to make the most of it.

Still, little untoward happened until the local potentate came off in his scruffy state barge. Then, a good deal happened.

Our CO broke out guard and band and manned the rail. This, by that time, had come to be routine and we went through the drill pretty much without thinking. It was old Adair who first noted the storm clouds, perhaps because he was most closely looking for them. He nudged the CO and directed his attention to our resident sheik.

That gentleman was showing every evidence of displeasure. His face glowered from under his headdress and he drew himself up to his full height, glaring as he did so at his approaching rival. He growled something to his guard and they unslung their rifles and ranged themselves along the lifelines, shoving our hapless matelots aside as they prepared themselves.

Instant alarm showed in the CO's face, as it might well do. Their Lordships had sent him to these benighted waters to make friends for His Majesty. It could not possibly be helpful for a King's ship to become the scene of battle between rival sheiks. It would be even less helpful to the career of the officer commanding that ship.

This must all have flashed through the CO's mind for he turned at once in all but abject pleading to Adair. Merchant Navy officers might not be gentlemen, but this one offered the CO his only hope for a solution. Certainly, there was nothing in Navy doctrines to cover the situation.

The shoreside sheik's boat was drawing steadily nearer, loaded to the gunwales with a comparable lot of brigands to our sheik's crowd, all loaded to the gills, of course, with rifles and daggers. Our sheik's lot were making unmistakable preparations for battle. The dry clacking of rounds being jacked into chambers rang across the deck.

The CO rushed to the side of our sheik. "I say," he cried. "You mustn't . . ."

He may as well have saved himself the trouble. There was the language barrier, for one thing, you see. The sheik shoved him aside and took up a position of command behind his men. Things were getting sticky indeed.

The CO was apoplectic. Mortals do <u>not</u> lay hands on Royal Navy captains. Not on Royal Navy captains' own quarterdecks, they don't. This, I think, was the crowning indignity thrust upon our poor CO but there was bloody naught he could do about it.

He turned again to Adair. "What's to be done, man?" he demanded. "You're the bloody expert. What am I to do?"

With the air of a man who has seen things go far enough, the old tramp skipper squared himself and approached our pugnacious sheik. The very picture of a Merchant Navy captain of the time, short, stocky, clad in funereal black from round-toed boots to squared hard hat, he spoke to the sheik in his own guttural tongue.

If anything, the sheik's face became even darker as he ranted at Adair for a moment or two, presumably going through an inventory of his resentments and becoming madder by the minute as he did so.

In the end Adair returned to our CO and reported. "The bugger says he's been insulted," Adair said. "He'll not abide such treatment."

"Insulted? Who the bloody hell insulted him?"

"You did," Adair said, calm as milk. "You still are doing so."

That was too much for our poor CO. He stood, mouth agape, looking first to Adair, then to our resident sheik. The finery of his full-dress rig made him look even more ridiculous than he must have felt at the time.

Adair then, with the air of a nanny making something clear to a backward child, explained. "You're manning the rail for yon bugger coming off the beach, you see."

"Aye," our CO said, completely discombobulated. "But I manned the rail for this bloody wog, too. What the bloody. . .?"

"The point exactly," Adair said. "Our fellow feels himself to be a cut or two above the one coming off yonder. He is insulted that you are doing as much for this fellow as you did for <u>him</u> yesterday."

"You're not serious?"

"Deadly," Adair said blandly.

"But that's ridiculous, man," our CO spluttered. "Manning the rail is manning the rail. What the bloody hell does he expect me to do?"

"I don't have a clue, Captain," Adair said. He glanced shoreward. "But yon boat'll be in range shortly. I strongly suggest you do something."

"But what do <u>you</u> suggest, man?" our CO spluttered again. "You're supposed to be the bloody expert."

"That's a different song than you sung in the wardroom, Captain. Seems to me you said something about the Navy being able to see to things without any help from the Merchant Navy. Seems like . . ."

"All right! All right!" our CO said. His surrender was abject. "What do you suggest?"

Adair savored his triumph only briefly. The boat from the beach was getting too close for comfort. He spoke behind his hand directly into our CO's ear so that those standing nearby couldn't hear.

"Do what?" our CO blurted. I've never seen a man's face reveal such consternation.

"Well, Captain, you can do as you like but that's what I would do. I don't know nothing else to try."

Our CO hesitated only a moment longer. An ominous order from our resident sheik to his riflemen did a good deal, I suspect, to hasten our CO's decision just then. He stepped clear of those of us standing about and drew himself to his full height to give one of the oddest orders I was ever to hear in what became a long career in His Majesty's senior service.

You will recall that the men were standing at their Man-the-Rail stations at the time. Our CO roared at the full strength of his considerable voice. "Hands! In Position! SIT DOWN!"

Well, I've seldom seen Royal Navy matelots taken aback, but I saw them taken well aback that time. All discipline aside, those in view of the CO turned and gawked their puzzlement. Even the Division Officers standing with their men didn't know what to make of the CO's command. The Arab riflemen along the lifelines were confused, as well, and looked to their sheik for help.

The CO took another hasty look at the approaching shore boat, then repeated his strange order with both tone and volume to allow neither misunderstanding nor hesitation.

"HANDS. IN POSITION. SIT DOWN."

And down they sat, looking silly, as you might well expect. The CO wasn't showing a great deal more dignity himself, but old Adair nudged him in the side, an indignity which would not have been allowed in normal circumstances, and nodded toward our resident sheik, who managed a benign smile over having so belittled his rival. Although I suspect he suffered a bit of frustration, as well, over not being to allowed shoot the bugger.

In short, that did it. Our sheik ordered his robed riflemen along the lifelines to stand down. They emptied their chambers and fell back to form a ragged rank behind their leader, obviously still well alert, but taking their cue from their leader to, as you Yanks say, "cool it".

At any rate, the sheik from the beach accepted the honors we rendered him, apparently not even noticing the sailors on their hams around the length of the ship. We were one of the first ships to visit the area and he probably had never seen the rail manned before. Not even we in His Majesty's Fleet had ever seen it manned that way, for that matter.

Whatever, it worked and no blood was shed. Once free of the local boy, we got underway and our resident sheik retired to his tent, content that his rival had received less in the way of honors than he had. Our CO and old Adair left the quarterdeck in what seemed mutually cordial conversation.

All I overheard from where I stood was our CO inviting Adair for a spot of the RN's yellow whisky and old Adair courteously refusing on the reasonable grounds that he had a perfectly good bottle or two of John Crabbie's best export Scotch in his kit, a product he fancied over the Navy's.

"Aye, and no reason, Jock," our CO said, "why we can't try the both of them. No point in making an uninformed decision, is there, now?"

And that is the way it ended. It had been rocky there for a while, but, at least in that instance, Royal Navy and Merchant Navy cooperated to a remarkable degree with, I am certain, a salutary result upon both.

ABOUT THE AUTHOR

Born in Oklahoma, Floyd Beaver grew up in the oil and Indian country of that state, far removed from the winds and the salt air he evokes in his stories of the sea. An early Wire Desk man for the Tulsa *Tribune*, he has remained an active semiprofessional writer through all the years since.

He enlisted in the United States Navy in 1938 and served throughout World War II on heavy cruisers, aircraft carriers, amphibious ships and British antisubmarine vessels. He left the Navy at the end of the war as a chief petty officer to complete his studies at the University of Tulsa.

After a brief stint on that school's economics faculty, he came to the San Francisco Bay Area. He worked in retail advertising and lived with his family in Marin County within walking distance of the sailboats he kept in Sausalito.

Of his published short stories, most are Westerns, drawn from his early life in Oklahoma's ranch and Indian country.

His later work was concerned more with the sea and the ships and men he had come to know there. It is this vicarious connection with a life now long gone which proved most therapeutic in making the frustrations of corporate life bearable.

His stories have been adapted for network radio and television.

He now lives in Mill Valley, California, and continues to sail his small black sailboat out of Sausalito's Clipper Yacht Harbor.